Touch of a Rogue

Touch of a Rogue

MIA MARLOWE

KENSINGTON PUBLISHING CORP.
www.kensingtonbooks.com

BRAVA BOOKS are published by

Kensington Publishing Corp.
119 West 40th Street
New York, NY 10018

Copyright © 2012 Diana Groe

All rights reserved. No part of this book may be reproduced in any form or by any means without the prior written consent of the Publisher, excepting brief quotes used in reviews.

All Kensington titles, imprints and distributed lines are available at special quantity discounts for bulk purchases for sales promotion, premiums, fund-raising, educational or institutional use.

Special book excerpts or customized printings can also be created to fit specific needs. For details, write or phone the office of the Kensington Special Sales Manager: Kensington Publishing Corp., 119 West 40th Street, New York, NY 10018. Attn. Special Sales Department. Phone: 1-800-221-2647.

Brava and the B logo are Reg. U.S. Pat. & TM Off.

ISBN-13: 978-0-7582-6354-4
ISBN-10: 0-7582-6354-6

First Kensington Trade Paperback Printing: March 2012

10 9 8 7 6 5 4 3 2 1

Printed in the United States of America

Chapter 1

The bed creaked out a merry rhythm of squeaks and scritches, like a chorus of tree frogs. The woman buried deep in the feather mattress moaned and gasped at the man's exertions over her.

Unfortunately for Jacob Aubrey Preston, he was not the man in the bed. Instead, he was under it, tugging his trousers back up, with nothing to show for his evening except a deeper acquaintance with dust balls.

When he and Lady Bothwell had heard her husband stomping up the stairs, he'd barely had time to dive beneath the slats. Lady B. had shoved Jacob's boots and walking stick after him a heartbeat before Lord Bothwell threw open the door to her boudoir with the announcement that he was fully tumescent and his wife must prepare herself forthwith.

Fortunately for Lord Bothwell, Jacob had prepared his wife quite well.

"Oh, Bothy," she said in a breathy tone as the creaking continued. "You're quite vigorous this evening."

Bothy? Jacob mouthed and rolled onto his stomach. The bottom of the mattress smacked the crown of his head as if in reproof.

"Well, I ought to be," her husband answered. "Just relieved

Lord Hampleton of two thousand shares of railway stock at the *poque* table this night."

"Oh, are they very valuable?"

Jacob imagined Lady Bothwell's rouged lips curved in a calculating smile. She was probably trying to figure the shares' worth in French millinery. The amount she had spent on her collection of bonnets would clothe a small English hamlet for a year.

Maybe two.

"At the moment, the shares are at the peak of their value," Lord Bothwell wheezed, clearly winded by his repetitive activity. "But I have it on good authority the principals in the company are quietly disposing of their holdings. I'll sell them all tomorrow before the market gets wind of it and the bottom drops out. Now do be quiet, madam, and kindly allow me to concentrate."

Jacob laid his cheek on the cool hardwood and sighed. At least he'd gleaned a valuable bit of intelligence from this ridiculous situation. He, too, held a considerable number of railway shares. Or rather, his brother Jerome did. But Jerome Preston, the Earl of Meade, took little interest in the actual running of the far-flung estate he'd inherited from their uncle.

At first, Jerome had been so tightfisted with his new wealth and position, he'd even cut off the previous earl's family from receiving badly needed support. However, his stinginess had bled into his investment choices as well and left him teetering on the brink of insolvency before Jacob had stepped in to help. He'd put the new earl's financial house in order and reinstated their aunt's support. Even now, Jacob couldn't let his brother manage the earldom's assets or they'd both find themselves light in the pockets in no time.

Jacob wished he could find a way to thank Lord Bothwell for the tip about the rail shares, but decided it would be deucedly awkward to explain how he'd come by the information.

The bed bounced for another thirty seconds by Jacob's pocket watch. Then Lord Bothwell emitted a sound rather like an old bullfrog struggling to stay atop a lily pad as the mattress shuddered to a halt.

Jacob waited.

Then he heard a whuffle, a grunt, and the beginnings of a stentorian snore. "Bothy" was enjoying the sleep of the just. Jacob propped his chin on his fist, wondering how long he'd be trapped beneath the bed.

Then he heard the rustle of sheets. The baroness lifted a corner of the counterpane and motioned for him to come out.

"He'll sleep till noon now," she whispered, knotting the sash at the waist of her wrapper. "We could use his chamber. It's just through that door."

Jacob swallowed hard. Granted, any man who thought simply saying "prepare yourself" constituted foreplay deserved to be cuckolded on principle. But after listening to the whole ghastly interlude with her husband, he feared he'd never be able to look at the lovely Lady Bothwell again without a chorus of frogs chirruping in his head.

"Charming as that offer is"—he whispered back as he slid out of hiding and tugged on his boots—"with regret, I must decline. I never romance a lady while her husband, however sound a sleeper he may be, is in residence."

Jacob had yet to be accosted by an angry spouse demanding satisfaction and he didn't relish beginning with Bothy. He felt little guilt about swiving another man's wife. He wasn't the one violating a vow after all, and a satisfied lady didn't cast her eyes elsewhere. But it went against his conscience to add insult to injury by embarrassing or, God forbid, killing a fellow in a duel over a wandering wife's dubious honor.

"Farewell, my dear."

He gave Lady Bothwell a peck on her cheek, then made for the French doors leading to a small balcony. Jacob threw his leg over the balustrade and climbed down the trellis, which was denuded of blooms with the first frost of autumn. He looked back up when he reached the bottom and blew a kiss to the lady whose ample bosom was in serious danger of escaping her wrapper as she leaned over to waggle her fingers at him.

"Tomorrow?" she whispered hopefully.

"I'll send word." He loped away through Lord Bothwell's fussy garden.

Unfortunately, the word would be "no, thank you." While Lady Bothwell fit all his criteria for a lover—enthusiastic, slightly jaded, and most of all, married—he wondered if he ought to rethink the last qualification. While a married lover freed him from the entanglements possible with a green girl, there were difficulties inherent in bedding another man's wife as well.

Perhaps if the lady's husband was on an extended voyage abroad . . .

Provided he sired no child, Jacob might even consider that he was doing the man a favor by keeping the home fires burning, as it were. He supposed he could keep a mistress, but it made no sense to spend the blunt necessary to support one. Not when whispered rumors of his bed skills brought a steady stream of ladies of quality sidling up to him at every soirée, ready for a dalliance.

He stepped out of the alley and onto the street. Gas lamps rose amid pools of yellow light, their bases fading into the low-lying fog along the thoroughfare. Jacob ploughed through the swirling mist, the slap of his soles on the cobbles the only thing dispelling the fanciful notion that he trudged through clouds.

Gray, odiferous clouds. Wind whipped around him. The fish-and-tar reek of the Thames was in rare form this night.

He passed by his brother's posh town house, a redbrick Georgian with white trim and wide granite steps leading to an entrance designed to impress. The earl always insisted Jacob was welcome to share the well-situated Grosvenor Square home, but he preferred to keep his own place.

It was all well and good for him to be privy to Lord Meade's business. However, he didn't need his brother's long nose in his. Most of Jacob's activities wouldn't bear close scrutiny.

The direct route to his town house near Leicester Square led him down an alley with no gas lamps at all. A gang of ruffians made to approach him, but he didn't slow his stride. Jacob carried a rapier hidden in his ornate cherry walking stick and knew how to use it. Last week he'd fended off a would-be thief and pinked him proper in the upper arm. He stepped into a shaft of moonlight pouring into the narrow way, grasping the platinum hilt, in case he needed to defend himself.

The gang stopped in mid-step as recognition widened their eyes. As Jacob pushed past them, they gave him a respectfully wide berth. Evidently, rumors of his bed skills weren't the only bits of intelligence circulating about Jacob Preston.

From the end of the block of unassuming town houses, he was mildly surprised to see an elegant equipage stopped before his red door. A crest with a boar and crossed swords was emblazoned on the side. He didn't immediately recognize the heraldic symbol. *In veritate triumpho* was etched above the device.

"I triumph in truth," Jacob translated. *Who in the world . . .* Then he clapped a hand to his forehead as the memory flooded back. He'd received a note from the dowager Countess of Cambourne a couple weeks ago announcing her intention to call on him for help on a matter of business while she was in London.

Probably another lonely lady hoping to entice him to her bed. Dowagers invariably had liver spots or warts or both, and Jacob didn't handle business for anyone but his brother, though he'd been known to dabble in a discreet investigation from time to time. Since Jacob made it a point not to respond to social notes that didn't interest him, the time Lady Cambourne specified for her visit had never settled in his mind. A quick glance up showed a light burning in his first floor parlor.

He pushed open his front door, swallowing back a curse. Who knew how long it would take to rid himself of the late caller? If he wasn't going to find a pleasing woman's bed, the least the Fates could do was allow him to find his own at a reasonable hour.

"Good evening, sir."

He scowled at the man who served as his butler, valet, and general factotum. Fenwick at least had the grace to look chagrined as he collected Jacob's coat, gloves, and hat.

Jacob's privacy was his most prized possession. When he hired Fenwick a few years earlier, he'd specifically instructed him that part of his duties included keeping unexpected and unwanted guests at bay.

"I see we have a visitor," Jacob said, glancing up the polished mahogany banister with a frown. Light from the parlor reflected off a long mirror hanging in the first floor landing and spilled down the stairs in jagged shards.

"Oh, yes, indeed we do." Fenwick attempted a cheerful smile to cover the dereliction of his duty. "The lady said as you were expecting her."

"Did I tell you I was expecting her?"

"No, sir."

"Then why is she still here?"

"Well, Lady Cambourne insisted upon waiting." Fenwick's

pale eyebrows nearly met over his watery blue eyes. "The countess is a . . . most persuasive person, sir."

"Hmph!"

"Sir, I took the liberty of looking the lady up in DeBrett's for you. Here are the particulars." Fenwick produced a much folded square of paper from his vest pocket, covered with his small, spidery handwriting.

"You have almost redeemed yourself," Jacob said, glancing at the information from the registry of the peerage. *Julianne Tyndale (nee True) Dowager Countess of Cambourne, wife of Algernon Tyndale, 8th Earl of Cambourne. No issue from the marriage. Widowed two years ago when the earl reportedly did away with himself.*

Jacob's brows arched in surprise. Unless a member of the aristocracy was despondent over gambling debts or losses in the market, it was rare for one of them to "shuffle off this mortal coil" ahead of schedule. He wondered which reversal of fortunes had sent the earl over the edge. Jacob resumed reading, glad he'd had the foresight to hire a literate fellow like Fenwick as his right-hand man, even if he occasionally let the rules of the house slide.

Lady Cambourne was formerly known as Julianne True of the Drury Lane Theatrical Company.

"I stand corrected, Fenwick. You have totally redeemed yourself. You obviously have more sources of information than I suspected. This last bit in particular could not have come from DeBrett's."

Fenwick grinned. "No, sir. I recognized her. Saw her play Lady Macbeth some six or seven years ago."

"So I'm assuming this is one dowager who doesn't possess three chins."

Fenwick shook his head and gave a nervous chuckle. "Couldn't blame Macbeth a bit. Every man in the theatre would have killed for her, sir."

Jacob smiled as he tucked the paper into his pocket. An attractive young widow waited in his parlor. Perhaps the evening wasn't a total loss after all.

But on second thought, money wasn't the only thing that could drive a man to an early grave. If what Fenwick said was true about the actress turned countess, perhaps the lady's husband *had* killed for her sake.

A black widow bore close watching.

Julianne checked her pendant watch for the umpteenth time, irritation sizzling in her belly. She smoothed the collar on her lilac bodice, flicking a speck of London's ubiquitous soot from the gray piping. The smart traveling ensemble bespoke her status as a wealthy widow in the final stage of mourning. The pale shade flattered her delicate coloring far more than the black she'd endured for the first two years after Algernon's death. Of course, even with the right hue against her skin, when frustration flamed her cheeks, the effect of a cool, collected lady of quality would be hopelessly lost.

And if Julianne knew one thing, it was the value of a first impression.

She looked up when she heard masculine footfalls on the stairs. Mr. Preston's servants crept about the immaculate townhome silent as wraiths. The heavy tread could only mean the man himself had finally deigned to arrive.

When the shadow of a man filled the doorway, she stood and tossed him a haughty glance. He stepped into the light of the gas lamp.

She noted with pleasure that Mr. Preston was exceedingly fine to look upon.

Of course, he would be. A man didn't gain the reputation for being a dissolute rogue without being charming, cynical, and blessed with armloads of masculine beauty. Jacob Preston possessed all three in sufficient quantities to overcome the combined scruples of a nunnery.

A shock of chestnut hair fell over his forehead above strikingly pale, almost silver-gray eyes. His fine straight nose divided a face of strong planes and angles, evidence of determination ingrained in his features. His lips turned up in a smile that was slightly crooked, dispelling the notion of perfect balance.

Good. She found small imperfections in a man attractive. Her experience in the theatre had taught her that perfectly sculpted males tended to be drawn to other perfectly sculpted males.

Jacob Preston was taller than most men of her acquaintance, with a corresponding breadth of shoulder.

She wondered if he was proportionate in other ways as well. Her body registered a response with a quick flutter under her ribs and a heightened sense of awareness that brought the masculine scent of bergamot and sandalwood to her nostrils.

Steady on, she chided herself. *This is about business, not pleasure.*

Still, Jacob Preston was devilishly attractive and perception was everything among the ton. Since she would likely be in the public eye while in London, it would enhance her standing to have a handsome man at her side. And she intended to keep Jacob Preston near her for as long as it took to accomplish her goal.

"Mr. Preston, I presume." She consulted her pendant watch again, though she knew perfectly well what time it was. Then she closed the silver filigreed cover with an annoyed snap. "I live in the country most of the year, so perhaps I'm not as well versed in city manners as I ought to be. But in Cornwall, it is considered beyond impolite to keep a countess waiting for three hours."

The man strode forward and made a correct obeisance over her gloved fingertips. "Your pardon, Lady Cambourne."

That was better. Julianne preferred to begin relationships, even those of a business nature, as she meant them to continue, with herself firmly in charge.

"As long as we're recounting deficiencies in our education, I too must confess to ignorance over country manners." His voice was a deep rumble, but he didn't boom as most men with bass notes tended to do. The low sound shivered over her like the purr of a lion in its prime. "For your future reference, my lady, in London it is customary *not* to call if one's intent to do so has not been acknowledged."

She narrowed her eyes at his insolence, but he seemed uncowed by her displeasure. In fact, the wretch's mouth twitched in a wider smile.

A sensual smile that sparked with recognition.

He'd probably seen her on stage. If she didn't need his help so badly, she'd storm out in a fiery scene that would put her Drury Lane days to shame. She realized suddenly that he hadn't released her hand, so she tugged it away.

"Are you this rude to all your potential clients?"

He stifled a yawn. "Only the ones who keep me from my bed." Then he skewered her with a penetrating gaze and she felt his animal heat sizzling toward her. "Of course, I'm never rude to clients who wish to join me there."

She cocked a brow at him. Why did men always assume actresses were ever ready for a quick tumble?

Besides, in matters of the flesh, she preferred to initiate an encounter. Julianne had been tempted to take a discreet lover during her mourning period, but she'd resisted. She wanted to keep matters simple. If she allowed a man in her bed, he might begin to contemplate marriage, and she'd have to cut him loose. She wasn't about to surrender the freedom of widowhood for the vacillating trifle of a man's affections.

Still, her belly tightened at Preston's suggestion and a quick flick of her gaze below his cut-away jacket revealed a more than satisfactory bulge in his close-fitting breeches. She turned her head aside, pretending fascination with the small Gainsborough landscape hanging above his fireplace.

Julianne was a sensual creature. She knew this about herself and embraced it, but she'd been so caught up in other more pressing matters since her husband's death, there'd been no time to find a suitable bed partner for a light dalliance. It seemed like ages since she'd been with a man. But this wasn't the time and Jacob Preston certainly wasn't the right man, if she intended to become his employer. She needed to regain control of this interview before her body began overruling her head.

"I'm sure you believe joining you in bed is a charming suggestion, Mr. Preston. Thanks to a subscription to the *London Crier*, I've heard tales of your amorous abilities even in distant Cornwall," she said dryly. "However, I discount such superlatives by at least half. And frankly, after meeting you, given the sensitive nature of my situation, I'm not sure you'll do at all."

His brows drew together into a frown. "Why not?"

"For one thing, I can't imagine the other things I've heard of you are true."

"And what things might those be?"

Now her lips twitched. By taking her business away, she'd increased his interest in it. Men were so predictable.

"According to rumors, you've solved a number of cases that baffled the best of Bow Street."

"That's true," he said with a smug grin.

"And you have a reputation for recovering items of intrinsic value . . . by means best left unexamined."

He gave a slight shrug. "You have the right of it, madam. If you want strictly legal means employed in solving your difficulties, I do have connections in Bow Street who might assist you."

Drat the man. He, too, knew the value of taking something away. "I wasn't speaking of legalities. I'm referring to means of inquiry which border on the fantastical."

His face hardened into a guarded mask.

"Of course, I put little stock in such rumors, myself," she said, depositing her oversized carpetbag on the marble top of a side table. "It is 1859, after all. I'd rather trust to science than some sort of gypsy fortune-telling."

"Rest assured, milady, I do not possess so much as one crystal ball," he said smoothly. "We've danced around the issue long enough. It's apparent that you have a case which requires my skills. Or you think you do. Perhaps you'd better tell me what it is."

He motioned her to a deep burgundy wing chair flanking the fireplace and settled into its mate once she sat.

"Actually, it's what *they* are. I have two commissions for you, if you feel yourself up to the challenge." She leaned forward slightly. "As you may know, the authorities ruled that my late husband took his own life."

"I take from your tone that you disagree with this assessment." He steepled his long fingers before him. "But why did they believe it was so?"

She retrieved her carpetbag and was gratified by the fact that Mr. Preston stood until she sat once again. His manners were improving by the moment. "Perhaps because his body was found in a room locked from the inside." She pulled a leather sheath from the bag. "With this dagger thrust through his heart."

Preston reached for the weapon, careful to hold it by the

embossed leather scabbard, not the hilt, she noticed. The haft was covered with swirling Celtic patterns ornamented with strips of gold and silver, studded with carbuncles and polished amber.

Preston took a handkerchief from his pocket and drew the blade from its home, careful not to touch the dagger with his uncovered hand.

She nodded approvingly. He understood that the oils from his bare skin might be injurious to such an ancient blade. Beneath the crosspiece, the lethal steel shone with iridescence in the flickering firelight. There was an indistinct pattern etched onto the blade as well that seemed to change shape as the light varied.

"Given the preponderance of evidence to the contrary"—he said as he eyed the dagger—"what makes you think your husband did not, in fact, end his own life?"

"The weapon itself," she said. "It's obviously a ceremonial blade, one of deep antiquity. My husband had far too much respect for history to misuse such an artifact in that way."

One of his brows arched in question. "Not because your marriage was deliriously happy and you can't imagine why he'd choose to leave you?"

She glowered at him. "The condition of my marriage is not your concern."

"It is if you wish my help."

"We had a . . . companionable marriage," she said finally.

"I assume he was much your senior."

"He was."

"How much?"

"Forty-five years." In truth, she was younger than Algernon's heir, a fact that rankled her stepson sorely.

"Sounds quite . . . companionable."

Preston's gray gaze traveled over her and she could almost

hear him calculating the worth of the union based on the cut of her clothing and the quality of the pearls and jet at her throat. But money and position weren't her only considerations when she'd decided to wed the earl. Lord Cambourne had promised her unheard of freedom in ordering her personal and financial life.

Lord Cambourne was smitten after seeing her onstage, but unlike so many others, he wasn't looking for a mistress. After a short courtship during which Algernon dazzled her with his wealth and title, showering her with the courtly attentiveness only older men seemed to possess, she'd agreed to leave the theatre and marry him. Julianne had known she'd probably not be accepted by his peers, but the fact didn't seem to trouble him as he'd long since retired from fashionable life.

They'd enjoyed a brief time of delight when his older body roused to her younger one with a last flare of passion. Then he seemed to remember his years, and their life together became one of shared enthusiasms.

Algernon had respected her intellect as much as he'd admired her beauty. He had allowed her to fund her pet charity, Mrs. Osgood's School for Girls, without restriction. He had even encouraged her to take a lover quietly, since he was unable to meet those needs, but she honored him too much to cuckold him, even with his permission. She understood his love of arcane weaponry and, because of her stint on the stage, was able to demonstrate the use of his acquisitions in little mock battles they both enjoyed. But her life of cherished freedoms had crumbled the day Algernon was found dead.

She had been fascinated by Lord Cambourne's collection of weapons, but she wished she'd never seen the dagger now in Jacob Preston's hand.

"You still hold your title," Preston said, turning the dagger in the light, inspecting the intricate whorls etched in the blade. "If you think you can afford to hire my services—and let me assure you I don't come cheaply—you obviously still have access to adequate funds . . ."

She schooled her face not to react. He didn't need to know her financial situation might shortly change. Worse, she wouldn't be the only one who suffered if it did.

"Why do you care if the world believes your husband's death was a suicide?"

"Because I know it wasn't," she said. "And because it would pain Algernon—I mean, the earl—to know that his body is not interred in consecrated ground."

She didn't intend to plead, but some men would not be moved without it. With no effort at all, she whipped up enough tears to set them atremble on her lashes without spilling over her lids and ruining her appearance.

"Please, Mr. Preston. This is the last good thing I can do for my late husband. I ask for your help."

He narrowed his eyes at her as if he were trying to peer into her soul. "Very well. But I can only go where the evidence leads. The motto on your coach says 'I triumph in truth.' If I discover your husband did—"

"He didn't."

"If the evidence leads us to a different conclusion, you must promise to accept it. Will you?"

She sighed and nodded.

"Now, what about the other matter?"

"You're holding it in your hand," she said. "That dagger is one of a set of six identical blades."

"And you know this how?"

She shot him a withering glance. "With all ancient artifacts, provenance is everything. My husband unearthed an illuminated manuscript, part of one at any rate, which describes this set of daggers and how they were dispersed in order to protect the weapons."

Jacob frowned at the blade he still held in his handkerchief-shrouded hand. "Protect the weapons? Usually one thinks of a weapon protecting its bearer, not needing protection itself."

"The manuscript hinted at magical properties in the blades, which my husband discounted, of course."

"What sort of magical properties?"

"Oh, the usual things one encounters in medieval texts. Special power over others, the ability to turn lead to gold, immortality to the bearer of the blades, those sorts of fantastical claims," she said, waving them away as unimportant. "Algernon was adamant about finding the missing pieces of the set."

"Let me guess," Preston said. "Because the magical properties would only be expressed if one possessed all six daggers?"

"Yes, but that wasn't my husband's motivation. He was a serious collector, devoted to history and—"

"And power, wealth, and immortality held no allure for him? What a paragon your late husband must have been," Preston said with a wry grin. "Let us assume the earl's motives were altruistic. Why do *you* wish to find the daggers?"

"My husband spent the last part of his life on this quest. He found and acquired five of the daggers. I would like your help locating the final blade."

"Again, why?"

"Because . . . it was my husband's desire to see them reunited."

"Not because you believe in magic?"

"Heavens, no!" Mr. Preston didn't need to know what she intended to do with the full set once she had it. She lowered her gaze and let the tears gather once again. "Call it a widow's way of dealing with her grief. Reuniting this set of arcane weapons was my husband's life's work. He was obsessive about it, particularly near the end. If I finish Algernon's quest, it will help ease the pain of our parting."

She was startled by the sound of soft applause.

"Brava, Mrs. True. Your thespian skills are as sharp as ever," he said sardonically. "As believable a grieving wife as ever I've seen."

She glared at him. "Why do you mock me?"

"Nonsense. I applauded, didn't I?" He rose and deposited the dagger on the mantel. "I will keep this for a time, so that I may study it."

Her irritation dissipated slightly. "Then you agree to help me?"

"Almost. There is a final requirement before I commit to this endeavor."

"If it's a question of payment for your services—"

"We'll deal with that later, after I've been successful," he said. "No, I need to know who I'm dealing with and you, madam, are an enigma."

"But I've told you—"

"Only what you wish me to know." He rubbed his chin as if pondering his predicament. "With most clients, a handshake enables me to get a sense of what's driving them, who they really are."

"All that from a handshake? And you claim to have no crystal ball," she said with a snort.

He leaned down and rested his large hands on the armrests of her chair, pinning her to the tufted back. "But in your case, milady, a connection of a more . . . personal nature will be required."

Of all the cheek! "You have an exaggerated sense of your own importance, Mr. Preston. I will not bed you simply to procure your services."

This time, he was the one who snorted.

"Why, Lady Cambourne, what a charming idea! But I wasn't suggesting a bedding at present. We hardly know each other. However, I must say I'm pleased with the direction in which your thoughts have turned. Believe me, you are not alone in your musings on the subject."

He ran the pad of his thumb over her bottom lip. "But no, all that I require of you at the moment . . . is a kiss."

Chapter 2

Her amber eyes all but spat fire. Indignation rose in a red flush from beneath her collar, kissing her lovely cheekbones with flame.

Lord, she was a beautiful woman.

She was also a talented actress, but not good enough to fool him. Jacob knew real irritation when he saw it. What annoyed a woman was a strong indicator of what was important to her. He'd felt her gaze flicking over him throughout the interview and knew she wasn't immune to a man's body. He'd caught her experiencing some unwidow-ish thoughts.

She wasn't upset over having them. Simply over being caught at it. Her sensitivity at how she was perceived surprised him a bit till he remembered an actress was first and foremost concerned with perception.

Undoubtedly that drove her to present herself with such stiffly correct posturing. She was driven to prove she deserved the respect due a lady of quality.

She crossed her arms beneath her breasts, pressing them together and lifting them slightly. Jacob's trousers grew tighter.

"You demand too much, sir."

"Perhaps." Jacob shrugged. "And perhaps discovering the

truth of your husband's death and finishing his life's work isn't so important to you, after all."

She drew a deep breath and released it in a single huff. "Oh, very well, if you must, you may have your kiss." She closed her eyes. "But be quick about it."

Not bloody likely.

Jacob would take as long as he needed. He leaned closer, so that his breath feathered over her lips. Her mouth tightened a bit at the corners. Whatever she thought he might learn from kissing her, she was determined to shield as much of herself as possible.

A lady with secrets, he thought with a grin. *Is there any other kind?*

He brushed her mouth with his, inhaling her scent. Most women favored overpowering perfumes, heavy with jasmine, rose and cloves. On Lady Cambourne, Jacob detected only a hint of camellia, a subtle, clean floral.

He slanted his lips over hers, creating a firm seal. She was doing her best to remain immobile, but as he traced the seam of her mouth with the tip of his tongue, he felt her softening like a dish of butter in the sun. She was undeniably sweet, soft and pliant.

All woman.

When her lips parted, he didn't rush in immediately. Instead he drew the breath from her lungs, then gently replaced it with his own. She leaned toward him by the tiniest of degrees. He suckled her bottom lip and she gasped, but didn't pull away.

She liked men. And based on that quick intake of breath, he'd bet the entire contents of his wallet she'd been without one for a while.

That was something he'd be pleased to remedy. He was just about to deepen the kiss, when she reached up and grasped both his lapels to pull him closer. Then Lady Cambourne thrust her little pointed tongue between his lips and started a teasing exploration of his mouth.

He'd been hard since he'd first suggested kissing her. Now his cock was like iron. The little minx dared him to make love to her mouth.

So he did, nipping and thrusting. She suckled his tongue and offered her own, giving as good as she got. She moaned into his mouth. The needy sound made his balls tighten almost painfully.

So many women in his experience were passive in their passion, waiting for him to waken them, to direct every bit of their tryst. Lady Cambourne would be a handful between the sheets, a woman who knew what she wanted and wasn't shy about demanding it.

He wondered what she'd do if he decided to test the sturdiness of that wing chair and hike up her skirt for a spirited coupling right there and then. Blood hammered in his ears at the thought.

Down, you rutting bastard, he ordered his cock. He couldn't afford to let himself be distracted now. Not when he still hadn't accomplished what he intended with this kiss.

He laid a hand on her neck, running the pad of his thumb along her jawline. Her skin was supple and silky, but he didn't intend to stop there. He slid his hand down to rest at the base of her throat, where he could feel her pulse fluttering like a hummingbird's wings.

Almost there.

Was it his imagination or did she arch her back slightly, thrusting her breasts forward?

Damn. If only those soft mounds were his aim.

Instead, Jacob splayed his fingers, letting the tip of his longest one brush the silver pendant watch pinned to her lapel. The precious metal had been humming to him in liquid tones since his hand first drew near. Now its song burst into his brain in full force, trilling and brilliant.

He couldn't remember a time when metal didn't speak to him. It was always the same when his bare skin touched any sort of lustrous chemical element. The voice of the ore came first and every sort of metal uttered a unique sound Jacob could hear when he was near enough. Delicate, musical notes indicated precious metals, with silver shimmering thinly and gold a warmer, more voluptuous tune. The song of steel was sharp-edged and strident. Iron's rough tones were ponderous and deep.

Of all metals, only platinum was silent before him. Since it was a restful substance, he surrounded himself with it as often as possible even though its rarity made it terribly dear. The platinum head of his walking stick had saved his sanity more than once when the voices of other nearby ores threatened to swamp his senses.

Then, after the metal's song, images cascaded through his mind, distorted into shards of shifting light, like a vision seen through a kaleidoscope. The history of the metal object scrolled past at blinding speed. Former owners paraded by. Disturbing events rose from the swirling mists of embedded impressions in the metal.

Along with the voices and the mental pictures came pin-points of pain stabbing his brain, but Jacob accepted them as the price for using his gift. He steeled himself not to shrink from it as the stings intensified.

Of course, Lady Cambourne's searing kiss was a good diversion from the chaos in his head. He hadn't yet plumbed the deepest secret the silver pendant watch could share—its wearer's emotions.

Jacob cupped the back of the countess's neck with his other hand to insure that the kiss would continue. She responded with a teasing nip of his bottom lip that sent his groin into pleasurable agony. He wished he could concentrate solely on the lady's delectable mouth, but he needed to move quickly to open his mind to his gift again.

He sought for a quiet center in himself, a good trick when the rest of his body urged him to action of a decidedly unquiet sort. He longed to wallow in the pure animal joy of a good hard swive, but he finally managed to drown out the riot in his trousers and felt Lady Cambourne's . . . guilt-tinged fear.

Deep-seated, jagged-edged, and unrelenting.

Jacob released her mouth and stood upright. His chest heaved, his body rebelling at breaking off the kiss. But he'd be damned if he'd continue kissing a woman with that much fear in her heart. He looked down at her, searching her face for evidence of the guilty panic he felt roiling off the silver pendant in serrated waves. Lady Cambourne returned his gaze with perfect calm. His assessment of her acting talent shot skyward.

He didn't think he was the cause of the lady's distress. Even so, Jacob sensed a wall rising behind her wide amber eyes. Whatever she was afraid of, whatever she was ashamed of, she didn't want him privy to it.

"Well, Mr. Preston," she said as she ran a fingertip along her bottom lip. It was only then that he noticed her breasts rose and fell as if she'd just run across Hyde Park with a pack of wild dogs at her heels. If he'd stayed connected with the silver longer, he suspected he'd have discovered she was also as deeply roused as he. "Did you learn what you needed to know?"

Actually the kiss posed more questions than it answered.

"Enough to know I will take your case, madam," he said, taking a step back to remove himself from the temptation to kiss her again. Not until he learned the source of that self-reproaching fear. "I will contact you as soon as I have discovered anything of interest. Please leave word of where you can be reached with my man Fenwick on your way out."

"I most certainly will not," she said. "If I am to be your employer, I'll dictate the terms of our agreement. You will not leave me dangling in the dark. I will accompany you during your investigations."

"Out of the question."

"Then I will seek another to assist me. One who doesn't make such unreasonable demands on his clients." She stood and retrieved the dagger Jacob had set on the mantel. It disappeared into her carpetbag.

"You didn't kiss me as if you found it unreasonable."

"Good evening, sir." She turned away, preparing to stride out.

"No, wait," Jacob called after her. The woman's portrait ought to appear in the dictionary beside the word *indomitable*. "Very well. You may accompany me. But I must warn you, milady, that a search of this nature often leads to . . . less than savory associations."

She rolled her eyes at him and lifted her chin a notch. "Mr. Preston, I used to be in the theatre. I promise you nothing we encounter will shock me."

"Point taken." His estimation of her pluck ticked up several degrees. "However, I must insist you leave that dagger with me at present."

Her brows drew together. "I'd prefer not to. It's quite . . . valuable."

Her hesitation made him wonder if its value was the only thing that concerned her about leaving it with him.

"All the more reason to entrust it to my care. I assure you that I have means to protect the dagger and it is essential that I have time to study its unique properties if I'm to find its lost mate." He held out his hand and after a few moments of indecision, she fished the leather scabbard from her carpetbag and placed it in his waiting palm.

"I will collect you first thing in the morning so we may begin," she announced.

"Make it second thing in the morning," Jacob said with a grin as he replaced the dagger on his mantel. "I rarely rise before noon."

Lady Cambourne didn't return his smile. "Nevertheless, you will alter your schedule to accommodate me, Mr. Preston. If I cannot discover the remaining blade by—" She clamped her lips tight to stop herself. "Suffice it to say that time is of the essence. Until tomorrow, then."

She headed toward the door, the gentle swish of her skirts a whispered farewell.

"Lady Cambourne, has someone threatened you over these daggers?" Jacob asked.

She stopped mid-stride. Jacob read increased tension in the set of her narrow shoulders, but she didn't look back at him so he could assess the answer in her features.

Cagey lady, but I'll take that as a yes.

"Good night to you, sir." She beat a hasty retreat.

Jacob watched from behind the parlor curtain as Fenwick saw her out to her conveyance and then returned to shut up the house for the night. No one else was abroad on the street, but as soon as the carriage rattled away, a small figure popped up from the shadows across the narrow lane. The urchin hotfooted it down the block and disappeared into a darker alley.

Legions of masterless boys prowled the streets of London. They were magpies with feet when it came to gathering information and useful for shadowing persons unaware. Jacob had several of them on retainer himself. Someone had taken a definite interest in the countess's activities.

Or his. Jacob had made his share of enemies in the halls of

commerce and working as his brother's right hand in background machinations within the House of Lords. But given the emotions he'd felt from Lady Cambourne, he'd bet the street rat was tasked with noting her whereabouts.

Turning away from the window, he massaged the bridge of his nose. Now that the pleasing distraction of Lady Cambourne was gone, residual pain from his contact with her silver pendant ached afresh.

He stared at the dagger resting on his mantel. Unfortunately, he wasn't done with pain yet this evening.

Fenwick appeared at the parlor door. "Will there be anything else, sir?"

"Yes, come back in half an hour. I suspect I will require assistance finding my bed."

The butler glanced at the dagger and nodded. Fenwick was one of the few souls on earth Jacob had taken into his confidence about his ability to extract information from metal. And one of the few he trusted to help him deal with the aftereffects of exercising his gift for a prolonged time.

"You'll be wanting a tonic, I expect."

Jacob nodded. "Easy on the laudanum, heavy on the whisky. Save the Glenlivet for another time." Might as well use inferior spirits because after extended contact with metal, he'd be in no condition to actually enjoy the drink. "You'll need to secure the dagger and its scabbard in the safe for the night once I'm finished with it. Do not leave it unattended for a moment."

"Very good, sir." Fenwick pulled the door closed behind him.

Jacob squared his shoulders and retrieved the dagger, careful to hold it by the leather scabbard. He pulled out his handkerchief and drew the blade, laying it on the escritoire in the corner, where the lamplight was stronger.

The dagger was beautiful in the manner of deadly things, elegantly formed and honed to razor sharpness. Now that he had time to study it, he realized the undulating design etched into the blade resembled a tree with branches spread.

The Tree of Life? he mused. Not likely on an instrument of death. *Perhaps a representation of the Tree of the Knowledge of Good and Evil, or the Norse World Tree, Yggdrasil.*

Jacob shook his head. He felt as though he'd seen this design fairly recently, but couldn't quite place it. Perhaps if he concentrated on the dagger's other properties, the meaning of the etching would become plain. He suspended his hand a half inch above the blade and let the ore sing to him.

Since the metal was an alloy, the sound of individual ores rose from an indistinct blur, like a choir warming up in myriad different keys. First came the low rumble of iron, followed by nickel's tinny voice. Cobalt, the element named for an evil spirit with a lugubrious cackle to match, joined the chorus.

Given that mix of metals, he'd lay odds the blade had magnetic properties. To test it, he picked a steel letter opener from the top drawer of the desk, careful to protect himself from direct contact with the handkerchief. No point in flooding his senses with metals to no purpose. Sure enough, the blade point chased the opener in jerky pivots when he held it close. The field was a strong one and seemed to grow in power the longer he tested it. He had to use both hands to keep the dagger from stripping the letter opener from his grasp and barely managed to yank it away before the blade whipped off the desktop in its lust to follow the opener.

It flew across the room and buried itself in the spine of his copy of *Cicero*, an old tome whose ink was heavily laced with iron. The ornamental hilt quivered with the force of the blow.

"Why in God's name would anyone want a magnetic blade?" Jacob could envision all sorts of unforeseen outcomes in the course of a fight. A magnetic blade might become firmly attached to any susceptible metal. The hand that wielded it could lose it to a lamppost, come to that.

Unless the purpose of this blade was more ceremonial than combative. The heavy ornamentation suggested as much, but the lethal edge was wickedly sharp. Jacob suspected Lord Cambourne hadn't even felt it slide between his ribs till it punctured his heart.

Jacob replaced the letter opener and retrieved the dagger. With a healthy respect for the unknown, he centered it on the desk again and brought his forefinger closer to the blade, careful not to make actual contact. The melodious tones of gold and silver peeled through his mind next, making this an odd alloy for a blade. They were too soft for weaponry, but he heard their presence in unusual abundance nonetheless.

There was something else there as well, a rustling sibilance on the edge of sound, but Jacob couldn't quite make it out.

He'd have to touch it.

He lowered his fingertips to rest on the cool surface and then jerked them back in reflex. It was iridium. A hard, almost unworkable metal he'd first encountered at Prince Albert's Grand Exhibition a few years ago. Men of science doubted its usefulness since it was unavailable in any but the smallest of quantities and possessed such a high melting point that common metallurgical methods were ineffective.

And yet long ago someone had discovered a means to meld it into this dagger and its five doppelgängers.

Jacob drew a deep breath. He'd learned as much as he could this way. It was time to bond with the dagger. He removed his jacket and rolled up his sleeves. Then he closed his eyes and laid his palm across the flat of the blade, leaning his weight on that hand to maintain contact.

And was sucked into a cold, dark hell.

Disembodied, he tumbled through pitch blackness, pin-points of light wheeling around him. Then he felt himself accelerating, faster than the fleetest steam engine, tight as a silent scream. He gained a sense of heaviness, of falling toward the blue and green orb that loomed ahead.

He shuddered into something he couldn't see. Flames licked around him, burning off dross in a fiery rendering. He was buffeted by hot wind, the sudden noise of flame and friction deafening after the silence before. He shot across an inky sky, trailing fire. Then an empty moor rose to meet him and he slammed into the ground, leaving a trench behind him and finally coming to rest in a smoking crater.

Jacob lifted his palm from the blade and was snapped back into his own reality. He grasped the desk with both hands to steady himself, half expecting to see smoke rising from his bare forearms, but real as it seemed, even his hand was not scorched by the vision. As expected, though, pain lanced his head.

So the metal was sky-born.

Offspring of a meteorite, his rational mind corrected. Still, its unusual origins explained some of its properties. He might try again later to discern how the ore was discovered and by what magic of metallurgy someone had fashioned it into the dagger.

But now he turned his attention to the hilt. It should tell him about the people through whose hands the dagger had passed. Before he reached for the haft, he settled into the desk chair, deciding it wiser to attempt such a melding while seated.

Jacob held his hand close, letting the haft speak to him. The hilt's composition was much less exotic than the blade. Common, in fact, but for the inlaid precious metals and gemstones. The jewels were silent to his gift.

If he needed to, he'd take the dagger to his cousin Viola. She had the same affinity for gems that Jacob did for metals, a quirky inherited ability that touched only a few of his relations as far as he knew.

His brother didn't possess it, he was certain. Jerome was a stolid sort, thoroughly grounded in the material world. The idea of perception beyond the normal senses made the earl scoff. Viola suspected some of their other cousins might have inherited the enhanced gift of touch, but the ability was freakish enough that none of them wanted it noised about. It wasn't something the Prestons discussed often, even among themselves.

But Jacob suspected the metals in this dagger would tell him all he needed to know without bothering Viola about the gemstones. With grim determination, he closed his fist around the hilt.

The old man leaned down, peering through a glass that rendered his eye bulbous and out-sized as he gazed at the weapon. He smiled, the satisfied acquisitive smile of the dedicated collector. He stroked the dagger on his massive desk, fingering the flat of the sleek blade as gently as if it were his lover's skin.

Then he wrapped his fingers around the haft and hefted its weight, making a few practice cuts in the air. He rose and cavorted about the room, an aged pirate with cutlass drawn. His years dropped away and his face lit up like a boy's on Christmas morn.

Then his face changed. His heavy silver brows beetled as the hand that held the blade began quaking. The tip of the dagger turned back, bending his wrist toward him.

Eyes wide, he extended his arm, trying to lock his elbow, but the joint gave way. He grasped the hilt with both hands, but the blade drew inexorably toward his chest. The man's mouth opened and closed, but no sound came out. His lips locked in a rictus of terror. A vein bulged on his forehead, straining with the effort of holding back the dagger.

He stumbled backward into his desk chair and lost his grip on the hilt. The blade zinged into his chest with the force of a cannon shot.

* * *

"Sir, please, sir. You must wake up." Fenwick's voice drifted down to Jacob as if he was lying at the bottom of a deep well. A hand clamped on his shoulder and gave him a shake. "You're bleeding, sir, all over the carpet. Mrs. Trott will be fit to be tied if I don't get that stain cleaned up before she sees it."

Jacob pried open one eye. He was vaguely aware that he was splayed on the floor instead of seated at his desk, with no notion of how he'd come there.

Fenwick's homely honest face peered down at him, pinched with concern.

"Ah, that's the ticket, sir. Let's get you up and see what's what. Mind the blade there. No hiding the rip in the rug, I suppose. That'll put Mrs. Trott on a proper tear and no mistake."

The dagger was standing upright near Jacob's armpit, its point buried in the Persian rug. Fenwick was right about how Jacob's housekeeper would react. Mrs. Trott's parents had given her the unlikely Christian name of Waitstill, but she wasn't the sort to suffer fools in silence. His housekeeper would have a conniption when she discovered the new defect in what she considered to be "her" carpet. In fact, all of Jacob's town house was Mrs. Trott's domestic domain, and for the most part, he was pleased to allow her that fantasy. As long as his home was spotless and his meals hearty and served on time, Jacob was content.

With Fenwick's help, he struggled to his feet. His tongue felt three sizes too big for his mouth.

Fenwick investigated the bloody rip in Jacob's vest and shirt, searching the skin beneath for the source of blood. He heaved a relieved sigh. "Only a scratch. Have you right as rain in no time, sir. Come now."

"No," Jacob whispered hoarsely. "Have to . . ." He fetched out his handkerchief and reached for the dagger again.

"Don't trouble yourself, sir," Fenwick said. "You tasked me with it. I'll see to that infernal thing presently."

"No!" he said with all the force he could muster. The dagger had killed Lord Cambourne. It had tried to kill him. Damned if he'd let anyone else handle it.

Even though his head was near to exploding, he shook off his servant and bent to retrieve the weapon. He slammed it into the protective leather scabbard and trudged across the room. With a touch on the secret spring behind the Gainsborough landscape over the fireplace, the painting slid to one side to reveal a platinum-lined wall safe. Once he secured the weapon, Jacob sagged against the fireplace, resting his pounding forehead on the cool marble mantel.

"Here, sir, I've brought your tonic." Fenwick pressed the drink into his hand and then positioned himself under Jacob's arm on the unwounded side to help him to his chamber.

Jacob upended the glass, waiting for sweet oblivion to deliver him from pain. He'd learned one thing at least. Lord Cambourne's hand might have been on the hilt of the blade that killed him, but he hadn't meant to use it to end his own life. Lady Cambourne would be gratified to know her husband's death was not a suicide. It was obvious from Jacob's vision that the poor man had no control over the blade.

Who or what did was another question entirely.

He flopped on his bed, letting Fenwick tug off his boots. Before he faded completely into the opiate cloud of his tonic, Jacob realized he'd learned another thing as well.

Lady Cambourne was right to be afraid. But why did she feel guilty as well?

CHAPTER 3

Jacob thrashed on his bed, slipping in and out of fitful, opium-laced dreams.

A shining cream-colored orb filled his vision. Subtle lights swirled in the hard nacre of the pearl button. He closed his teeth over it and bit it off.

Lady Cambourne laughed. He spat the button out and went for the next one, marching down the front of her bodice as they rolled together on his capacious bed.

"No," she said, palming his cheeks to turn his face away. "Let me undo them or my modiste will have a field day gossiping with her friends about how I lost my buttons."

"Be quick then," Jacob said.

Or maybe he only thought it. Words were slow to form on his tongue after taking his tonic. His dreams were just as bumfuzzled. It was hard to be sure whether this *was* a dream or whether Lady Cambourne was actually there with him, writhing on the sweat-soaked linens. Either way, his need to see more of the countess's skin was fast becoming more important to him than determining the reality of the encounter.

As quickly as she undid the buttons, he peeled back the fabric of her bodice.

Her breasts rose in soft mounds above the lace at the neck of her all-in-one. The fabric was sheer enough that her dark areolae showed through, beguiling shadows around the pointed tips. He bent and suckled her through the thin linen.

She clutched his head to her, murmuring incoherent encouragement.

Even with the fabric separating them, she was the sweetest thing he'd ever tasted. Her flavors burst on his tongue—honey and treacle and spun sugar.

But he wanted more.

He turned her around to face away from him, none too gently, and yanked at the laces of her bodice. His fingers were too large, too clumsy, and he fouled the cords in a hopeless knot.

He growled in frustration, skimming the surface of consciousness. Her voice called him back to the poppy-laced deeps.

"Use the dagger to cut them," she suggested.

He and Lady Cambourne were suddenly no longer in his soft bed. They were somehow standing in his parlor and the safe's door hung open at an odd angle, like a drunkard clinging to its hinges trying to remain upright. A chill crept over him as the dagger began to sing.

He stopped his ears against the weapon's summons, focusing on the call of his cock instead.

"No, milady," Jacob said. "We'll manage without using the blade."

He kissed her while he tugged the undergarment down far enough to free her breasts. They were plump and soft and fit his hands perfectly. When he thrummed her nipples, her whole body hummed in response. He smelled the color of her skin, tasted the sound of her sighs. His hand found the slit in the crotch of her all-in-one.

She was slippery as a mossy well. Warm and fragrant as a hothouse orchid. He plunged a finger in to gather her nectar. She shuddered when he stroked the right place, delight making her chant his name.

"Aubrey."

Not Mr. Preston. Not even Jacob. She called him Aubrey in breathy, loving tones. No one had ever used his middle name except his mother, and then only as in "Jacob Aubrey Preston, you young scamp, just you wait till I tell your father."

He decided he liked it this way much better. It gave him license to think of her as Julianne instead of "milady." The way she said his name made it seem as if she knew him, and not just the parts he wished her to know, but all of him. His weaknesses, his strengths, his honor, and his shame—he was laid bare by that simple "Aubrey."

And yet he felt accepted.

But then from the corner of his eye, he saw that the dagger was no longer in the platinum-lined safe. It lay like an ill-wish between the fire irons of his hearth, the lethal tip pivoting from one to the other in time with Jacob's heartbeats, steady as a metronome. The tree on the blade swayed as if caught in a stiff wind. An oak in a gale.

A Druid oak.

The connection bubbled up to his conscious mind and lodged there. He groaned, tangling the bed sheets as he rolled over to seek his dream once again.

He walked the countess backward and pinned her against the wall, so he wouldn't have to look at the dagger. If it came nearer, his unprotected back would be in its malevolent path, not hers. The lady made a soft, needy noise and arched against him.

He shoved the blade from his mind.

She hitched a knee over his hip and rocked her pelvis, coating him with her slick dew.

"If I don't take you now, I'll die," he gasped.

"Don't die."

He lifted her, poised himself at her entrance. Her gaze locked with his, her eyes sloe-lidded and languid. Balls clenched, he began to lower her by inches on his hard length, watching her mouth go passion-slack as he filled her. He felt her heartbeat between her legs, pulsing around his cock, her life's blood flowing around him, through him.

He wanted to go faster. He wanted to draw out their loving. He wanted time to collapse on them and leave them suspended in aching need till they both came in ragged waves from sheer wanting.

There was a loud pounding in the distance. Someone was calling his name. And they weren't calling him Aubrey.

He lowered his mouth to hers, determined to ignore the voice, and slid the rest of the way into her velvet channel. She made a sound of surprise and pleasure in his mouth and licked his hard palate with the tip of her tongue. It tickled a bit and they laughed together, the secret laughter of lovers who recognize how ridiculous lovemaking is and how deadly serious at the same time.

Two souls in one joined body, two hearts in peril because the only thing sure in this world was that their joining could not be forever.

Then Jacob heard the dagger's voice again, but nearer now. It was clear of the scabbard, flying through the air like a loosed crossbow bolt. Headed straight for them.

Lady Cambourne screamed.

Julianne pounded on the bedchamber door, but there was no response. "Mr. Preston, I insist you open at once or I'm coming in, whether you will it or not."

"Your ladyship, I beg you. It would not be seemly," Fenwick said, trying in vain to insert himself between her and his master's chamber.

"Is it seemly for your employer to keep me waiting again?" Julianne glared at him until he stepped aside. "Mis-ter Preston!" She rapped her knuckles sharply on the door between each syllable.

A low bellow came from the room, the feral noise sounding more like the guttural cry of a bull standing at stud than something torn from the throat of a man. Fenwick's eyes went round and he jumped farther away from the door. Julianne grabbed her chance, turning the crystal knob and pushing it open.

"Mr. Preston, I—"

Words failed her. Jacob Preston was standing on his bed, legs spread, knees flexed and fists clenched. His red-rimmed eyes were wild as a stallion's, his hair sticking out at odd angles like a startled hedgehog. His brows were lowered in a gladiator's frown. He looked ready for the fight of his life.

Except for the fact that he was naked.

And fully roused, further reinforcing Julianne's earlier impression of a bull at stud. She'd seen some impressive male members in the past, but this one rendered the others pale and flaccid by comparison. Fully engorged, Jacob's length and girth were beyond her experience. His ballocks were drawn tight, nested in chestnut curls at the apex of taut thighs.

She forced her gaze away from his groin, traveling up his torso to his well-muscled chest and forearms. Clearly, Mr. Preston didn't spend all his free time in gaming hells and brothels. A man didn't acquire that sort of muscular development without regular strenuous work. But there was a blood-soaked bandage near one brown nipple, so perhaps he regularly participated in bar fights instead.

Julianne met his ferocious gaze and wondered if he could even see her. His bloodshot eyes were unfocused and darting. She didn't think he was drunk. If this was the aftereffect of too much alcohol, she doubted he'd sport such a formidable cockstand.

She sniffed the air and thought she detected a subtle, cloying odor mixed with whisky fumes.

Opium, she thought with disgust. The upper crust complained about the way gin had enslaved the masses but were blithely unconcerned by their own addiction to laudanum. How was Jacob Preston to be of any use to her if he woke with a head full of poppy each morning?

"Oh, dear, oh, no. Oh, my lady, you've ruined me. He'll

have my guts for garters, sure as there's snot on the face of an urchin," Fenwick fretted from behind her in the doorway.

"Don't despair, Mr. Fenwick. It's not your fault your employer is an opium fiend."

"Oh, but he's not usually . . . I mean, you don't understand—" Fenwick began, then seemed to reconsider arguing with a countess. He slipped away, murmuring something about fetching that sovereign English remedy for all ills—tea.

The opium fiend in question rested his bleary-eyed gaze on her and blinked slowly. Then Mr. Preston gave his head a vigorous shake, like a water spaniel emerging from an algae-coated pond.

"G'morning, Julianne," he said, his speech far clearer than she expected it to be. He seemed to have shrugged off the ill-effects of his night of drugged indulgence with surprising quickness.

She stiffened her spine. "I have not given you leave to use my Christian name."

One corner of his mouth kicked up. "If a woman's staring at a fellow in his altogether, you can't blame the man for assuming she's given him leave of some sort." Heedless of his nakedness, he stepped down from the bed and stomped over to the washstand. Then he leaned over the basin while dumping the contents of the pitcher over his head. "We'll take it turn and turn about. You may call me Jacob. Or Au—well, Jacob will do for now."

"I'll do no such thing." His buttocks were as tight and firm as his thighs, Julianne noted despite herself. His long legs were lightly dusted with the same chestnut hair as his head.

He toweled himself off, sleeking his hair back like seal's fur. Then he grinned at her. "You will call me Jacob if you want to know what I discovered about your dagger last night."

Her fingers curled into impotent fists. The man made her

want to hit something. Mostly, his cocksure face. "What did you learn?"

His brows arched, clearly waiting.

The name curdled on her tongue till she spat it out. "Jacob."

"There. Was that so hard?" He still was. His cock pointed toward her merrily. "You know, Fenwick's a thoroughly capable chap, but it's much more satisfying to wake to a pretty face like yours. Makes a man glad to be a man."

"Yes, well . . ." There was certainly no questioning his masculinity. She looked away, aware he'd caught her gawking at his male attributes. "Perhaps you'd do me the decency of covering yourself."

"Haven't seen one angry in a while, eh?" he said as he ambled toward the bed and pulled off a sheet to wrap around his waist. "But if we want to be sticklers for decency, Julie, may I point out that you're the one who burst into *my* bedchamber? And I distinctly remember you promising that you're not easily shocked."

"I meant about whatever we might discover in the course of our investigation," she reminded him, trying not to react to the diminutive "Julie." She refused to give him the satisfaction.

"Does that make this a social call then?" He cocked a brow at her. "I like the sound of that."

"You're insufferable." The sheet slid down on his hips, revealing a thin strip of dark hair starting at his navel that widened as it disappeared into the bulge beneath the linen at his groin.

"Yes, I am, aren't I? Too bad you need my services, but there it is and no help for it. Ah! Here's Fenwick with your tea and, if there's a God in heaven, my shave." He ran a hand over his stubbled jaw. "A nice close shave makes a man utterly civilized."

Julianne perched on a small chair near the window while Fenwick poured out a steaming cup for her. "In your case, I suspect it would take a good deal more than a shave."

"Now, now," Jacob said. "Is that how friends speak to each other?"

"We are not friends."

"Yet," he said with cheer as Fenwick draped a silk banyan over his broad shoulders. Jacob dropped the sheet and inadvertently gave Julianne a final look at his private parts, quiescent now, but still of formidable size, before he knotted the sash at his waist. Then he settled into the only other chair in the room while Fenwick stropped the straight razor.

"What did you learn about the dagger?" When he didn't answer immediately, she added, "Jacob."

He flashed a quick smile. Then he assumed the tortured expression men adopt to flatten the angles of their face for a shave while Fenwick lathered his cheeks with foam.

"For one thing, I can offer you the comfort that I'm certain your husband didn't take his own life."

She blinked in surprise. "How were you able to prove that so quickly?"

"I didn't say I could prove it. Simply that I know it. He was murdered. Without question. We'll get to the issue of how and by whom later."

While it was gratifying to find another soul who agreed with her about Algernon's death, evidence that he hadn't killed himself would have been much better. "I assume we'll need to go to Cornwall for that, so you can examine his study."

"I already know what happened in his study."

"How do you—"

"That's none of your concern," he said briskly. "What I

don't know is the precise mechanism of how the deed was done and at whose behest, but you're right. We will need to eventually return to your husband's home. Am I correct in assuming the other daggers are there?"

She nodded.

"In a safe?"

She shook her head. "But no one will ever think to look for them in their present location, I assure you. When the time is right, I will explain." When he started to protest, she held up her hand. "I've not demanded to know how you came by your knowledge of my husband's death. I was warned your methods might seem mysterious. I ask you to extend me the same courtesy."

"Fair enough. Let us make a pact. Mysteries are allowed, but no lies. What we share with each other must be the unvarnished truth," Jacob said, rising as Fenwick wiped a dab of soap from his earlobe. "The etching on the blade is the symbol for the Ancient Druid Order. Today, you and I will visit the old chaps and see if we can find a true believer among the poseurs and fakes."

"Druids?"

It seemed the height of anachronism in Queen Victoria's thoroughly Christian England to imagine the existence of a group dedicated to that ancient pagan practice.

"My husband received a number of letters from . . . oh, I can't remember the name of the fellow now, but the letterhead was from the Ancient Druid Order." When she'd gone through her husband's correspondence after his death, she'd found several missives from someone connected with the Order. She'd assumed it was merely a club of some sort, not a serious religious group. "He kept asking most insistently for the earl to come to London to speak to their group about his collection of daggers."

"Hmmm," Jacob said. "A name would have been helpful, but the fact that your husband received those letters means we're on to something. Did the earl contact them first or they him?"

Julianne cast about in her mind, trying to remember the contents of the letters. "It's difficult to say. When I was going through Algernon's things, my mind was . . . preoccupied. I missed him. I thought reading his papers would help me through a difficult time. These letters were very esoteric, very scholarly in nature, so it's hard to say which of them initiated their common interest in the daggers."

"He never visited the Order, I assume."

"No." One more letter came after Algernon's funeral, still urging the earl to visit. She'd sent back a short note explaining that her husband was deceased, and received a stilted note of condolence with no further mention of the daggers.

Then as her period of mourning drew to a close, the other letter came, the cold, business-like one, from a gentleman who wished to remain anonymous. He made an offer that seemed the answer to all her problems. Could there be a connection?

"Druids," she repeated softly. "Algernon said the daggers were old, but I never dreamed—"

"Oh, the metal is far older than the Druids," Jacob said with confidence. "But I hope we'll find someone who's familiar with the lore about them among the members of the Order. Fenwick, see what you can discover about where this group meets, who its leader might be."

"Right-o, sir. I'll send for a runner straight away." Fenwick gathered up the tea service.

"Oh, and while you're at it, contact Mr. Marleybone and tell him to sell all my brother's railway shares. Today, if possible."

Fenwick nodded, disappeared out the door, and turned toward the back staircase. "Should have something for you within the hour."

"That quickly?" Julianne said. "Your Mr. Fenwick is a man of many talents."

"He is that." Jacob chuckled. Of course, it also helped that several Bow Street investigators owed their most public successes to Jacob's private assistance. He wasn't shy about calling in favors when the occasion warranted.

His brows drew together. "Be warned. Once we peel back the social club aspects of this group, I suspect we'll find a core of adherents with some . . . bizarre rituals and private activities."

"Theatre people live for bizarre ritual," she quipped.

"Not like this. At least I doubt it. These sorts of groups usually have a . . . primitively sensual component. You'll have heard of the Hell Fire Club, I expect."

Lily Parks, who served as a prop mistress for Drury Lane Theatre, told her once about attending a meeting of the Hell Fire Club back when Lily was still young enough to "trod the boards." Lords and their ladies, members of Parliament, and judges used the Hell Fire Club as an excuse to throw off convention and commit acts of lewd and flagrant immorality. Surely the person who'd sent Algernon such dry, intellectual letters wouldn't be involved in that sort of thing.

"The Hell Fire Club is no longer in existence," she said.

"No, but the spirit of the club lives on, and I suspect it has found a new incarnation in some faction of the Druid Order. I'd bet my best shirt on it." His gaze sizzled over her in unspoken lust. "If we commit to this course, once we're in with these people, we won't be allowed to bow out gracefully. You have your title and wealth. Be sure you want to risk your reputation for the sake of this search before we proceed."

Julianne swallowed hard. She'd always have the title of

dowager countess. Her stepson had no control over that, but now that her mourning period was all but finished, he could wreck havoc with her finances and personal freedoms. Unless she produced all six daggers for her mysterious buyer by mid-December, her choices would dwindle considerably. A title wouldn't buy bread, wouldn't clothe her and put a roof over her head, or keep her promises to the ones who were depending on her.

The fact that she could claim a "milady" wouldn't help Mrs. Osgood and the foundlings under her care one bit. Julianne knew what it was to live hand to mouth. She couldn't bear to see the school for orphaned girls she'd founded crumble and its residents thrust back onto the unkind streets of London.

Her stepson was committed to beggaring her if she didn't marry some horrid little backwater baron who was a friend of his from his days at Eton. So she considered her remaining options with a practical dispassionate eye.

Julianne loved the theatre, but she couldn't go back to that vagabond life. Besides, her years of playing a convincing ingénue were dwindling fast. She'd seen plenty of leading ladies end their days sewing costumes for others in near-sighted poverty. She wouldn't settle for that.

She had the education and style to be a top-tier courtesan, but if she wouldn't surrender to a loveless marriage, she'd also be no man's plaything, something to be used and cast away on a whim. She'd be her own mistress.

Reuniting the daggers was the only way to bring about that happy state. Her anonymous buyer was prepared to part with a king's ransom for them. But, once she reached London, another note in the same handwriting had been left for her at the Golden Cockerel with terse instructions that if she missed the deadline, all deals were off.

This was her only chance. She'd endure whatever she must

for a season in order to live as she wished for the rest of her life.

"My mind is made up," she said. "We proceed as planned."

"As you will," he said with a nod of grudging respect. "Now I suggest you repair to the parlor." His smile turned wicked. "Unless of course, you'd like to help me dress. We could practice for our sojourn among the pagans."

She hurried out of the chamber, his masculine laughter chasing her all the way down the stairs.

Chapter 4

"The countess come to town by coach, just like ye said she would." The ragged boy swiped his nose on his sleeve and continued with his tale. "Then she settles into the Golden Cockerel, y'know the one, that fancy new inn hard by Victoria Station. After that, she visits a few shops for gewgaws and such and—"

"You related all this to me yesterday," Sir Malcolm Ravenwood said, wondering if the boy possessed sufficient intelligence to be a useful tool. His gazing ball could have told him as much, and without the odor of unwashed boy stinking up his study.

"Aye, guv, so I did. It just helps me to remember things if I start at the beginning, y'see." The boy's eyes rolled up and right as he searched for the thread of his story again. "And when ye gave me that note for the lady, I nipped over to the inn and left it for her, like ye said. Then I found her again after that, taking tea with some old biddy from Drury Lane. And then, the lady goes to Blue Gate Fields."

Malcolm frowned. "What's a countess doing in that part of town?"

The boy shrugged. "She spent a bit of time at a house hard by St. George's Chapel. All full of girls, it was." He made the small grimace of distaste for females only boys too young to have hair on their balls could manage. "Mighta been a school. It looked to be in better shape than the other houses on the block. Them girls was all dressed alike when they come out to bid her good-bye. Made over her something fierce, so they did."

Malcolm considered this a moment. He hadn't expected it of a former actress, but obviously, Lady Cambourne was a benefactress of the school.

Good. People who championed an altruistic cause were easy to manipulate if that cause was threatened.

"Then the lady makes for a house off Leicester Square," the boy said with a triumphant grin.

The grin faded when Malcolm continued to stare at him without comment.

"It were a Mr. Preston's house. I got the name straight from his housekeeper." He shifted his slight weight from one foot to the other. "And a fresh bun from the kitchen when I asked could I sweep chimneys for her."

"Preston, hmm?" Sir Malcolm repeated, wondering why the name tickled his memory. *Could it be the rakish brother of Lord Meade?* Jacob Preston's only talents of note were betting consistently on the right side of wagers at White's and wenching his way through the unhappy wives of the Upper Ten Thousand. "Was the man's name Jacob Preston?"

"Aye, guv, that's the one. The lady"—he pronounced the word as if it were "li-dey"—"were there a long time, waiting on him, I fancy, as the gentleman hisself come along much the later." The urchin bobbed his head like a sparrow on a window ledge, as if that nervous tick added veracity to his words. "And then she come back early to his house again this morning. Then the lady and the gentleman bundled off in her fancy coach together, thick as thieves, so they were."

Malcolm drummed his fingers on his desk, setting the

wings of the stuffed bat on one corner atremble. "Where did Lady Cambourne and Mr. Preston go?"

The boy eyed the bat with suspicion, as if he half-expected it to leave its wire perch and flap around the room. "Well, your worshipfulness, I'm fair fast on me feet, but even I can't outrun a pair of bays."

When Malcolm scowled, he hurried to add, "But I did hear the gent tell the driver as they wanted the King's Arms Tavern, off Oxford Street. Once I heard that, I nipped off straight here. I thought as ye'd want to know directly."

The boy held out a grimy paw. His lips thinned in a tight, hopeful smile.

Malcolm fished in his pocket and came up with two coppers. He flipped them across the desk. One rolled off before the lad could nab it and he was forced to scuttle on his knees after the coin. He came up with both of them, grinning and thanking Malcolm as if he'd been given diamonds and pearls.

"There's more where that came from for a lad who can keep his mouth shut and his eyes open. From now on, you may ignore the whereabouts of the lady. Watch Preston. I'll expect a daily report."

The boy nodded vigorously. "Aye, ye'll have it, sir. I'll watch 'im like a hawk."

"Don't let him know he's being watched. No more hanging about the kitchen door hoping for scraps. You'll attract someone's notice that way." Malcolm narrowed his eyes till the boy seemed to shrink into his grubby collar.

Power was useless if one was hesitant to employ it, and Malcolm rarely hesitated. Grown men had been known to cower under one of his silent curses. He wasn't surprised to see the boy's thin hands shake as he surreptitiously made the sign against evil alongside his trembling flanks.

"N-no, sir, I won't let no one see me."

"Good. Now go."

The boy took to his heels. Malcolm's lips twitched in a satisfied smile. Properly motivated by enough fear, the lad just might be able to outrun a pair of bays.

Malcolm stood and looked out his gothic arched window. His home was on the Penton Rise, so from his top floor vantage point, London spread out before him, its spider-leg streets stretching in all directions. If Jacob Preston was headed for the King's Arms, he'd likely already made the connection between the daggers and the Order. That tavern was their regular public meeting place.

It wouldn't be right for Preston and the countess not to be met by someone who could send them in the correct direction, so Malcolm threw on his cloak and descended four flights to the street. He'd call on Lord Digory, the nominal head of the Ancient Druid Order, and offer to stand the old windbag to a midday pint.

And if they should fall into chance conversation with a countess from Cornwall and a rogue from Leicester Square, Malcolm would be in perfect position to take his enemy's measure.

Oh, he meant to use Lady Cambourne and her associate, right up until they uncovered the remaining dagger. But there was no doubt in his mind that they were the enemy and not to be trusted beyond that.

When a person spent too much time near a thing of power, it called to them, drew them to it with silken cords, making it impossible to part with. Surely Lady Cambourne had already been in contact with the daggers long enough to realize they were more than simply interesting artifacts.

Perhaps her husband had even explained their true function before his tragic demise, Malcolm mused as he pushed through the knots of people crowding the narrow streets around St. Paul's. He'd learn more once he arranged for Lord Digory to be his unknowing shill for this morning's outing.

* * *

The yeasty smell of bread and beer greeted Julianne's nostrils as Jacob held open the door to the King's Arms for her. The interior of the tavern was dim, the wooden benches and booths dark with age. Decades of soot stained the stone face of the massive fireplace along one wall. Nearly every seat was filled with rough-edged patrons hoisting pints or falling to their trenchers with gusto. Evidently, the quality of fare offered at the venerable establishment was beyond the common in both food and brew.

Curious eyes raked over her and she realized there were no other women in the tavern who weren't wearing a serving apron. Several men nudged their neighbor with an elbow as she passed by. Julianne felt decidedly overdressed for the King's Arms in her mauve merino wool skirt and bodice with its smart cream rosettes. She'd have caused less stir if she were still wearing the horrid black crepe of deep mourning. No one looked twice at a woman in widow's weeds.

She gave herself a stern mental shake. When did she ever fear making an entrance? She raised her chin and strode forward into the gloom.

Jacob steered her to an empty booth in the far corner and ordered shepherd's pie and ale for them without consulting her. Julianne bristled a bit. She was his employer, not his companion. He ought to defer to her more. The serving girl deferred enough for all three of them, dimpling prettily when Jacob smiled at her. She scurried away to do his bidding with a saucy flip of her skirt.

Julianne scanned the sea of faces. There were burly, stub-nosed workmen, spindly shopkeepers and ink-stained clerks with scarves wound around their necks against the autumn chill. An odd assortment, but none of them looked as if they'd have a scholarly interest in a set of Druidic daggers.

Julianne imagined more than a few of the laborers would know how to handle one in a brawl, though.

"How will you be able to tell if there's anyone here who—"

Jacob cut her off with a wave of his hand when the serving girl returned with frothy mugs in each hand.

"Pulled that meself, so's it'd be fresh. Your pie'll be up in a bit, sir. I do hope everything's to your liking." The girl leaned forward, offering him a long look down her low bodice. As an afterthought, she tossed a glance at Julianne. "Yours too, ma'am."

Julianne decided the girl was fetching in a speckled pup sort of way. And as annoying as one who'd just piddled on the floor.

"Thank you, m'dear, but you should address her as 'milady,'" Jacob said. "This is the Countess of Cambourne."

The girl's eyes widened and she dropped a quick curtsey. "Begging yer pardon, milady. We don't generally get no quality folk in here, except some o' them Dru—" She stopped herself by worrying her bottom lip.

Julianne smiled thinly at her.

Jacob leaned toward the girl confidingly. "Were you about to say Druids?"

The girl cast a quick glance toward the tavern's owner and nodded. Then her gaze dropped, as if she wished to guard her thoughts. "Yes, sir, I was about to say . . . them."

"In that case, I'm wondering if you could help us with something."

"O' course, guv. Anything," she gushed, obviously hoping for a change of topic.

The chit's expression turned positively puddingheaded. By her breathy "anything," Julianne suspected the girl really meant she was ready to bear Jacob's children.

"So it's true that the Druid Order frequents this fine establishment from time to time?" Jacob said.

"Aye." The wary look was back, like a doe sensing menace in the thicket, but not quite able to identify its source. "It's not their regular day, ye understand."

"No, I suppose not, but I'm wanting to make their acquaintance," Jacob said. "Do any of the members drop by at other times?"

The girl shrugged and then nodded. "When they take a notion."

He laid a coin on the table. "If any come in while we're here, if you could point me in their direction, there's another guinea in it for you."

She scooped up the coin, her cornflower blue eyes glinting with renewed interest. Her broad smile returned. Clearly whatever trepidation she felt over the Druids' occasional presence could be overcome with the right amount of money. "If I see any of those gents, I'll be sure to tip ye the eye."

Jacob's gaze followed her for a moment as she flounced away.

"That's not all she'll tip you," Julianne said, irritated that the thought of Mr. Preston tumbling a barmaid made her feel so waspish.

"But it'll do for the present," Jacob said with a wicked grin as he hefted his pint. "To the success of our endeavor, milady."

Julianne clinked her mug with his. "To our *timely* success." The note her anonymous buyer had left for her at her inn was unequivocal. The deadline for delivering the six daggers was set in stone.

But that wasn't the only thing she found troublesome about the note. The fact that it came to the Golden Cockerel for her at all, and within only a few hours of her arrival in London, meant someone was aware of her movements. She glanced around the common room again. She didn't catch anyone at it, but she couldn't get over the sensation that someone was watching her.

She decided to return the favor, marking each newcomer who pushed through the front door. After a few minutes, a pair of gentlemen who stood out from the normal clientele entered the tavern.

The shorter one was dressed in a fashionable walking suit, though the horizontal stripes on his gray trousers did nothing to add the illusion of more height. However, the felted beaver top hat more than made up for that oversight. The little fellow seemed to be arguing with his more imposing associate, gesticulating wildly as he spoke.

Julianne swallowed back a smile. She suspected the man would be mildly entertaining in the manner of all those who are addicted to the sound of their own voices.

She didn't watch him long. After a second glance, his companion was far more interesting. Tall and broad, the man was easily Jacob Preston's match for size. But while Jacob was dark, this man's pale blond hair was all the more striking because he wore only black, topped by a rather theatrical cape instead of a double-breasted frock coat like his friend.

His features were sharp and raw-boned, his nose handsomely hawkish. Deep grooves were carved between his pale brows and his jaw seemed solid as granite. Then he smiled at his smaller friend and his face changed from that of a brooding demon to a beneficent archangel. Still warlike in countenance, but now blessed with the quality of lightness as well.

Julianne's belly fluttered slightly in response to the sight of a singularly attractive man.

"Find someone you'd like to tip the eye?" Jacob said as his gaze swiveled from the newcomer to her and back.

"Of course not. I'm simply trying to discover if one we seek might be here." Julianne buried her nose in her ale, pleased to discover it was rich and yeasty as warm bread. She was saved from further explanation when the girl returned with their pie. Its wholesome aroma reminded Julianne she'd skipped breakfast. She forked up a bite of the flaky crust and steaming gravy. "Delicious."

Jacob pulled a three-tined fork from his vest pocket and did the same. The white metal didn't shine with the same patina as silver, but neither was it rough pewter, like the forks the tavern had provided.

"Do you usually bring your own tableware when you dine out?" she asked.

"Always."

"Why?"

"A friend of mine is studying to be a physician. According to George, there are tiny little beasts called 'germs,' so small we can't even see them. He says that's what causes sickness in London, not the foul air of the Thames. At any rate, George claims these germs live everywhere, moving from person to person like minuscule lice." Jacob looked around the room at their salt-of-the-earth dining companions. "At least, when I bring my own fork, I know whose mouth it has been in."

"Ugh! Trust you to ruin my meal."

"Nonsense. I'm sure yours is fine. George has been known to be wrong about a good many things. Eat up."

Because the delightful smells had made her so hungry, Julianne did—but only after she scrubbed her fork with her coarse napkin for the space of about a minute.

In case this George person was right about tiny little beasts called germs.

Chapter 5

"Your money's no good here, Digory," Malcolm said, plunking down sufficient coin on the bar. "This one's on me."

"Much obliged, Ravenwood." Lord Digory stopped talking long enough to quaff down half his drink. It left a foamy mustache on his protruding upper lip, which he licked clean with a smacking sound. "Lady Digory is being swayed by those pestilential temperance busybodies. There's not a drop of spirits in the house. She still allows me wine with dinner, but I ask you, what's the world coming to when a man can't have a wee dram in the comfort of his own parlor?"

"In that case, we'll make the next round whisky," Malcolm said, signaling to the barkeep. "Make it your best single malt, Tobias, and step lively."

The man scuttled behind the bar where the better bottles were kept. The light-skirted barmaid passed by Malcolm and his companion without a second glance, intent on following her employer.

Malcolm had considered the wench a time or two when the Order met at the tavern. She was comely enough in a raw sort of way. He preferred women with more polish himself, but she'd be an adequate vessel for some of his adherents when the next clandestine gathering was scheduled.

"Tobias," she said, half-whispering, but Malcolm was keen enough of hearing to make out her words. "We got us a real honest-to-God countess in here this day."

"Where?"

"In the back booth."

Lord Digory was pontificating about the evils of the temperance movement again to everyone in general and gaining several "Hear, hear's" and nods of approval from the surrounding patrons. Malcolm was free to let his gaze and his attention wander.

Even in the dimness of the tavern, he could tell that his glimpses of Lady Cambourne in his gazing ball had not done her justice. She was fine-boned, delicate as china, with large, speaking eyes and a waiflike point to her chin that made a man want to shelter her. The curve of her bosom made him want a number of other things.

She was exquisite. It was easy to see why the old earl had overlooked her somewhat tawdry background to make her his countess.

She'd do just as well as a queen.

The barmaid's urgent whisper interrupted his thoughts. "I was wondering have ye any of them fancy biscuits left?" she said to Tobias. "I'm thinkin' we ought to give her and the gent she's with a bit o' something extra just for dressin' up the place. If they likes us, they might bring in more of her snooty friends and ye can raise yer prices."

"Check the pantry." Tobias reappeared with a bottle of Glenlivet he had to dust before opening, and poured up two jiggers for Sir Malcolm and Lord Digory. The baron clinked his drink with Malcolm's and downed it in one gulp. He signaled for another.

When the girl reappeared with a tray of sweets, Malcolm

grabbed her arm as she passed. Her eyes flared for a moment when she recognized him, and then she cast her gaze to the tips of her slatternly shoes.

Did she somehow sense what he'd like to do to her at the next gathering of his secret sect? he wondered. He'd even make sure she enjoyed some of it. The line between pleasure and pain was a blurry one. It needed to be crossed on occasion in order to be certain where one was.

"Did I hear you mention that a countess is with us this day?" Malcolm asked.

She nodded.

"Her name," he said, tightening his grip on her forearm.

The girl winced and rolled her eyes. "The Countess of . . . Can . . . Cambore."

"Cambourne?" he supplied helpfully.

The girl nodded with vigor and tried to wiggle out of his grasp.

"Cambourne!" Lord Digory lifted his snout from the jigger long enough to repeat the name, then knocked the contents back with barely a sputter. "Why, that was the fellow who was in possession of those ceremonial daggers, wasn't it? Of course, it was. I have a memory like a steel trap. The old earl might not have been one of us, Ravenwood, but by gum! He knew his history. Pity he did away with himself." Digory glanced around the room. "I should so like to meet her."

"She's right over there," the girl said with a toss of her head. Lord Digory lifted his foppish lorgnette, a throwback to an older age, and peered in that direction. "The lady's with that handsome bloke in the corner. I was just after takin' them this plate o' biscuits."

"We'll take it," Malcolm said, wresting the tray from her hand. "Come, Digory. You can give the lady your personal condolences."

"Yes, by all means. Quite."

The baron adjusted his jacket, trying to make it hang straight over his paunch and failing miserably. The fashions of the day were unkind to Lord Digory, a fact of which he seemed blithely unaware as he strolled toward Lady Cambourne.

The man sitting with the countess rose as they approached.

Jacob Preston. He might be accepted in higher circles than Malcolm could aspire to, but only on his brother's account. Despite his wealth and privilege, Preston was a mere commoner.

Far beneath a knight of the realm, Sir Malcolm thought with understandable smugness. Even though Preston was on his feet, there was no deference in his gaze. The way he stood, shoulders back, hands fisted, it was more a challenge than an expression of respect and polite self-deprecation.

Cheeky bastard.

In a vague, disconcerting way, Malcolm recognized a bit of himself in Preston. The man seemed to sense real power didn't lie in rarified titles, but he probably didn't know what Malcolm did. Power was in the air, in the elements, waiting for an adept man like himself to harness and use it.

When Lord Digory reached the dim corner, he sketched a courtly bow.

"The Countess of Cambourne, I presume. Allow me to introduce myself. I am Baron Digory, but you might recognize me better as head of the Ancient Druid Order. I believe your husband and I were onetime correspondents. At your service, milady."

He bowed once more over her proffered hand as she thanked him.

"And may I also present my associate?"

Digory's manners always became more stilted when a bit of whisky warmed his belly.

"Sir Malcolm Ravenwood." Digory waved his hand in Malcolm's direction.

With barely a nod of acknowledgment to either of them, Preston plopped back down and returned his attention to his trencher.

"May I offer my sincerest sympathy for your loss, countess?" Digory said.

"You're most kind."

Her voice was low-pitched, sultry even. Malcolm remembered she'd been an actress before her marriage, a good one by all accounts. She obviously still knew how to charm an audience. She introduced Jacob Preston, who barely looked up from his pie. Then once Malcolm presented the tray of biscuits, Lady Cambourne invited Digory and Malcolm to join them.

"Not wishing to seem indelicate"—Lord Digory began and then blundered ahead without the slightest hint of delicacy in any case—"but would you still happen to be in possession of those daggers about which your husband and I corresponded?"

She glanced at Preston, who appeared to be preoccupied with stuffing overly large bites of mutton and potatoes into his mouth. "Yes, I still have them."

"Unusual that your husband didn't see to it the daggers went to his heir," Malcolm said. For a man not to hand such power on to his son was unconscionable, but the manner of the earl's death proved he had no magecraft in his soul. Perhaps Cambourne hadn't known the full extent of the daggers' strength.

Until the end.

"My stepson has no interest in such things," Lady Cambourne said briskly. "The weapons remain in my keeping and I'm looking for more information about them. My husband was so taken with the set, you see. It eases the pain of his parting for me to continue his interests. I've engaged Mr. Preston to assist me in my search."

Jacob Preston looked up for a moment and bared his teeth in a wolfish smile. Then he shoveled another bite into his mouth and washed it down with a large swig of ale without adding a thing to the conversation.

"A commendable way to honor the earl's memory," Digory said. "Perfectly understandable, my dear. Is there any way I might be of assistance?"

She glanced at Preston as if expecting him to take the lead, but when he didn't, she plowed ahead. Malcolm thought he detected irritation glinting in her large brown eyes.

"I'm sure a gentleman of your scholarship is steeped in the lore surrounding this sort of artifact," she said. "If you could share any information you might have about the set of daggers, I would be most grateful."

"Actually, I meant since they can only be a reminder of your sorrow, the Order would be pleased to offer you something for them and take them off your hands."

"Oh, the daggers aren't for sale," she said quickly.

Care to wager on that? Malcolm thought.

Digory puffed himself up, a nattily dressed little toad of a man. "I would like nothing better than to aid you, but the rules of my Order constrain me. To be honest, Lady Cambourne, the lore of the Druids is forbidden to the gentle sex."

If she was offended, she hid it well. Her smile was intoxicating. "Oh, I quite understand, Lord Digory, but surely a man of your considerable enlightenment is aware of the changes in our modern society concerning what's appropriate for my gender." She leaned toward him, and Digory seemed to melt a bit. "Why, a petition was even lodged in the House of Lords urging that august body to grant universal suffrage for women—"

"Eight years ago and nothing has been done with the petition to date," Malcolm said stonily. If she wanted information about the daggers, he'd make sure she had to come to him.

She flicked her gaze toward him, barely concealing her annoyance over his statement of the obvious. Proud, intelligent, and blithely unaware how powerless she really was.

How lovely it will be to humble her, to teach her the way of things and make her beg in quivering need.

"Lord Digory, in view of the unique nature of the artifacts in my possession, surely you'd make an exception just this once. If we might be able to attend one of your meetings—"

"Impossible."

She fiddled with the jaunty slant of her bonnet, adjusting the bow near one ear. "In case you're unaware, before I married Lord Cambourne, I was an actress of no little talent. I could come disguised as a man and I promise you, no one would be the wiser."

Lord Digory laughed. "Forgive me, my lady, but no one could mistake one of your delicacy and beauty for anything other than a woman, no matter how well disguised."

"I'll bring one of the daggers for your membership to examine." Tears made her eyes glisten like amber, and she reached across the table to lay a slim, gloved hand on Lord Digory's forearm. "Please."

Digory screwed his mouth to one side and made a small noise of frustration. "I greatly fear I'm unable to comply. But I'll tell you what I can do. A week from this Saturday, Lady Digory and I are hosting a little soirée at our home. The members of the Order are allowed to bring their wives to this sort of event. There'll be dinner and dancing and then when the ladies retire to the parlor, Mr. Preston can join the gentlemen for port and cigars. It won't be the same as a regular meeting of the Order, you understand, but a great many things of interest will come up for discussion then, I assure you. Especially if Preston brings the dagger with him."

Lady Cambourne sighed in frustration. "But my lord—"

"We'd be delighted," Preston said, those few words the first indication he could do anything with his mouth besides chew. He wiped his fork on his napkin and stowed it in his vest pocket. "Come, my lady. It's past time for your appointment at the modiste and now you'll need a new ball gown, no doubt."

Lord Digory smiled indulgently as they took their leave. "What do I always say, Ravenwood? Women are all the same. As easily distracted as children and all it takes is a bit of French lace. Suffrage for women indeed!" He shuddered. "Unthinkable."

Malcolm watched them leave, wondering at the rather unusual behavior of Mr. Preston. Taciturn and surly in the company of his betters, then lifting a fork from the King's Arms, of all things. He was either a very odd duck, or he wanted them to think he was and so underestimate him.

"Yes," Malcolm agreed with a frown. "Unthinkable."

Jacob gave the driver the name of the mantua maker's shop favored by the fashionable. Julianne bit her lip to keep from countermanding him. Admitting she was a bit light in the pockets might make Jacob reconsider his decision to help her.

She hoped she could afford a new gown without having to pawn some of her jewelry. She hadn't worn anything but the pearls and jet for a long while, but she'd brought some of her good pieces to London with her, just in case. She hated to part with them for an unnecessary extravagance like a ball gown.

She was relying on the more costly pieces Algernon had given her to tide her over if she couldn't find the last dagger in time. Her ruby necklace would support the work of Mrs. Osgood's school for a couple years, so she didn't count that piece in her available stash of portable wealth.

"You were no help at all in there," Julianne said through clenched teeth as soon as she and Jacob bundled back into her coach. "I might as well have had a sack of potatoes beside me. You left me to do all the talking."

"So I could do all the listening," Jacob said smoothly, rapping on the ceiling of the coach with the head of his walking stick to signal the driver they were ready to go. Then he drew the coach curtains, leaned back, and shut his eyes. "A man's ears close when his mouth is in motion. He's busy thinking about what he'll say next instead of listening to the other fellow."

He made sense, but she didn't want to admit it. "Well, a woman has more experience in listening while she speaks because if she didn't, she'd never get a word in edgewise. And what about that Sir Malcolm thinking the blades should have gone to Algernon's ruddy heir? As though my stepson gave two figs for his father or anything he cared about. Algernon would spin in his grave if he knew—" She bit back the rest of what threatened to tumble out. "All right. If you were listening so intently, what did you hear that I didn't?"

"That Digory is willing to bend the rules for you by inviting us to an event normally reserved for members only. This will work to our advantage."

"How so?" She wished he'd look at her. It was disconcerting to converse with a man who might drift off to sleep at any moment. "I'm still relegated to the parlor for tea and tedious talk with the women while you—"

"Do what you hired me to do," Jacob said. "Do you think I won't share every bit of what I learn there with you?"

"Won't Digory be expecting you to and not be as forthcoming on that account?"

"I think that depends on how much he wants to see the dagger." The coach was a small one and Jacob's shoulders were uncommonly broad. He opened his eyes, sat up straight, and draped an arm around her over the back of the seat so they fit together more easily on the forward-facing squab. "I won't be as quick to offer it up as you were."

She eyed him narrowly. "If you wanted me to do something differently, you might have said so."

"Never mind. You did fine, Julianne. Truly." His hand grazed her shoulder in soft slow circles. She ought to make him stop but it felt so wickedly good. Agitation drained out of her with each small caress.

"But if the dagger is to leave your safe, I want it with me," she said with emphasis.

"Fear not." He slipped a finger under her chin to turn her face toward him. "The dagger isn't going anywhere. It will remain in the safe."

"But you said—"

"We'd be delighted to attend his soirée." He leaned closer and she inhaled his male scent, rich with spicy bergamot and sandalwood. "I didn't promise to bring your dagger. He only assumed I would. Among my less than savory associates, there is a skilled artisan who can create a reproduction for us. Your actual dagger will be in no danger."

His gray eyes darkened from ice to burnished pewter as he gazed down at her. His mouth was so close she could almost taste it. She swallowed with difficulty.

It wasn't the dagger that was in danger just now. It was her determination not to become involved with a man who was in her employ.

"But if he learns the dagger isn't the real one, then . . . then how will you pry any secrets from him?"

"My associate is very good at what he does, but if by some chance Digory is smarter than he looks, I'm not without a bit of skill myself. How does anyone learn another's secrets?" He brushed her lips with his and pulled back. "I'll have to make him want to tell me what he knows."

Heaven knew, he was making her want. The memory of

Jacob's kiss from last night was burned in her mind. His breath warmed her slightly parted mouth. She flicked her bottom lip with her tongue. Then she leaned toward him, closing the distance between them, and kissed him back.

She hadn't meant to. It was just that he was so close and male and so vibrantly alive. He made her body remember what it was like to feel real.

There was a time when she'd felt real only when she was onstage, where she might slip off the skin of the poor, common girl who was born in Cheapside and become anything—a goddess, a temptress, a murderess, or a whore. Each night, she tried on other selves as a person might try on a set of clothing. She lived and sometimes died in their most harrowing moments and emerged from the side stage door in one piece when all was said and done.

It was as if her life outside the theatre—the grubby little rented rooms, the endless travel to the next town, the playhouse politics and jealousies—was the fantasy. The only words that tasted true in her mouth came from the script, the only real passions were the ones she indulged in character each night, twice on Saturday counting the matinee.

In some ways, becoming Algernon's countess was the best role of her career. But it was only a role.

Jacob's mouth on hers was real. This kiss wasn't scripted. It just happened. The way her blood pounded in her ears when he kissed her wasn't contrived. No audience was hanging on every move waiting to see what happened next. His hand on her skin—

She realized he'd unbuttoned her bodice without her being aware of it and now traced the lacy edge of her all-in-one peeping above her corset. Her nipples hardened at his finger's nearness. His mouth traveled along her jaw and down her throat. He kissed his way across her shoulder bone.

He slipped a finger under the lace and brushed her nipple

with his fingertip. Desire shot to her warm, moist center. She sucked her breath over her teeth.

Her body flared to raging life as he kissed his way down to the hollow between her breasts. He untied the bow on the neckline of her undergarment with his teeth and peeled back the linen to bare her pink nipples just above the heavy boned corset. He closed his lips over one and suckled her.

The jolting coach faded around her.

She'd had lovers before her husband. What actress hadn't? She'd had a briefly satisfying time with Algernon when he was able to keep his vow to "worship" her with his body. After he died, she'd been tempted to welcome a man to her dowager's bed.

But she'd never wanted anyone with as much white-hot longing as she wanted Jacob Preston.

She slid her hand inside his jacket, down the front of his shirt and vest. A man's warmth radiated through the fabric. The image of his naked body rose in her mind. His chest was rock hard.

She suspected another part of him was too.

But before her hand drifted lower to find out, Jacob stopped paying skillful homage to her breasts and raised his head.

"The coach has stopped. We must be there." He began re-tying the bow at the neck of her all-in-one.

Her mouth gaped. "Is that all you can say?"

His gaze sizzled into hers. "What do you want me to say? That I'd rather lift your skirts and swive you senseless than continue to work on your case?"

He slid a hand under her petticoats and hoops and ran his palm up her leg. The thin linen of her undergarments was no shield against the shivers that trailed in his fingers' wake.

"It would be the truth," he admitted.

Her core throbbed. He covered her sex with his hand, holding her hot mound. A fingertip found the slit in her undergarment and slipped into her wet cleft. She closed her eyes and bit the inside of her cheek to keep from moaning.

"Shall I tell the driver to take us around Hyde Park a few times?" he asked, his voice a sensual rumble in her ear.

She ought to say no. She ought to remember her late husband. She ought to keep in mind what would happen if she didn't find that other dagger in time. But when Jacob's fingers moved slowly over her delicate parts, all she could do was feel.

"Driver," she heard Jacob say as if from a great distance. "Three trips around the park, if you please. And . . . take your time."

Chapter 6

The coach's shades shut out the world and threw them into partial darkness, but she didn't need to see anything. Jacob's mouth covered hers, swallowing the needy little sounds that tore from her throat. His wicked hand was back between her legs, discovering all her secrets, laying her soul bare with each stroke.

Julianne wouldn't have stopped him for worlds. She spread her knees wider, hitching one over his lap, to give him complete access.

"Lord, you're so sweet," he said, his voice hoarse with need. He released her mouth and started back down to her breasts again. She untied the bow before he got there and lifted her breasts a bit so more of them would be free of the restrictive corset.

He sucked her nipple in rhythm with the rocking coach, in rhythm with his hand on her slit. She tilted herself into his fingers.

Heat. Friction. Warm wetness. She was slick and swollen, aching for him. Desire licked over her in tingling lashes.

He circled her nipple with his tongue while his thumb circled her sensitive spot. She made a small noise of distress. He slid a long finger into her. His thumb continued its maddening game.

She reached down and cupped his groin hard. Through the flannel of his trousers, his balls tensed under her touch. Then she ran her palm over his hard length from root to tip with no gentleness at all.

He growled with pleasure and fastened his lips around her nipple, tugging at her needy flesh. He found the right spot between her legs and stroked her toward her goal with a few deft flicks. She was there before she knew her peak was about to surge.

The wave of release came so fast, it crashed over her without warning. Her entire body shuddered with the force of her inner contractions, her limbs bucking. She seemed to leave her house of flesh momentarily, tossed high into a realm of pure light. Then she slammed back into her body as the last ripples shivered over her, spent and gasping.

When the capacity for rational thought returned, Jacob was kissing her again, his mouth soft on hers.

Coaxing her back from wherever she'd been.

Now it was her turn to send him there. Her lips curved in a feline smile, she moved to the seat opposite him, tugged off her gloves and undid the first button at his waist.

The interior of the coach smelled slightly of her faint camellia and strongly of the sweet musk of sex. Jacob's body responded to both scents. Julianne's voluminous skirts didn't allow him a peek up them, not with all the layers of petticoats and hoops, but her lovely breasts were still on display as she worked with concentration on his trouser buttons.

She was a wonder.

He wanted to tell her so, but he was hesitant to say a word, lest he break the spell. His tongue clung to the roof of his mouth as she made short work of the fastenings on his drawers.

His man Fenwick, who'd never been lucky in love, claimed all women were part witch. Had Julianne hexed him with silence? When her fingers found his bare flesh, Jacob decided he didn't care if she had.

His cock sprang free of his clothing, but she wasn't content until she'd exposed his scrotum as well. He watched her face while she studied him. Her mouth hung slack as she slid a questing fingertip around his balls, making every wiry hair stand at full attention. She ran her knuckles between his testicles and up the full length of his penis, pausing to thumb the rough skin just beneath the head.

Jacob shuddered with pleasure and willed the pressure in his shaft to drop. Despite his best efforts, a pearl of fluid formed on his tip. He reached over to stroke her breasts. Her nipples tightened, ripe pink berries.

"You're beautiful," he whispered.

"So are you."

She lifted her skirts and climbed onto his knees, settling herself near his groin. With all the hoops and petticoats bunched between them, it was a good trick, but the tickling warmth of the curls between her legs finally pressed against his shaft.

Thank God for the French.

They might be England's perennial foe, but they were geniuses when it came to women's undergarments. The fellow who designed the all-in-one to have an open crotch should be awarded a knighthood at the very least.

The coach hit a pothole that sent both Julianne and him airborne for a moment. They came back down hard with the stiff busk of her corset smacking his top lip and her breasts settling on either side of his nose. His lip stung, but the rest of him was jubilant.

Jacob laughed, deciding it was a fair trade, and covered her breasts with kisses. When he scraped his teeth over her nipple, she made little mewling sounds of pleasure that sent his groin into near spasms.

"Much as I'm enjoying this, we'd better get down to business," she said with a small chuckle. "Hyde Park isn't that large."

She shifted her weight and the tip of him slipped through the slit in her all-in-one. He didn't enter her, more's the pity, but he was close enough for the wetness of her arousal to coat him. He bit his lip to keep from spilling his seed like a callow lad.

"Oh, you're bleeding a bit." She leaned forward and kissed his injured lip softly.

"Guess that corset of yours was laying for me." He licked his top lip and tasted the coppery tang of blood.

"It's not so bad." She reached into her reticule and pulled out a handkerchief to dab the bit of broken skin. "But it may swell later."

"I know something that will take my mind off my injury." He rocked himself under her.

She sent him a perfectly wicked smile and tilted her hips, luxuriating in her own arousal.

Finally, a woman who knew the joys of her body and reveled in them as much as he did.

He wasn't sure God listened to lascivious prayers, but whatever he'd done to deserve this, he hoped the Deity would show him what it was so he could be certain to do it again. Soon.

Julianne reached between them and guided him into herself.

"Angel woman," he breathed as she engulfed him in her hot tight channel. His hips rose to meet her but because of their position in the coach, she set the pace.

Her eyelids drooped as she moved on him, losing herself in her own pleasure. Soft light filtering along the sides of the coach's window shades showed her pink-tipped breasts to devastating perfection. They spilled over the lacy but implacable corset, bouncing joyously as she moved. She raised her arms to steady herself with splay-fingered hands on the coach ceiling.

Jacob reached between them to spread her labia and circle her clitoris, silently blessing George. His physician friend had lent him the medical texts where he'd learned the proper names for a woman's parts and their many delightful uses.

Her head fell back, her bonnet hopelessly askew. She arched her spine in pleasure, her rhythm ticking up.

Jacob groaned.

He thrummed a nipple with his other hand, then slid down to press her hips more firmly onto him. What he wouldn't give for a bed so he could spread her out and torment her properly.

Then Julianne began some torment of her own.

She stopped suddenly, looking down at him with hooded eyes, an unspoken dare raising her brows.

Forget angel woman. Now there was a succubus on his cock, promising pleasure and bringing him to the brink only to deny him. Jacob almost pleaded with her to continue, but it wasn't in his nature to beg. Instead he started stroking her, teasing featherlight touches that had her panting in short order.

She moved on him again and he resumed the pressure she seemed to need. A low feminine growl of desire escaped her throat.

He tried to smile at her, but knew it was more of a grimace. His aching erection made a true smile impossible. He was close, perilously close. He needed to pull out but he wasn't ready to sever their connection yet. If he could only feel her come around him, know he'd served her well before he let himself find release.

Julianne leaned forward to kiss him. Their tongues played against each other, a warm, wet joust, as they pushed on toward the pinnacle. He arched his hips up, pressing into her as deeply as he could and she cried out.

Her first spasm began, fisting around his cock while he teetered on the brink of losing control. She pulsed hard. Rolling contractions in her inner walls made her whole body shudder. When he felt the first spurt of his semen rushing upward, he lifted her off him, snatched her handkerchief and covered himself with it.

He pumped steadily for about half a minute, eyes closed in the fierce pleasure of release. Even when it ended, his breathing was still ragged. His heart rate slowed from a gallop to a canter.

As wonderful as part of him felt, another part felt . . . cheated somehow.

He didn't know why that should be. He always withdrew at the crucial moment. It was the gentlemanly thing to do.

Why did it feel so wrong this time?

Julianne slid over to the opposite seat, smoothed down her skirts and fiddled with her bodice. She covered her breasts and tied the lace over them in a neat bow. She struggled to do up her buttons. Her cheeks were flushed.

"Here," he said softly. "Let me help."

"I'm perfectly capable of fastening my own buttons," she said, her voice tight.

Did she feel it too, that odd sense of loss? For a brief moment, they'd been more than the sum of their combined parts, but now they were separate, their souls safely locked in their own houses.

"I know you can do it yourself." He reached over to slip the last button deftly into its hole with a flick of his fingertips. "But why should you have to?"

She expelled all the air in her lungs in a long huff. "I owe you an apology, Mr. Preston."

He chuckled. "I think under the circumstances you'd really better call me Jacob, don't you? And what the devil are you talking about? You've done nothing that requires an apology. On the contrary, I think we both owe each other a bit of thanks."

"No, I must. It was unconscionable for me to . . . to take advantage of you like that."

"What do you mean?" He rearranged his own clothes as the coach made a lumbering turn and slowed. He stuffed the soiled handkerchief into his pocket. Mrs. Trott would read him the riot act for it, but he was accustomed to his housekeeper's scolding. "Feel free to take advantage of me any time you wish. I do not feel the least abused, I assure you."

"But you're my employee. I have never . . . well, it was most unseemly of me," she said stiffly. "I apologize if you felt obliged to—"

He stopped her with a finger to her lips. "First, I never do anything because I feel obliged. Second, I'm not your employee. Consider me your partner in this endeavor, if you must, but that is as far as I'll allow. Since we've yet to come to any agreement about payment, there's no question of my being in your employ."

She batted his hand away, her cheeks darkening with embarrassment.

The direction of the conversation was making him testy. Usually his lovers were only too quick to hang on his neck and beg him to name the time for their next assignation. Julianne merely scooted farther away from him each time he leaned toward her.

"Ours is supposed to be a professional arrangement." She

adjusted her bonnet and retied the bow with jerky movements that threatened real violence to the delicate laces. "This"—she waved a hand vaguely—"this changes everything."

An alarm bell jangled down Jacob's spine. Now he remembered why he'd always insisted that his lovers be married women. Was Julianne the sort who believed sexual congress outside the bonds of matrimony must be remedied by an immediate plunge into leg-shackled martyrdom?

He wouldn't have thought so.

"How does this change everything?" he asked suspiciously. The coach shuddered to a halt and Jacob figured they'd reached the modiste's shop again.

"If we surrender to our baser natures whenever the urge strikes, it will divert us from our purpose, and we haven't the time for it," she said, shooting him a look worthy of a spinster governess. Jacob could scarcely believe she was the same woman who'd ridden him with wild abandon only a few moments ago. "And besides . . ."

"And besides what?"

"If you must know, it changes the balance of power between us. Regardless of whether or not you feel yourself in my employ, you are acting at my behest. How can I expect you to take direction from me properly if you . . . if we . . ."

"What makes you think I ever intended to take direction from you?"

"You accepted my case."

"Perhaps because I thought it would be the quickest way under your skirt," he said with a grin, hoping to lighten the tone of the conversation.

Her hand flew so fast, he didn't see it until her palm connected with his cheek.

"How dare you!"

Damn! The vixen had slapped him.

"With very little effort at all actually," he said, heat rising on his neck. "You certainly didn't make me beg. Can you deny you wanted this as much as I did?"

She pulled back her arm for another swipe at him, but he caught her wrist this time. Good thing too. Her hand was balled into a fist for a ringing punch instead of a ladylike slap.

"Get out of my coach," she ordered.

"No."

"Then release me at once. I won't remain in your company for another moment."

"Fine. Leave." He leaned back so she could climb over him if she wished. "But if you go, you'll never get your dagger back. I'll consider it payment for services rendered."

Her eyes narrowed to glittering slits. "I will scream and the driver will come to my assistance."

Jacob shook his head. "He'll be on my side."

"Blast it all, you're probably right. Men always stick together." Her face crumpled. She folded her arms across her chest, quivering with rage. "I can't afford this kind of distraction. There's too much at stake."

A distraction? Was that all their heart-stopping joining was to her?

"You don't understand. How could you?" she muttered. "You're a man."

"A fault for which I cannot be blamed. Perhaps you'd care to take it up with my Maker, since it's obvious you feel yourself His equal," he said. "You've been reading Wollstonecraft, haven't you?"

He wasn't the least surprised when she nodded. The writings of Mary Wollstonecraft put all sorts of odd notions in women's heads.

"But she didn't tell me anything about men and my smaller place in the world because of them that I didn't already know," Julianne said.

He rolled his eyes. "You've neatly damned half the race. I ask you, what's wrong with being a man?"

"Nothing." She snorted. "The world believes the sun rises and sets on a pair of ballocks. Don't you think I'd change my gender in a heartbeat if I could?"

He blinked hard at that. "In God's name, why?"

"No matter how mean he may be, a man is still captain of his own fate," Julianne said. "You've never had to be at the mercy of others."

"I fail to see how—"

"Are you treated as if you were an imbecile or a child, incapable of understanding the simplest matters of business or scholarship?"

"No."

"I am. You saw it for yourself in the way Lord Digory treated me in the King's Arms." She spat the words out. "Have you been used as a plaything by members of the opposite sex?"

He might be able to answer yes to that, but since he didn't begrudge the women who sought him out, it didn't seem as if he'd experienced the same distress over it she obviously had. Her eyes were wells of hidden hurts, but no tears came. He decided the best course was to remain mute.

What had happened to this woman to make her so bitter?

She sniffed and pressed her palms against her cheeks in an effort to lower her high color. "Are you able to enter into business for yourself without the assistance of others?"

"Yes, of course."

"I can't. If I wish to invest my own funds, I have to hire a man to carry out my wishes," she said. "Suppose you marry. Will you forfeit all rights to your own property?"

"No."

"A woman does." She glared at him as if he were the source of all the inequities she named. "And if you do find a way to support yourself, as I did in the theatre, do you know what it is to fear you'll lose your hard won place to someone younger, prettier, or more willing to spread her legs for the director and his friends?"

She didn't meet his gaze any longer, though he doubted she saw the tufted velvet seat back at which she stared.

"When you were a child, were you ever—" She stopped herself with a hand to her mouth. Her shoulders quivered and her eyes were unnaturally bright, but she still didn't cry. She drew a deep breath and mastered herself.

If she'd only continued, he suspected he might have learned the source of her guilty fear.

"That's not important now." She met his gaze, her eyes clear. "Here is it, baldly then. I only want the freedom you enjoy merely by virtue of your gender. However, my stepson demands I marry a man of his choosing or he'll cut off my allowance altogether. I'll have nothing."

"Many women find comfort in marriage," Jacob said. "Your own marriage to the earl does not sound as if it were unbearable."

"It wasn't, but the man my stepson expects me to accept is a swine with two feet," Julianne said. "I will not exchange my freedom for the dubious hope of comfort. I have a buyer for the set of daggers, but only for the full set. It is a sufficient sum for me to keep myself comfortable for the rest of my days. But I must deliver them all by December fifteenth."

Her shoulders sagged. "The truth is if I cannot find the last dagger and sell the set, I will not even be able to pay you whatever you intend on charging me."

She stared at the white-knuckled fingers clutching her skirt.

Gently, Jacob took one of her hands and smoothed out the tension in her fingers. "Well, then. That gives me all the more incentive to help you, doesn't it?"

She looked up at him. "There's no need to go to the modiste's. I can't afford a new ball gown."

"My credit is good."

"There, you see. This is precisely what I mean. Things have changed between us already. You feel as if you have to take care of me simply because we . . ."

"Because we gave each other a bit of ourselves?"

The words surprised Jacob as they came out of his mouth. He'd always seen sexual congress as an extremely pleasurable, but ultimately animal act. For the first time in his life, he allowed that something else, something much deeper, might have passed between him and this woman with whom he'd joined his body.

He raised her hand to his lips and pressed a lingering kiss on her knuckles. "Julianne, I have no desire to change you. I want you to remain as independent as you wish and I'm committed to helping you acquire the means to do so. If that means a new ball gown, I expect you to accept it in the spirit with which it's offered. Will you do that?"

She searched his face and nodded. "Thank you, Jacob," she said, palming the cheek she'd so recently slapped with her other hand. "You do understand, after all. But with all that's at stake, I'm sure you agree we simply have to make certain this sort of lapse in judgment doesn't happen again."

"I can't promise you that." He circled her knuckle with his thumb. In fact, he could almost guarantee that now they'd been intimate, it was bound to happen again. Frequently. "I've never been particularly sensible about that sort of thing."

She tugged her hand away with gentleness and pulled on her gloves. One corner of her mouth turned up in a wry smile. "Then I guess I'll have to be sensible enough for both of us."

Chapter 7

There were myriad things to do before the night of Lord Digory's soirée. The French modiste Jacob took her to see did miracles with a length of silk moiré. Nevertheless, Julianne had to endure several fittings for her new rose-colored gown before Jacob pronounced it worthy of her. She couldn't rightly complain since he was paying the considerable bill, but the man certainly believed in getting his money's worth.

Or perhaps he simply enjoyed seeing how much he could make her blush with merely the heat of his gaze during those fittings. Julianne felt each flick of his gray eyes. When his lingering gaze touched her shoulder, her waist, the curve of her breast with unabashed admiration, he set her skin dancing from across the room.

She suspected the wicked rogue knew full well he was doing it too.

They visited the artisan who'd been hired to create a believable substitute for the real dagger. His work was exceptional and should fool the most skilled examiner. When the replica was finished and Jacob laid it beside the real one, Julianne couldn't be certain which was the original, though Jacob was adamant that he could tell them apart.

"The fake blade has a magnetic charge, but it's much

weaker than the real dagger," he'd explained. "It was important to include that feature, in case the members of the Druid Order know to look for it."

Jacob also took her to meet his fencing coach, an expert in weapons of all kinds, but the man had never heard of the set of Druidic daggers. And he had no notion why anyone would fashion magnetic blades.

When the last day of her half-mourning passed, her stepson sent a missive ordering her to return to Cornwall immediately. She sent the coach back empty instead.

Jacob decided it would be best if Society believed he was courting her. It would explain why they were seen together with such regularity and should distract any who might take an interest in their search for more information about the daggers. So, they attended lectures on Egyptian hieroglyphs and gallery openings for fledging painters. They strolled through the Crystal Palace to view the remains of Prince Albert's grand exhibition, seeing and being seen by all the right people.

There'd been no repeat of the wild coupling in the coach. Now that Julianne's equipage was rattling back toward Cornwall, she was careful to insist that she and Jacob hire only open air barouches for their traveling needs. Jacob demanded she allow him to foot the bills for their search, and since she was short of funds, she agreed. She didn't really feel guilty about this added expense for him. It was his fault for being such a temptation. The man ought to pay for his devastating charm and all-too-amazing sensual skills.

By night, they attended the theatre, and one evening, Julianne arranged to meet the prop mistress, Lily Parks. She'd taken tea with her when she'd first arrived in London and hadn't expected to do it again. Her life on Drury Lane felt as though it had happened to someone else. She and Lily had run out of conversation fairly quickly.

But even though she and Jacob made the rounds of all the

fashionable places and crossed paths with many people she'd met when she'd first wed Algernon, Julianne received no invitations from the *haute ton*. She was lonely for some feminine companionship and Lily's was a friendly, if unfashionable, face. So they met again in one of the few coffeehouses that allowed unescorted female patrons.

"You made the *London Crier*," Lily said, shoving the tabloid across the small table. "You and that fancy fellow you've been keepin' company with."

"Really?" Julianne scanned the short article.

> We note, with unconcealed pleasure, the return of Lady C. to London society. This one time actress-turned-countess has always been entertaining, both on and off the stage, and one wonders what new scandals the merry widow has in store for our fair city.
>
> She's been seen in close company with a certain gentleman, the notorious Mr. P., a fellow with high connections and low sensibilities. Our gentle readers will recall his many amatory exploits and the warnings we have issued about the cad in previous columns. Well-bred young ladies would do well to take warning should Mr. P. decide to desert his current paramour, Lady C., and roam the haunts of the ton once again.
>
> But in light of the Earl of C's untidy demise, one feels one should sound a note of warning to Mr. P. as well. Let the lessons of the animal world guide you, Sir.
>
> A black widow feeds on her unwary mates.

Julianne flipped the damning paper over with so much force, her china cup rattled in its saucer. No wonder Society's doors remained closed to her.

"Good review, what?" Lily said between sips of her chocolate.

"It's absolutely scurrilous. I should sue for defamation of character."

"Nonsense. They're talkin' about you, ain't they? That's all a review is good for," Lily said with a dismissive wave of her heavily veined hand. "Didn't you always say it don't matter a fig what they say so long as they talk about you?"

"But this isn't the theatre, Lily," she said with a frown. "This is my life."

"Same thing, dearie. Only difference is when you're off stage, you can play more fast and loose with the script." Lily popped a petit four into her mouth, wrapped up three more in her napkin, and secreted them in her disreputable bag, along with one of the silver teaspoons.

Julianne sighed. She should have met Lily in a less posh establishment where the temptation wasn't so great for one with light-fingered inclinations. Then she wondered if Lily feared for her place in the theatre. Once Julianne sold the daggers and set up her own pension, she promised herself she'd look into providing for Lily and those like her on Drury Lane who didn't have much laid by for their advanced years.

"And speaking o' the theatre, when you coming back to us?" Lily asked.

"I'm not coming back."

"Sure you are. Once a body gets greasepaint in the blood, there's no way to get it out." Lily leaned forward confidingly. "I heard rumblings that Mr. Farthingale is hankering to do Othello and word is, he knows you're in town and thinks as you'd be the perfect Desdemona."

Wonderful. She could look forward to being strangled by a jealous husband nightly.

"What d'you say?" Lily urged. "Mr. Farthingale says you'd pack the house."

Undoubtedly, she would. It wasn't every day a dowager countess trod the boards. The *ton* would come from morbid curiosity, and leave satisfied that Julianne had finally learned her true place.

"You already know the role, I'd wager." Lily's wheedling tone was starting to dance on her last nerve.

Julianne knew Desdemona. Every word. During her days in the theatre, when she wasn't in rehearsal for one role, she was studying others she intended to take up one day. Once, her life onstage had been the only source of truth and beauty, the only real thing in a world of fakes, and she dove headlong into it.

But that was before she met Jacob Preston, she realized with a jolt. Before she started to . . . need him.

She groaned inwardly. No. She couldn't allow it. Her dependence on Jacob was a temporary thing. Once she had the daggers and made the sale, she'd cut him loose with a substantial payment for his time and trouble. She wouldn't owe him anything.

"O' course, maybe you're thinking of taking up another role," Lily said with a shrewd wink. "Mrs. Preston, perhaps? A good-lookin' bloke, that and with more than two coppers to rub together in his pocket, I'll warrant."

"No, Lily," she said with firmness. "Mr. Preston is certainly a fine diversion, but I don't intend to marry again. Ever. Men make women . . ."

"Happy?" Lily offered.

"Weak," Julianne corrected. And she would never be weak again if she could help it.

Contemplating weakness brought something Jacob had

said during their first conversation bubbling to the front of her mind. She leaned forward and lowered her voice, lest she be overheard.

"Lily, do you remember when you told me about going to the Hell Fire Club?"

Lily laughed, a rough cawing sound. "I'm not likely to forget it, am I? Lord, that takes me back. Did I tell you the honorable Charles Fox was there? Fancied me, he did. You should have seen 'im when he—"

"Never mind about that," Julianne interrupted. The couple at the next table had cut their eyes toward Lily for the third time. Julianne continued in a whisper and hoped her friend would reciprocate. It would be too embarrassing to be asked to leave this establishment because Lily had no sense of propriety. "What I want to know is if there are any clubs of that ilk still about in London?"

Lily's gray brow arched. "The Hell Fire's gone, o' course, but there are rumblings of another," she said softly. "I just hears snatches, you understand. They wouldn't take an old crone like me in, that's for sure."

"What do you hear?"

"Well, the Hell Fire Club was mostly about folk doing what came naturally. Oh, a few were unnatural too, I suppose, but it were all about having a rip snorting time. And there was always a few who fancied a good paddling, which I guess don't do a body harm if everyone's agreeable to it. But one of the girls in the chorus—Mina Pitt, it were—she went to this new club and she told me . . ." Lily's voice dropped to such a low whisper Julianne had to lean forward to catch her words. "Well, the further you get into it, the more it's about whips and chains and some sort of religious mumbo-jumbo instead of a bit of harmless swiving. Not my cup of chocolate, that's for sure, but it takes all sorts, they do say."

Lily tipped up her cup and drained it to the flaky dregs.

"But trust me, you don't want anything to do with this new bunch, dearie," she said, swiping her mouth on her sleeve. "After she went to this new club a second time, Mina didn't come back to the theatre. I never saw her again."

Julianne left a generous tip at the coffeehouse to cover the spoon that Lily absconded with, and returned to the Golden Cockerel. She'd allowed herself plenty of time to dress and prepare for Lord Digory's soirée. The inn would provide a lady's maid to assist her for a price, so she'd arranged for one. Since the bodice of her new gown fit like a second skin, she couldn't lace herself tightly enough to fit into it without assistance.

She'd chosen the Golden Cockerel for its extra amenities and reputation as a haunt of the Upper Crust. After that horrible piece in the *London Crier*, she realized she needn't have bothered. They'd never accept her no matter where she stayed or what she did.

Since she'd lived hand to mouth a time or two, Julianne knew what it was to squeeze a copper till it squealed. The extravagance of such a high-toned hotel now chafed her thrifty soul. Especially since it meant she'd had to pawn the lovely little ruby ring Algernon had given her in order to pay the bill.

When she entered the opulent lobby, she was surprised to find Jacob there. He was ensconced in one of the wing chairs by the common room's fireplace. His long legs crossed, he was sipping tea and, much to her chagrin, reading the latest edition of the *Crier*.

"You're early," she said, wondering if he'd run across the article about them yet.

"I thought you might require my assistance," he said pleasantly, flipping the paper to the next page.

"Thank you, no," she said in an embarrassed whisper, still

begrudging the extravagance of hiring a temporary servant. "I've already engaged a lady's maid for the evening."

He folded the paper neatly and tucked it under his arm as he stood. "I'm not here to help with your toilette, but it's a charming idea. Wish I'd thought of it."

Her face heated as if with fever. She could have kicked herself. There was something about this man that made her say the most ridiculous things.

"I daresay, barring the hair dressing, I'd have made an admirable abigail for you," he said with a grin. "But alas, I'm only here to escort you to your room."

She blinked in surprise. "That's neither necessary nor appropriate."

"Maybe not appropriate, but definitely necessary." He took her arm and led her toward the staircase. "One of my boys says there's a fellow snooping about this establishment."

"One of your boys?"

"I hire a number of them to be my eyes about town. I tasked one to observe you whenever I'm not with you."

Maybe that accounted for the prickles between her shoulder blades whenever she was out and about. "You should have told me."

"It might have changed how you behaved. Unfortunately, I'm not the only one interested in your comings and goings. My lad, Gil, says the man he's been watching sneaked into the hotel this afternoon. Based on his dress, Gil is certain the fellow is not a guest." Jacob stopped at the landing. "If he's still in your chamber, I'd rather you not meet him alone."

In my chamber? Julianne lifted her skirts and scurried up the rest of the way. Her heart sank when she saw the door was ajar. Her hand was almost on the knob when Jacob pulled her behind him, laying a warning finger to his lips.

Stay back, he mouthed. Then he gave the door a swift kick

and burst into the room, brandishing his walking stick like a cudgel.

"It's all right," he said after a few moments. "He's gone."

But someone had definitely been there. All the drawers in the chifferobe were turned out, her lacy undergarments tossed about. The bedclothes had been yanked off and dumped in a pile in the middle of the room. The mattress lay askew, half on, half off the bed frame. One of her pillows had even been gutted, its feathery innards lying in downy piles.

"Is your jewelry missing?" Jacob asked.

"Hang the jewelry," she said, making a beeline for her traveling trunk. The lid was propped open and all the little compartments had been rifled through, but nothing seemed to be missing. Her sapphires set in silver, the emerald choker, the ruby pendant big enough to choke a horse were all where she'd left them. With relief, she found her ivory cameo in the bottom of the trunk. It was yellow with age and the tin setting was thin and misshapen, but she'd had it as long as she could remember. It was the least valuable piece in her collection, but if she had to part with her jewelry to support herself, it would be the last to go.

Clearly the man was after something else. She depressed a hidden lever in the trunk, praying he hadn't realized it had a false bottom. She eased a bit of ribbon from the tight side joint and gave it a slight tug.

"Oh, thank God." She breathed a sigh of relief. "It's still here."

"What is?" Jacob stood over her to see what she had.

"The manuscript." She lifted the fragile sheaves of parchment and carried it to the dressing table to make certain it hadn't been damaged. "Remember I told you provenance was the most important thing about establishing the authenticity of ancient items? This manuscript is what Algernon used to discover the whereabouts of the five daggers."

"I had no idea you'd brought it to London with you. You should have told me about it," he said gruffly.

"It might have changed the way you behaved," she parroted back to him. Careful to touch the delicate sheaves only on the upper corner, she turned the pages of the ornately worked book. It had suffered no new damage.

"Eighth century?" Jacob asked, peering over her shoulder at the fantastical beasts writhing in the margins of the handwritten codex.

"Late seventh, Algernon said."

She stared at the text, but since it was in Latin, she couldn't read a word. Given her haphazard education, she counted herself fortunate to be able to read English. But there was an illustration on the front piece that showed six daggers. With typical medieval disregard for perspective or relative size, the blades surrounded a human figure bedecked with light in the guise of gold leaf. For that reason alone, she knew there was another dagger to be found.

"After my husband studied this, he traveled about Britain for a good half year, visiting various sites and odd wayside shrines. When he returned, he had five daggers in his possession."

"Why only five, do you suppose?" Jacob asked.

She turned the manuscript over to show him that the bindings were frayed and the back cover missing. "The manuscript has been vandalized at some point in the past, split in two. Algernon thought it was divided for the same reason the daggers were separated from each other—to keep them safe from discovery."

"Has it occurred to you that some things are best left undiscovered?"

She frowned up at him. "It crossed my mind. Especially after Algernon died. But even if I didn't complete the set of blades, it would not bring him back." And selling the set would help her and the children of Mrs. Osgood's school beyond knowing. "I'm hoping Lord Digory or someone else among the Druid Order has the rest of the manuscript. Algernon believed he'd find clues to the whereabouts of the last dagger in the remaining text. Perhaps we could arrange for an exchange or—"

"No," Jacob said. "It's important that no one learns you're in possession of this manuscript."

She looked around at the disarray of the room. "I suspect someone already knows."

"Maybe not," Jacob said. "The fellow who ransacked this place might have been looking for the daggers themselves."

"But I'm sure Lord Digory knows about the manuscript. He mentioned it in his letters to Algernon and seemed almost as interested in that as he was the blades. If he has the rest of the manuscript, why shouldn't we try to rejoin the pieces?"

"If they have the second half, wouldn't they also have been able to find the missing blade?" Jacob asked.

"I don't know," Julianne said. "It was only Algernon's guess that the location of the final blade was in the last half of the book. The text is not straightforward. Maybe the Druids simply haven't figured out how to decipher the clues."

"That may not be the problem," Jacob said, narrowing his gaze at the final page. "The first part of the text is in Latin. This near the end is in some other language."

It was all curving lines and squiggles to her. "Can you read it?"

"No. It's not Greek, either, which exhausts my knowledge of ancient languages. But we have more pressing issues at the moment." He crossed the room to give the bell pull a hard yank. "We'll need some help to pack you up. It's not safe for you to remain here. You are removing from this hotel immediately."

"And where am I going?"

"I have plenty of room in my home."

"Out of the question." She didn't have much of a reputation to begin with. She'd have none at all if she stayed at Jacob's town house.

He snapped his fingers as an idea struck him. "Then I'll take you to my cousin, Viola," he said. "Lady Kilmaine, I mean. You'll like her. Her husband Quinn is a decent chap as well. They'll be delighted to have you."

After the article in the *London Crier* denouncing her as a black widow, Julianne took leave to doubt that.

"Did you have a chance to read all the paper today?" she asked. "If not, I direct your attention to the *on dits* on page three."

"I saw it." He snorted. "In case you didn't notice, they were no more charitable toward my sins than yours. Though I can't fault them for accuracy, at least on my account."

"In light of all this, what makes you think your cousin would welcome me?"

Julianne could count on one hand the number of genuine female friends she'd made over the years. There'd been too much jealousy. Too much scrabbling for the same limited means. During her stint in the theatre, they were all jostling for the same role.

Or the same director's bed.

Once she married Algernon, the women of his class were either benignly neglectful or openly scornful toward her. She wasn't sure she hadn't preferred the latter. At least she knew where she stood with the ones who delivered direct cuts. The ones whose voices were soothingly bland while they smiled their thin pasty smiles were the ones who made her knees knock. Arrows that came without warning sliced deepest.

"Viola doesn't put any stock in such things," Jacob said. "She's not the sort to care what others think. And you shouldn't either."

Julianne wished she didn't have to. Thumbing her nose at the world and living exactly as she pleased without fear of what another's censure might mean—that was real freedom.

That was what the six daggers meant to her.

She picked up the nightshift that the vandal had flung over a chair and tried to fold it. Her hands trembled so, she gave up and stuffed it back into a drawer. Obviously someone else wanted the daggers just as badly as she did. Her belly spiraled downward.

"If someone has been following me and is willing to risk breaking into my room, giving me hospitality might endanger your cousin."

"Don't trouble yourself on that account," Jacob said. "Did I also mention that her husband Quinn is a very handy fellow to have at your back in a tight spot? Lord Kilmaine served with distinction in Her Majesty's military. You'll be safe as houses with them."

When had she ever been safe, really? Her history with men was as dismal as her list of feminine friendships. Nothing lasted. In her most torrid affairs, nothing remained after the flame burned out. Even Algernon, her stalwart rock, had left her in the end.

Jacob would be no different.

He put his arms around her and kissed her forehead. "What's this? You're trembling." He hugged her tightly. "Don't worry. You'll be perfectly safe. I'll stay at Viola's home too just to make certain."

She leaned into him, her crown tucked beneath his chin. His heartbeat against her cheek was steady, comforting.

She was used to Jacob's nearness setting her insides aflutter. One look, one glancing touch, and her body leaped into a state of heightened sensual awareness. This calm center of safety was new.

And deceptively dangerous.

No, no, no, something inside her screamed. *You can't need anyone like this.*

If life had taught her anything, it was that she could only rely on herself. Needing someone was an unacceptable risk.

If she needed Jacob Preston, she didn't think her heart could take it when he left.

And she knew, eventually, he would.

Chapter 8

"This gown is simply gorgeous." Lady Kilmaine ran a slim palm over the rose silk laid out on the bed so the shimmering fabric wouldn't wrinkle. Jacob's cousin had not only welcomed Julianne heartily as a guest in her elegant Mayfair home, she'd made every effort to show herself friendly. "You have wonderful taste."

"That's Ja—Mr. Preston's doing," Julianne said from behind the dressing screen. "He chose the pattern and the material for the gown. I'm afraid I've been rusticating in Cornwall for the last few years and couldn't be trusted to make a stylish choice."

"Understandable. It's difficult to remain fashionable while in mourning." Her hostess cast a sly grin toward her. "So, Lady Cambourne, my cousin is 'Jacob' to you, is he?"

Julianne bit her tongue. She couldn't afford to reveal so much to Lady Kilmaine, even if she did seem friendly. "Please don't put any stock in that informality. We've been spending so much time together, it seemed trifling to insist he call me by my title all the time. It is only natural for me to use his Christian name as well."

"Oh, I'm so glad you feel that way. I wish you'd call me

Viola. Honestly, Lady Kilmaine sounds . . . well, rather barbaric, doesn't it?" She smiled as if they were sharing a private joke at her husband's expense. "If the title hadn't come with such a devastatingly handsome man attached, I'd happily chuck it in the river."

Julianne couldn't help returning her smile. "Of course, I'll call you Viola. And thank you again for your hospitality. But you're wrong about Jacob and me. I know the *ton* believes we've formed an attachment, but actually, your cousin is . . . my partner in a business endeavor. He's helping me settle a final matter regarding some of my late husband's possessions."

It was strictly the truth and she felt she owed Viola some justification for the time she and Jacob spent together, even though she wasn't quite sure how to classify their relationship herself. Mention of the old earl should put her further off the scent.

"Hmmm." Viola's sharp-eyed gaze narrowed in speculation.

"I'm not at liberty to discuss the particulars, of course—" Julianne's words were cut off as Viola's abigail cinched her corset so tightly half the air was forced from her lungs. She grabbed another breath to finish her thought. "There's nothing between Jacob and me but mutual respect and business."

One of Viola's brows lifted in a delicate arch. "Quinn and I were . . . mutually respectful business partners to start with too." Then she wandered over to the dressing table. "Oh, these are lovely emeralds." Viola stretched out her fingers to touch them, but drew back at the last moment.

"Try them on if you like."

The maid fetched the rose gown and helped Julianne slip it over her head, letting the voluminous skirt fall in shining waves over the crinoline. Then the maid took up the hooking tool and started fastening the long row of small porcelain buttons that followed the line of Julianne's spine.

"Oh, no, I never wear emeralds," Viola said. "I usually make do with a ribbon around my neck. If the occasion requires more finery, I never wear any other stone but jet."

"Mourning jewelry?"

Her hostess shrugged. "I find those stones restful, but I can well imagine you're tired of them by now. Since your mourning has passed, do you think you'll wear the ruby this night? It would suit the gown."

Julianne stepped out from behind the dressing screen and caught her reflection in the long silvered looking glass. Jacob was right when he'd insisted she needed a new gown. She'd packed some of her old ones, but in the two and a half years of her mourning for Algernon, fashion had moved women's waistlines several inches lower, dipping into a startling low V in front that pointed toward her sex and accentuated it. The skirts had belled out to even wider sweeps. The mirror told her the style of this new gown showed her figure to good advantage.

"Oh, even better." Viola clapped her hands together. "The gown was lovely on the bed. It's spectacular on you. Jacob will be utterly helpless."

"I don't want him helpless. Honestly."

"Give us a moment, will you, Maggie?" Viola said to her maid. The girl dropped a curtsey and slipped out the door.

Here comes the truth, Julianne thought. *Now that the servant is gone, Lady Kilmaine will reveal what she really thinks of having a black widow in her house.*

"Jacob is my cousin and I care for him deeply," Viola began.

"And you don't think I'm right for him. I understand. That's why I want to assure you that—"

"No, I think you're splendid for him," Viola said. "I'm more worried about him being worthy of you. He does have his . . . quirks."

"Such as?"

"Has he told you about—well, that's none of my business, I suppose, but I just want to make sure you realize he's not trying to be difficult. At least not all the time," Lady Kilmaine said with a grin. "It's because he wrestles with such a difficult ability."

A difficult ability. Is that what they call being catnip to the rapacious she-cats of the Upper Crust nowadays?

The *Crier* had made sure everyone knew about Jacob's "amatory exploits," but Julianne hadn't expected his cousin to speak so cavalierly about them. She kept her eyes downcast. It wouldn't do for Viola to realize Julianne knew full well the extent of Jacob's considerable abilities. The mere thought of their lovemaking in the coach made her body weep with fresh longing for more of him. "Yes, I've . . . heard about his ability."

"Oh, I'm so glad he confided in you." Viola sank onto the end of the bed. "It's a heavy burden to bear alone and his sensitivity is more complicated to avoid than my own." She put a hand to the ribbon at her throat and smiled, as if that explained her odd words. "His gift is a blessing and a curse. I worry for him because it seems this modern world of ours is 'metals mad.' Everything is all steel and steam. I don't see how he bears it."

Julianne schooled her face not to react to this strange turn in the conversation. Clearly, she'd misunderstood. When Viola mentioned Jacob's ability, she did not mean his bed skills.

"On the one hand, using his gift opens up a world of information not easy to obtain by other means," Viola said with an upraised palm. She lifted the other to suggest a tipping scale. "But nothing comes without a price."

"A price?" What on earth was she talking about?

"You don't know about the sick headaches then? How like a man." Viola rolled her eyes. "Never wanting to show weakness."

"Is Jacob ill?" He seemed in robust health. Too robust, if

his body's reaction to her each time they were alone together was any indication.

Viola's brows drew together and she cocked her head to the side. "Well, it appears I've said either too little or too much. So he's careful to hide the headaches."

She must know about Jacob's opium use, Julianne reasoned. If he was plagued with headaches, perhaps that excused an occasional bleary-eyed walk through the poppies. Barely. Laudanum was responsible for so much of the pain in Julianne's past, it was hard for her to justify its use at all. "As far as I know, he's only used laudanum once since we met."

"Only once? He's doing amazingly well, but then he's always been strong. I managed to keep away from opiates myself, but as I said, the source of my sensitivity is more easily avoided. If I hadn't discovered how jet and silver could act as a shield for me, I, too, might eventually have relied on laudanum to control the adverse effects of my gift."

Gift. Sensitivity. Shield. Viola didn't appear mad. Her wide hazel eyes were clear and untroubled, but her words made no sense at all.

The hall clock on the lower level chimed the hour.

"Oh, goodness, I've kept you talking when you need to finish getting ready. I'll send Maggie back in to dress your hair, shall I?" Before Julianne could answer, Viola hugged her impulsively. "I'm so very glad my rogue of a cousin has found someone like you."

Lady Kilmaine was gone before Julianne could respond. The viscountess's kindness disarmed her. The bizarre conversation disturbed her. And the idea that Jacob had some sort of malady brought on by a mysterious gift dismayed her beyond words.

Half an hour later, Julianne descended the stairs to the foyer where Jacob was waiting. He didn't hear her soft tread, so she was able to look her fill of him without being caught doing so. She drank him in, as if he were some deliciously decadent and frothy syllabub. Her insides fizzed at the sight of him.

The man was an eyeful in street clothes. In formal attire, he was blinding. The cut of his dark frock coat emphasized the breadth of his shoulders. The gray brocade vest echoed the gray of his dark-lashed eyes, and flashed with the same glinting light. The studs on his collar were the same shiny polished metal as the head of his walking stick. From his artfully tousled mane of chestnut hair to the tips of his polished hessians, Jacob Preston was the picture of sartorial splendor.

He didn't look like a man with a mysterious, debilitating "gift." Lady Kilmaine must be mistaken.

When he heard her approach and looked up, his gaze seared her with masculine approval. She nearly melted into a puddle on the landing. Somehow, she managed to descend the rest of the stairs without tripping.

"I'd tell you you're ravishing, Julianne," he murmured as he slipped a velvet cloak over her shoulders, "but I fear I'd give myself ideas."

The way her belly cavorted about, her body would welcome a good ravishing from him.

He popped a beaver top hat on his head, emphasizing his already considerable height, and placed a hand on the small of her back to shepherd her out the door. Even through the layers of her cloak, gown, and corset, her spine welcomed that proprietary touch.

"Oh, an enclosed coach," she said warily, as he handed her into the equipage he'd hired for the evening. It was one thing to admire a fine looking man and even revel in the way her body surged with life in his company. It was another to be in such a tempting situation with him. "I thought we'd agreed on using barouches."

"It's too cool for an open air drive now and will be even colder by the time we return," he said as he climbed in behind her. He rapped on the ceiling and they lurched forward. "Alas! Our destination is too close for a reprise of our last enclosed coach ride. Unless, of course, you fancy a few trips around the park again."

Julianne scooted as far as she could toward the opposite side of the small coach. She succeeded in creating only a finger-width of space between them.

"Regardless of how close or far we are from our destination, you and I decided not to give in to our baser natures again," she said, tight-lipped.

"You mean *you* decided not to," Jacob said. "I haven't stopped thinking about it."

He took her hand between his. Even though their skin was separated by his soft kidskin and her silk gloves, her body remembered his touch in exquisite detail. When his fingertip slipped into one of the eyelets at her wrist, the thin skin there rioted in pleasure. He undid the pearl button over her pulse point and brought her wrist to his lips.

"Can you honestly tell me that coach ride hasn't crossed your mind?"

After he kissed her wrist softly, he flicked his tongue over the small patch of exposed skin. Then his warm breath feathered across it.

Pleasure rippled up her arm.

"I remember every detail," Jacob said. "I remember how your skin smells, how soft your breasts are, how responsive. Did you know your nipples are the exact color of the flesh of a pomegranate? And ever so much sweeter between my lips."

Under her heavy boning, her nipples contracted into tight buds. He was still stroking her wrist in small circles, but she seemed to feel his fingertips brushing her sensitive breasts instead.

"When I can't sleep, I think about you by night, Julianne. I imagine undoing every bit of lacing, popping every button, and laying you out naked on my bed." His voice rustled over her like a piece of worn velvet, soft and decadent. "Would you like to know what I'd do then?"

She didn't have enough breath to answer, so she simply shook her head.

He ignored her silent no.

"I'd touch you very slowly, every bit of you, front and back. Every hill. Every valley."

His finger still massaged her wrist, but now she seemed to feel his touch along each rib, over the dimples of her spine down to tease slow circles above the crevice of her buttocks. She scarcely noticed that he'd slipped another button from its loop to expose more of her inner forearm.

"Then I'd kiss you," he said.

He brought her wrist to his mouth again and this time, he sucked the bit of charged flesh. Now she imagined his hand dipping between her legs to find her swollen, wet and ready for him. She closed her eyes in bliss.

"I'd kiss you everywhere," he whispered.

Good heavens . . . everywhere! Her insides churned with warmth and a dull ache. The low throb that had started between her legs when he first began stroking her wrist now had become a determined drum beat.

Even . . . everywhere?

"In my imaginings, you enjoy my intimate attentions quite a bit," he said, tugging off one of his gloves. "Do you think you would?"

Everywhere. She swallowed hard. She'd had her share of lovers, but no one had ever kissed her . . . *everywhere.* "Did you enjoy it?"

"More than breathing," he assured her and lowered his mouth to claim hers in a hot kiss.

Chapter 9

The carriage rumbled over the cobbles, sending vibrations through the padded seats. How easily they'd fallen into the rolling motion of the coach last time. How easy it would be to do it again.

She couldn't get enough of him. His tongue teased her mouth, dipping in shallow, then plunging in deep. She suckled him, welcomed him. He scraped his teeth lightly over her lips and her breath hissed in.

Would he kiss her like that *everywhere*?

She imagined Jacob's mouth on her there. Kissing, sucking, licking. The thought made her light-headed. Her thighs parted slightly of their own accord.

Then she felt his hand under her skirt and it was no mere thought. He was sliding past her knee, up her thigh, on his way to . . . *everywhere.*

Oh, the wretched, blasted . . . His fingers found the slit in the crotch of her all-in-one . . . *blessed man.*

She should have realized from her days in the theatre this could happen once he started to recount his nighttime fantasies. Every actor knew what the mind imagines, the body makes real. It was why she was utterly spent at the end of each performance. She'd lived a lifetime in the space of a few hours and her body didn't know it was pretend.

Jacob's talk of what he would do to her naked on his bed made her body respond as if he had already done it.

"Julianne." When he broke off the kiss to press his mouth on her cheeks, her closed eyelids, her temple, the way he said her name still echoed in her mind.

It only seemed right for her to respond with his. She murmured his name, chanted it.

He made her want. Outrageous things. Indecent things. Filthy, wicked, lovely things.

His fingers whipped her to aching fury. Her body tightened, coiling in on itself seeking release, as her mind wandered a dark hallway with only one exit.

In her other affairs, she'd held a portion of herself apart, a solid inviolable core no one had ever touched. Jacob wouldn't allow it. She couldn't hold back under his relentless onslaught. Bit by bit, little pieces of her dropped away and she was helpless to pull herself together enough to shelter that exposed bit of her soul. A whimper escaped her lips, a helpless needy sound.

Jacob growled in response as he drove her forward.

Harder, faster, she pleaded silently.

Julianne balanced on the edge, teetering for a few heartbeats, then her body loosened its last hold on reality and she fell headlong into Jacob's fantasy. His mouth was everywhere and she bloomed beneath it.

She came undone under his imagined intimate kiss. Her inner contractions made her whole body shudder in release. She called out, louder than she should as the coach rattled along, but she couldn't help it. She practically sang Jacob's name as her insides continued to pound, all the shattered bits of her flying away.

His kiss and deft touch drew out her climax, extending the bliss far longer than she'd ever dreamed possible. Just when she thought it was subsiding, a fresh wave started and she jerked with renewed inner spasms.

Then finally the madness began to recede and there was only his soft kiss, gentle on her lips now, and his warm hand holding her mound through the thin linen of her undergarment. Her cheeks were damp with tears squeezed from her tightly closed eyes. Somehow, all the pieces of her that shattered during her release had reassembled into a glowing whole.

She was shaken, but perfectly at peace. Balanced, but undone in ways she'd never imagined.

Then Julianne realized with a start that the coach had come to a halt.

"Are we there?" she asked shakily.

"Oh, I think it's safe to say one of us was there and back again." Jacob grinned and pressed a kiss to her forehead. "But yes, we've also reached Lord Digory's town house. Don't worry. We haven't been stopped here for more than a few minutes."

A few minutes! Anyone walking by might have heard her cry out *in extremis*. She pushed at his arm so he was no longer cradling her sex in his palm.

"It's all right, Julianne," he said softly, as if she were a spooked mare. "Take the time you need to collect yourself. All the best people come fashionably late to these sort of things, you know."

"Whereas I've come much too early." The words were out of her mouth before she thought better of them.

Jacob laughed. "Is that a joke? I didn't think you had it in you."

"No, it's not a joke," she snapped. He'd invaded her mind with his imaginings and exposed her soul. Why did he act as if nothing of importance had happened? As if only her body was involved? "Why did you do that to me?"

"With you," he corrected. "Not to you. And I don't recall you protesting. I knew we wouldn't have time for more, but it gives me pleasure to share your sensuality, Julianne."

A curl had escaped her coiffure. He smoothed it back behind her ear.

"This is going to be a challenging evening," he said softly. "I thought if you could start out feeling relaxed, it would be easier for you."

Relaxed? In truth, it was more as if he'd primed the pump. Even though she'd experienced a life-changing release, an empty ache still throbbed in her womb. She needed Jacob inside her. If her body had its way, she'd order the driver to take them three times around the park again.

Maybe four.

Then his words sank into her brain more clearly. He seemed to think she was a nervous, flighty woman who must be handled.

"So you did this simply because you thought I . . . needed it?"

Something in her tone must have sounded a warning.

"No, no, it's not like that," he said. "Hang it all, Julianne, I just wanted to touch you. Why must you make everything so complicated?"

He smoothed down her gown and put his glove back on. When he lifted the coach shades, she saw a steady stream of couples entering Lord Digory's gaslit double doors.

"If you're finished being difficult, do you think you're ready to go in now?" he asked, a rasp of frustration in his tone.

"Of course," she said, even though she suspected her knees would be wobbly.

Difficult, he says. She'd show him difficult.

* * *

Jacob usually declined offers to dine because he couldn't very well pull out his platinum fork at someone else's elegantly set table. Lord Digory's silverware had a rich patina, a classic design, and a long memory. Its pealing voice sang in Jacob's head each time he lifted the soupspoon to his mouth.

He'd have a splitting headache by the end of the night, but there was no help for it. The silver didn't have anything of importance to share with him, but images of past diners washed over him without relief. He tried not to wince. Julianne was doing her best to keep up the dinner conversation, but he had little to contribute. Jacob would be useless so long as he was fighting the metal around him.

Good thing the replica of the dagger tucked inside his vest was thoroughly sheathed in leather or he'd be in serious distress.

"The thing is, Lady Cambourne, most people have the wrong idea about Druids. We're not so much a religious order, per se, as adherents to a philosophy," Lord Digory said after the soup course was cleared and the fish arrived. "There's nothing the least barbaric or fantastical in our code. We simply believe in living in harmony with nature rather than bending it to our will. Mark my words. Steam power will be the ruination of this age."

Jacob was close enough to the head of the table to hear the conversation with their host and near enough to keep an eye on Julianne. She was seated to their host's left with Jacob kitty-corner across the broad table from her. Lady Somerset, a portly, but pleasant matron with a distracting ostrich feather nodding above her turbaned head, was on Lord Digory's right, Jacob's left. It was an ideal arrangement, and if he'd been able to bring his own tableware, he'd be enjoying himself hugely.

Except for the presence of Sir Malcolm Ravenwood directly

across from him, Jacob was well pleased with the situation. He couldn't place his finger on it, but something about the silent, brooding man made his hackles rise.

"Do you mean to say that your Order condemns progress, my lord?" Julianne asked.

She studiously avoided meeting Jacob's eye. Still miffed at him, he supposed, though why she should be was a complete mystery. He'd pleasured her without thought of taking his own. What more did the woman want from him?

He ate a bite of bread that accompanied the fish, thankful to set the silver aside for a bit.

"One must have a care for the common man. How can one call it progress when all these machines throw countless laborers out of work?" Lord Digory said, waving his soft hands loftily.

Given the lack of calluses at the base of his lordship's pudgy fingers, Jacob would lay odds Digory had never engaged in labor of any sort.

"So you're rather like the Luddites of a generation ago, then," Jacob said. That movement had turned violent when unemployed laborers destroyed the new machines that had replaced them. The government responded to the Luddites' vandalism with fierce repression and more than a few executions for machine breaking.

"Oh, no!" Digory exclaimed. "We're not a bit like the Luddites. We eschew violence. Reason is the cudgel with which we shall effect change."

Sir Malcolm's lips twitched before he lifted his glass of pale pink wine to them. The man might be Lord Digory's right hand within the Order, but Jacob suspected Ravenwood would be much more at ease with violence than reason.

Jacob swiped his mouth with a napkin and caught a faint whiff of Julianne's intimate scent still imprinted on his hand.

He drew a deep breath and the niggling residual pain from his contact with the silver receded.

Why did women spend so much on expensive fragrances when no smell devised by perfumers went to a man's head as quickly as the scent of a woman's healthy arousal?

He sent her a wolfish grin and a becoming flush crept up her alabaster neck. Did she realize he could still smell her sweet musk?

She must, for she shot him a withering glare and turned to Ravenwood. "Is Lord Digory's goal of peaceable change your aim as well, Sir Malcolm?"

"His lordship is head of the Order, Lady Cambourne," Ravenwood said.

Not a straight answer, Jacob thought.

"My late husband was quite a student of Druid history, though he didn't embrace its teachings." Julianne directed her speech to their host once again. "I gathered from him that the Romans made Druidry illegal back when they occupied the British Isles."

"Quite true," Digory said.

"I confess to a bit of confusion then. Since there haven't been any practicing Druids for hundreds of years, how do you know what the philosophy entails? Oral traditions are strong in many cultures, but I've never heard of any Druid folk tales," she said with a disarming smile. "Is there by chance . . . oh, how shall I put this without seeming blasphemous? . . . a Druidic equivalent to written scripture?"

Lord Digory was quaffing the wine in his green-tinted goblet and sputtered in surprise at her question.

He must know of some sort of manuscript, Jacob decided. Whether it was the second half of Julianne's text remained to be seen. A scowl flashed over Sir Malcolm's features, but he recovered quickly.

"This is far too serious a subject for such lovely company," Ravenwood said.

Julianne was determined to worry the issue like a terrier with a rat. "But Sir Malcolm—"

Jacob overturned his wineglass in a seeming accident, sending the rosy liquid across the gleaming damask tablecloth toward Sir Malcolm. Ravenwood leaped to his feet to avoid the spreading stain.

"Well, that was clumsy of me. So sorry. Seems I'm always bumbling where I shouldn't," Jacob said, shooting Julianne a warning glance. They'd learned what they needed to know. Pushing for more now would only put Lord Digory on edge. While the servants buzzed around the table trying to sop up the mess, Jacob turned to Lady Somerset. "Seems to me I heard your daughter Honoria will be making her come-out next Season. Am I misinformed?"

A matron with a marriageable daughter, whether she was the wife of a secret Druid or not, could always be counted upon to wax poetic over the charms of her offspring.

The topic of conversation was officially changed.

After supper, the company moved to the third floor, where Lady Digory had arranged for a small string ensemble to play the prescribed dance tunes. Julianne was presented with a gilded dance card with her partners already penciled in. Since she'd arrived with Jacob, she would dance the Grand March with him.

Her joints still felt achy and loose after the tussle in the coach. It left her feeling vulnerable. Dancing with Jacob was an equally dangerous endeavor. Being so close to him, moving beside him in rhythm, her hip against his in light touches, made her body prick to full awareness again.

Good manners prohibited them from partnering again until the final number. She was heartily relieved.

"I'll see you for the last waltz," he said, when the strains of the march ended. Jacob surrendered her to a balding viscount who led her through a jerky polka and compounded his faux pas by complaining loudly over the music about the deficiencies of the second violinist.

When the strings began a waltz, Sir Malcolm appeared by her side.

"I believe this is my dance, Lady Cambourne. May I have the honor?"

"So it is, Sir Malcolm." She curtseyed and mouthed the correct response. "The honor is mine."

He bowed slightly over her fingertips and took her into the proper position. Her hand disappeared into his large one. In short order, they were tilting and twirling around the room. For such a big man, Ravenwood was remarkably nimble on his feet. Unlike her other dance partner, this handsome fellow was quiet enough to qualify as surly.

"I hope you weren't put off by my questions at supper," she said. "It's simply that I find the whole idea of reviving Druid practice so fascinating."

Sir Malcolm looked down at her, his dark eyes unreadable, but compelling. "The Order is uncommonly strict about feminine involvement."

"And you agree with that?" she asked. "It never fails to amaze me that Englishmen who swear fealty to their queen, whom they may never actually meet, can't discuss the simplest matters with the ladies they routinely see every—"

"I didn't say I agree with keeping women from the mysteries of Druidism."

She arched a brow at him. "So there are mysteries after all? I thought it was merely a philosophy."

"To some perhaps." Sir Malcolm's gaze flicked to their host

who was holding court in the corner with a pair of matrons whose dancing days were long past. "You were right at dinner. There is a sacred text extant."

"I suspected so," Julianne said. "That must be where Lord Digory acquired his love of nature and distaste for steam power."

"To my knowledge, Lord Digory has not read the entire text," Sir Malcolm said. "But even if he had, everything is open to private interpretation within our Order. A man follows his conscience."

"Some might argue that conscience is a Christian idea." Julianne realized with a start that she enjoyed this verbal joust with Sir Malcolm. Most men would tell her not to trouble her pretty head with larger issues. Some might even laugh at her for expressing an opinion on something other than flower arrangements or dinner menus.

"All people have an inner voice which prompts them to act or not, regardless of creed," Sir Malcolm said. "The conscience, if you will, is a product of a man's beliefs and the texts he holds sacred."

"That makes sense," she said as he led her through a graceful under arm turn. "So tell me, Sir Malcolm, what do you hold sacred?"

"Power. Power to live as one wishes."

It was as if he'd read her secret desires. That was exactly what the sale of the Druid blades would bring her. She wouldn't be forced into a loveless marriage, wouldn't be beholden to her stepson for support, wouldn't have to stop supporting Mrs. Osgood's school. No one would rule her destiny. She would own herself.

"I must warn you, a fair reading of the Druid text shows us its teachings are not for the faint of heart," he said, not missing a single step in their circular route around the dance floor.

"Some of us aren't content with mere philosophy. We seek to breathe life into the Old Ways."

"Indeed?" Her heart rate increased several notches. "Are you suggesting that there is an Order within the Order?"

"Exactly. But those who seek admission to our sect must be unafraid to harness the real power of the Druids." He leaned down to whisper in her ear. "Women are welcome to our rites. In fact, they are essential to the mysteries."

Mysteries. Rites. The words smacked of the religious gibberish Lily Parks had warned her about when Julianne asked if there was a successor to the Hell Fire Club.

"How very egalitarian of you to include the weaker sex," she said.

His lips twitched. "I assure you none of our women may be called weak."

They continued to dance in silence for a few bars. As they moved about the floor, she caught a glimpse of Jacob with his partner for the waltz, the attractive young wife of a Member of Parliament.

Jacob had been sure a splinter group existed within the Ancient Druid Order. She wished she could ask him what to do now that it seemed she'd discovered an adherent to the fanatical faction, but she couldn't even catch his eye.

Nothing ventured . . .

"How might one join such a group?" she asked.

"One does not join. One is initiated." He stopped dancing and pinned her with a penetrating gaze. There was something feral, something proprietary about the way he looked at her. Her gut clenched in response. "Do you wish it?"

Oh, Lord, what now? She didn't see any other way to learn more, so she nodded. "Where do you meet?"

He put a finger to her lips to silence her.

"You have no need to know that. You will be contacted," he

said cryptically. "I understand one may find you at Lord Kilmaine's residence at present. Do you intend to remain there?"

"For now." Jacob had moved her from the Golden Cockerel only that afternoon. "How do you know where I'm staying?"

"The mysteries provide ways of knowing that are beyond your imagination," he said. "Be ready two nights hence. And be prepared to come alone."

CHAPTER 10

After another hour of indifferent quadrilles and reels and one truly ghastly mazurka, Julianne was finally paired with Jacob once more for the last dance. However, she couldn't chance telling him of her conversation with Sir Malcolm lest they be overheard by nearby dancers.

Then the party split up along gender lines. The men disappeared into a lounge fragrant with cigar smoke and fortified wines, and the women retired to the proper parlor. Most of the women took tea, but a few accepted cordials laced with laudanum "to calm their nerves" after the dancing.

It never failed to amaze Julianne that women were judged too weak to drink Madeira or port, but were offered an addictive opiate as a matter of course. Perhaps these sheltered ladies had never seen what poppy could do, how it could so warp the minds of those who craved it that they'd do anything, sacrifice anyone to have it.

Lady Somerset, who sank onto the settee next to Julianne, accepted a cordial from Lady Digory. The vile smell of laudanum was only partially disguised by the other ingredients in the drink.

Julianne's heart fluttered, a reflexive panic triggered by the sickly sweetness. She buried her nose in her teacup and pushed the spiderweb of memories away. No good could come of retracing those distant steps.

Instead, she concentrated on making proper approving nods and "mm-hmm's" while the ladies around her chatted about the latest shipment of lace from Brussels or which fashionable gentlemen were really far too light in the pockets to be considered eligible for their daughters' hands. One would never guess from the mundane conversation that their husbands were discussing anything out of the ordinary over their smokes and claret.

Perhaps that was truly the case. Lord Digory's interest in Druidry seemed as scholarly as Algernon's had been. The goal of living in peace with nature seemed naïve, given the rapid advances in industry. The way Lord Digory lived showed he thoroughly embraced modern comforts, brought to him courtesy of that industry he eschewed. Julianne judged him eccentric, but harmless.

Sir Malcolm's sect did not seem nearly as tame. Ambition sparked in his eyes when he spoke of their mysterious rites. Those who sought power didn't generally have such a benign goal as living in harmony with the natural world.

Jacob would be showing them the replica of her dagger now. She hoped it would fool Lord Digory and encourage him to share whatever he might know about its mate's whereabouts.

She was less sanguine about fooling Sir Malcolm.

"Well, what did they say about the blade?" Julianne asked once she and Jacob had thanked their hosts and climbed back into the waiting coach.

"Digory was enraptured by it," Jacob said. "He wanted to study it, so I told him he could keep it for a week."

"Do you think that wise? He might discover it's a fake."

"How? Unless he has a real one in his possession, which I

doubt. He was quite taken with the scrollwork and engraving, but there was no sense of recognition in his eyes," Jacob said, rubbing the bridge of his nose as if he were trying to smooth away the frown lines that deepened between his brows.

Lady Kilmaine had mentioned her cousin's sick headaches. Julianne wondered if Jacob had the beginnings of one now, but since he'd taken such pains to hide the infirmity from her, she couldn't show sympathy.

"I'm satisfied he's not seen the dagger's like before," Jacob said.

"Not even an illustration of it?"

"I didn't get the sense that he has the other half of your manuscript," Jacob said, neatly following her train of thought without her needing to explain. "Or if he did, that his section contained a picture of the daggers as yours does."

"What about the other men?"

"The others parrot whatever Digory says as if they haven't a brain among the lot of them." He snorted in disgust.

"Sir Malcolm too?"

"He's a different case." Jacob cast a sideways glance. "I gather you think so too. You certainly seemed intent on him while you were dancing."

She hadn't caught Jacob glancing her way a single time while she danced with the Druids. Apparently he'd taken more notice of her than she'd thought. "If I didn't know better, I'd say you sound a bit jealous."

"If I didn't know better, I'd admit that I am." He shrugged, his gesture in opposition to his words, and stared out the coach window as London rattled past them. "What were you and he talking about?"

"The existence of a sacred Druid text," she said with smugness. "He confirmed it."

Jacob turned back to her. "What else?"

"He told me about his secret sect, the Order within the Order, as it were. You warned me we might find a nest of true believers in the mix of poseurs. Sir Malcolm seems to be their head," she said. "What would that make him, an Arch Druid, you think?"

"I doubt they have a pope," Jacob said dryly. "I suppose failing that, your friend will have to be satisfied with Arch Druid."

"He's not my—" Julianne clamped her lips shut, refusing to be drawn into an argument. Instead, she told Jacob what she'd gleaned about the Order within the Order—the fact that it involved mysterious rites, accepted female initiates, and didn't particularly long for harmony with nature.

"I'm not surprised," Jacob said, dragging a hand over his face. Julianne recognized the gesture as an attempt to soothe away pain and her chest constricted in silent empathy. "He seems the type."

"If by that you mean he's charismatic, attractive, and intelligent, I have to agree. Sir Malcolm is a natural leader." She enjoyed a brief surge of triumph when Jacob scowled at that. Perhaps he really was jealous. "If Lord Digory is aware of the existence of a partial manuscript, Sir Malcolm all but confirmed that he's not read it. His ideas about the goals of Druidism are entirely beneficent. Sir Malcolm takes a much different view. I don't know why he makes such a show of standing behind Lord Digory."

"Classic misdirection," Jacob said. "Digory is his straw man. Ravenwood runs the show, yet remains in the shadows. I'm surprised you're so taken with him."

"I'm not." She bristled at him and immediately regretted being so prickly when he raised his hands in mock surrender.

"All right," he said. "Where do we find Sir Malcolm's unholy little sect?"

"We don't," she said. "It appears they find us. Or rather they find me. I've been invited to their gathering two nights from now."

"Well, that's something," he said, removing one of his gloves and rubbing his palm on the head of his walking stick. "It would make sense for them to keep whatever text they regard as 'sacred' in the place where they perform their rites. Once we're there, we'll be able to search for the other half of your manuscript."

"There is no 'we.' The invitation was quite pointedly for me alone."

"I'm sure it was," he said. "But that's out of the question. You have no idea what you may be getting into."

"I'm not a child. I knew from the outset that finding the last dagger would not be without risk."

"But this is beyond risky. It's lunacy."

Regret over being prickly faded in an instant. Jacob was treating her as if she were incompetent, helpless. Sir Malcolm had said the women of his Order were not weak. They were welcome. Essential, even.

"I did not hire you to counsel me on where I may go or not go. I hired you to find the dagger," she told Jacob. "You are not my keeper."

"I beg to differ," he said. "You hired me to help you. Consider keeping you from doing something foolish an added bonus."

"On the contrary, the only foolish thing I've done this night happened right here in this coach." She folded her arms across her chest and looked out the opposite window to avoid the sight of his damnably handsome face. "And I'm not likely to repeat it."

"Now listen here, Julianne—"

"No, you listen." Suddenly she knew exactly how to throw

him off. "Your cousin told me you live with a difficult ability. I don't think she meant you have a hard time keeping your nose out of other people's business, though you seem to struggle with that as well. What was she talking about?"

The coach passed from shadow to light as they clattered by a street lamp. For a moment, she caught a glimpse of his wary expression before they were plunged back into shades of gray.

"It's nothing," he said flatly.

"She said you have terrible headaches whenever you use your 'gift,' so it doesn't sound like nothing to me."

His lips tightened into a thin line. It was more than annoyance. The man seemed to be in genuine pain.

"What exactly is this gift, Jacob? And don't you dare try to tell me it's what dangles between your legs."

It was a low blow, but he'd started this row. She hadn't grown up in Cheapside and clawed her way to center stage on Drury Lane without learning how to fight dirty.

"You misunderstood Viola."

"No, I didn't," she said evenly. "She said her sensitivity is easier to avoid than yours. Since you're about as sensitive as a bull in a china shop, I can't imagine what she means, but the look on your face tells me you know exactly what she was talking about."

"Not now, Julianne," he said, squeezing his eyes shut.

"Why? Because your head hurts?" Just because she hadn't caught him using opiates since that first morning didn't mean he hadn't. Her aunt had been sneaky about her addiction at first too. "Have you considered the reason it hurts might be because you've abused laudanum so long, you now need more in order to feel normal?"

She knew he wasn't to blame for the devastation laudanum had left in her past, but she could still smell the cordials the women at Lord Digory's home had sipped so blithely. Opiates had cost her so much. They were the beginning of her long empty road. Like phantom pains from a missing limb, the lonely ache still throbbed in her chest.

Jacob frowned at her. "I rarely take a tonic. Only when absolutely necessary."

That was how it always began for an opium addict. First, it was rarely. Then on occasion. Finally the addict couldn't imagine a day without it.

The first morning she'd arrived on Jacob's doorstep to begin their search for the dagger, his eyes had been red-rimmed, bleary with the remnants of drug-induced oblivion. Even then, she'd recognized the signs.

She simply hadn't expected to care.

Usually, she had to work hard to manufacture a few tears. Now they trembled on her lashes without having to stir them up. Didn't he realize what laudanum could do to him? She kept her face turned carefully away from him as the coach shuddered to a halt.

Without a word, he climbed out and handed her down. They walked in silence to Lord and Lady Kilmaine's door and were greeted by the thoroughly competent butler. The man took their wraps and politely asked Jacob if he'd like a drink before retiring.

"Whisky," he said wearily and the man disappeared to do his bidding.

"Don't forget to add your poppy juice," Julianne muttered as she headed for the stairs. She knew she was being spiteful but she couldn't seem to help it. The old wound had been pricked and nothing would stop it from bleeding.

"Julie, wait."

She stopped on the second riser, her stomach roiling. She might be swayed if she looked into his pain-riddled eyes, so she didn't turn back to face him. She didn't want to hear his excuses. He was weak. She despised him for his weakness.

And despised herself for caring.

"I'll tell you about my gift," he said softly.

She held her breath.

"But you have to tell me something in return," he continued.

"What do you wish to know?"

"Why you're so afraid all the time. And so guilty."

She rounded on him. "I am not."

How could he know about the remorseful panic that always clawed her gut?

He approached her, the difference in their heights obliterated by her perch on the stairs. For the first time, she was able to meet his gaze without looking up.

"You hide it well, I'll give you that," he said. "I suppose it's part of what made you such a good actress, but it's there just beneath the first layer of your skin all the same."

She lifted her chin. "I'm not afraid of you, if that's what you're thinking."

"I almost wish you were." He laughed mirthlessly.

"I'm willing to go to the secret Druid rites. Doesn't that prove I have courage?"

"I didn't say you weren't courageous. I said you were afraid. You can't rightly be the first without the second." He cupped her chin with gentleness. "What happened to you, Julianne?"

The temptation to bare her past made her lean toward him slightly. He seemed like a solid rock, but if Jacob used poppy, she knew that would change. She couldn't bear to see another person she cared about and counted on disintegrate before her eyes.

The butler appeared behind Jacob with a tot of amber liquid balanced on a salver. The man cleared his throat discreetly.

"Your drink is here," she said, pulling away from him. "Do

you keep your vial of laudanum hidden in your walking stick or is it secreted with your shaving accoutrements?"

"Neither."

He was probably lying. All opium fiends kept secret stashes and lied about their whereabouts. She couldn't bear to hear another word from him. It hurt too much.

"Good night, Jacob."

Julianne skittered up the stairs before he could stop her.

CHAPTER 11

Jacob sat in his cousin's dark parlor, nursing his whisky. Damn it all, Julianne was right. If he'd been home, he might have told Fenwick to add a healthy splash of laudanum to his drink. He'd certainly earned it.

The evening had been a cacophony of metal voices. First, the silverware on Lord Digory's immaculate table wouldn't stop trilling in his head. Then later in the smoking room, he'd been expected to handle not only the replica of the druid's dagger he'd brought to the dinner party, but also a number of other arcane blades in Lord Digory's collection.

Each of Digory's swords and sabers had its own gruesome stories to share. Jacob was forced to bear up under them in stoic silence while pain lanced his brain. Only being able to rest his hand on the platinum head of his walking stick on occasion had given him the teeniest bit of relief.

The worst of it was he'd learned very little for his pain.

Julianne had actually advanced their cause more by wangling that invitation from Sir Malcolm. Not that Jacob would allow her to attend a gathering of the secret sect alone. If he couldn't make her see reason, he'd simply follow her. It certainly wouldn't be the first party he'd attended without benefit of an invitation.

That decision made, he drained the last of the spirits. The pounding at his temple subsided from anvil strikes to imperial gongs.

If a bit of opiate could reduce it further, what was the harm? It wasn't as if he used laudanum without reason.

God knew he didn't enjoy the wild, disturbing dreams the poppy gave him. All he wanted was for the pain to stop. To feel normal after a siege from his decidedly abnormal gift.

Not that it had been much of a gift this night.

Rain pattered against the windowpanes, further dampening his mood, but he heard no other sound in the dark house. Everyone else was in bed, without a bleeding cannon going off in their noggins at regular intervals. Even Julianne surely rested, despite her constant internal panic.

He wished he knew what really drove her. Not just what motivated her to find the missing dagger, but what was behind her guilty fear.

Then it occurred to him that there was a way for him to find out, even if she wasn't willing to tell him.

"Well, old son," he muttered to himself. "As long as your head hurts anyway, you may as well make it worth your while."

Jacob pulled off his boots so his tread would be silent and headed up the long staircase. If Julianne caught him spying on her, she'd be furious. But hell, she wasn't exactly thrilled with him at the moment in any case.

It was worth the risk.

Fortunately, the door to her chamber had been recently oiled. The latch was silent when he turned the knob. Jacob had always been cat-eyed and sitting in the dark parlor with his whisky for the better part of an hour had further sharpened his vision.

Julianne lay on her side in the big bed with one delicately arched foot peeping from beneath the counterpane. Her hair was plaited in a long loose braid and her lips were parted in the relaxation of sleep. She looked much younger, much more vulnerable than the Julianne who'd reviled him at the foot of the stairs.

More welcoming too.

She stirred, rolling onto her back. Her breasts rose and fell beneath her thin nightshift. If he climbed under the cool sheets with her, would her sweet body drive the shards of metal from his mind?

He turned away from her before she could distract him from his purpose and moved to the dressing table, where her jewelry lay in a neat row.

Not the ruby he'd watched dangle in the hollow between her breasts all night. It was too fine and too dear. Jacob suspected the precious metal around that stone would hold only memories of her late husband. Same for the emerald choker.

The thought of Julianne having a husband, late or otherwise, churned his innards.

He scrutinized the jewelry again. It would have to be something old, something she'd had for a long time. He nearly overlooked the cameo since it was carved ivory and wouldn't yield any secrets to him. Then he noticed it was set in thinning tin. The back of the pin was dented and much scratched.

He lifted the piece with his thumb and forefinger, careful to touch only the ivory. Then he sank to the floor, crossing his legs, Hindu-fashion. He could usually control how much information a bit of metal sent him by breaking off contact. If he was actively seeking answers to an open-ended question, it meant baring his mind to whatever the ore chose to send. For however long it chose to send. Prolonged contact with metal meant he'd probably lose consciousness.

May as well sit lest I fall, he reasoned as he settled the tin back of the pin into the center of his palm.

* * *

Two girls huddled together on a lumpy mattress, shivering visibly. Both should have had the apple cheeks of youth. Instead unrelenting want had scraped the excess flesh from their faces, pointing their chins and chiseling their cheekbones. Dark smudges, like day-old bruises, bloomed beneath their oversized brown eyes.

They were obviously sisters.

The bigger one put one of her thin arms around the smaller one. Neither seemed warmed by the gesture. Their breath puffed into the cold room as if a pair of small dragons had taken refuge amid the threadbare blankets and pillows.

Jacob wrapped his arms around himself, feeling the bone-chilling cold along with the children in his vision.

The younger girl sniffled a bit.

"Auntie will be back soon," the other said, patting her shoulder. "And she'll bring us something to eat."

"Turkish delight would be nice, wouldn't it, Mary?" the littler one said.

Jacob sensed she'd had it once in her young life and he imagined since that time, the child felt anything worth having was "fine as Turkish Delight." Her lips turned up hopefully, and he recognized the small smile as Julianne's. Even though she was painfully thin, he saw, in nascent form, shadows of the beauty she'd become.

"I'd settle for an orange," Mary said with practicality. "Or a lime."

Jacob's own mouth began to water as his gut hollowed with their hunger. It was always so when the mental pictures were this vivid. Sometimes, he lived the vision, smelling the smells, feeling the touches, seeing events through the eyes of the shades encased in the metal's memory. He counted himself lucky when he was simply a watcher of the shadows of what had come before instead of being cast as an active participant.

Then the door burst open and a blast of frigid air followed a woman with a red shawl through the portal. The girls started toward her, but stopped dead when a man in a disreputable hat tromped over the threshold after her.

Unlike the hungry children, the man had not missed many meals. Jowls hung by either side of a thick-lipped mouth and when he narrowed his eyes, they nearly disappeared into his flesh like piggy slits.

He gestured toward the girls. "These them?"

The woman nodded, her face strained. She swiped her reddened nose on her sleeve. "Just the one, you said."

He reached for the younger girl, but her sister flung herself between them.

"Leave Julie alone."

The man pushed the older girl away and glared at the woman. "You said she'd come quiet like."

Julianne scrambled back till her bony spine was pressed against the iron headboard. She bared her teeth in a small growl. It was clear she wasn't going anywhere, quiet-like or otherwise, with that man. Not if she could help it.

But he didn't heed the warning and when he reached for her again, she bit him. Blood bloomed in a small crescent on his beefy hand.

The man swore and backhanded her. Julianne's eyes rolled up in her head and she collapsed like a marionette whose strings had been slashed.

"I'll take the other one this time," the man said, sucking at his wound. He handed the woman a brown bottle that she clutched to her chest as if it were her firstborn. "If you want more in a month, you'd better beat some sense into the little one. Come on, you."

He grabbed Mary's hand and dragged her into the night, heedless of her sobbing and pleading.

The woman slammed the door on the child's voice and, with quaking hands, unstopped the brown bottle. A medicinal stench flooded the room, one Jacob recognized. She upended the opiate, not waiting to mix it with anything that would cut the vile taste and make it more palatable. The woman chugged several swallows. She sank into the corner, dark liquid staining her lips. Her eyes glazed over in mellow haziness and her hands stopped shaking.

Julianne moaned, but the woman didn't rise to tend her. Finally, the child pushed herself upright and looked around.

"Where's Mary?" Her small voice quavered like a willow in the wind.

The woman didn't answer. She simply took another swig of the laudanum.

Julianne's eyes went wide. "You let him take her. You sold her for that bottle."

She leaped up, skittered to the cupboard and tore through a basket filled with rags the girls were tasked with weaving into rugs. From the bottom of the rubbish, she came up with a cameo in her fist.

"Half a mo'," the woman said, trying to force the trinket out of Julianne's grip. "What's that? Been holdin' out on Auntie Nell, have ye?"

"It was Mother's. You can't have it." Julianne jerked her hand away and ran straight to the door. "I'll buy Mary back with it." She slipped under her aunt's lunging grasp, her treasure still in tow.

Julianne ran into the night, disappearing into the shadows, crying out her sister's name.

Pain knifed through Jacob's mind and he seemed to be two places at once—still seated on the floor at the foot of the adult Julianne's bed in his cousin's posh town house and also padding after the young Julianne down a rubbish-strewn lane. He stretched out his hand toward her.

"No," he tried to warn the phantom in his head, but his voice wouldn't work. The man would never agree to return her sister for an old scrap of ivory. He'd only take Julianne too. *Don't go*, he mouthed in impotent silence.

He didn't think he'd made any noise, but the little girl seemed to hear him. She whirled around, still clutching the cameo to her flat chest, and stared past him into the darkness. The whites showed all the way around her enormous brown eyes. Her face was taut with fear, both for her sister and herself.

She was alone in a city that ate its young. And she knew it.

Jacob watched her turn and run from him, her shadowy image growing ever more thin and vaporous until she faded completely into the mist of time.

A fresh blade of pain sheered through his head and Jacob's vision waivered, tunneled, and finally winked out like a snuffed candle.

The loud thud jerked Julianne from a sound sleep. She lay in the soft bed, holding her breath, listening intently in case the sound came again. Rain peppered the small rectangular windowpanes. She heard the occasional creak of the house settling on its foundations, but there were no more bumps in the dark.

Then very slowly, she became aware of the sound of someone breathing, soft and rhythmic. Her gaze darted around the room, but no intruder skulked in the corners.

Then someone groaned like a wounded boar.

The sound came from the foot of her bed. She sat up slowly, trying not to allow the linens to rustle more than necessary and crept down to peer over the footboard.

A man was curled into a snug ball, his knees drawn up to his chest and his arms raised to trap his head between his elbows. He moaned and pressed his elbows together as if his skull were a nut he was trying to crack.

Julianne couldn't see the man's face, but she recognized the cut of his coat and was tempted to offer to crack his head for him.

"Jacob Preston," she hissed. How dare he compromise her in his cousin's house by sneaking into her bedchamber. "What are you doing here?"

He rolled onto his back and stared up at her, without the

slightest hint of recognition in his eyes. Alarm jangled up her spine.

"What's wrong?" She scrambled off the bed and knelt beside him.

His mouth moved but she couldn't make out the words. She bent down to press her ear close.

"No," he whispered over and over. "Don't."

Viola had hinted at some mysterious ailment and now Julianne saw the truth of it firsthand. Jacob was ill. Terribly ill.

When fresh pain made him grimace, Julianne's heart ached in sympathy.

"No, Julie," he repeated. "Don't go."

He still looked past her as if his eyes couldn't focus. She wrapped her arms around him, pulling his head to her chest. "I'm not going anywhere."

He slipped his arms around her waist and clung to her. His great body shuddered and another groan of pain escaped his lips. Then his head fell back and he lapsed into unconsciousness.

Suddenly, Julianne didn't give two figs what anyone thought about the propriety of finding a man lying at the foot of one's bed.

She called out for help at the top of her lungs. If she woke the entire household and ruined her reputation for all time, she didn't care one bit.

CHAPTER 12

If anyone was surprised to find Jacob unconscious at the foot of Julianne's bed, they gave no sign of it. His cousin Viola and her husband Quinn took charge of matters immediately. Quinn and his valet lifted Jacob's inert form and carted him off to his own bed.

Viola sent Julianne to the kitchen to roust the cook, who gave her some smelling salts and a decanter of wine. By the time she returned to Jacob's chamber, the valet had stripped him and settled him in bed. His cousin used the smelling salts in order to rouse him enough to take a glass of wine.

Jacob didn't try to speak. He merely did as Viola bade him, meek as a lamb. Then he sank back into the pillows, his face pale and drawn, his eyes closed.

"There," Viola said. "Dinner parties are always so difficult for him. The silverware, you know. Perhaps he'll sleep now."

"What happened to him?" Julianne asked. Lord Kilmaine seemed to understand what Viola meant about the silverware for he nodded grimly. Julianne suddenly remembered that Jacob had brought his own to the King's Arms, but it still made no sense. "How could using someone else's fork and knife result in these dire straits?"

"Ordinarily, it wouldn't be this bad. He says silverware

rarely has anything of importance to share. More of an irritant than anything. If I didn't know better I'd say he—oh!" Viola noticed one of his hands was balled into a fist. She uncurled his fingers and pried something from him. "That's what he was doing in your chamber. This is yours, I collect."

Julianne took the cameo from her. "What did he want with this?"

"So I guess it wasn't the silverware at the dinner party that devastated him this evening. That cameo is what happened to him." Viola shook her head. "The foolish man. I warned him about this, but would he listen?"

"Warned him about what?'

"About using his gift to spy on someone."

Julianne's brows tented in a frown. "What are you talking about?"

"Obviously there's something about you he wished to know and either you wouldn't tell him or he simply wished to bypass discussing the matter." Viola rolled her eyes. "Men are like that sometimes."

Her husband Quinn raised his hands in mock surrender. "Leave me out of this. I'm going back to bed."

"I'll join you soon." Viola called after him with a smile of promise that told Julianne theirs was a happy marriage. Then Lady Kilmaine looked back at her cousin, whose dark brows were drawn in pain even in sleep, and shook her head. "Jacob should have known better."

"Better than what? You're talking in riddles," Julianne said. "How could my cameo make him this ill?"

"Oh!" Viola stared at her for a moment and then put a hand to her mouth. "So you don't know, after all. Oh, I feel so stupid. From our previous conversation, I assumed he'd told you everything. Oh, dear. This is really something you should hear from Jacob."

"Viola, please. As you said, men often like to skip over talking about things. Why don't you just tell me?"

"I suppose I shall have to now." Her hostess huffed out a long breath. "Jacob has the gift of touch."

A ripple of agreement surged through Julianne's body, but she realized Viola couldn't possibly mean his ability to undo a woman, body and soul, with only his talented fingers.

"Some people are exceptionally keen of hearing. Others have eyes like hawks. What Jacob and I have is a little like that, but . . . more so." Viola sank onto the foot of her cousin's bed. "You see, the things we all surround ourselves with take on a bit of us as we use them. Our lives leave an imprint on the objects."

Julianne blinked in surprise. She'd never heard such an outlandish idea, but didn't want to offend her hostess by saying so.

"And if an item can be imprinted, it stands to reason that there is a way to retrieve the impressions. That's what Jacob and I do. When I touch a gemstone, or when Jacob touches metal, we are able to glean more information from it than most. We tap into the object's memory, if you like," Viola explained. "We see visions, remnants of the object's past, snippets from the life of the current owner. Jacob can even sense emotions swirling around the metal."

Julianne stroked the old cameo in her palm. "So when he touched this he . . . did what?"

"It looks as if you've had that piece for quite a while. Plenty of time for it to collect memories," Viola said. "Jacob was probably using it to peep into your past."

Julianne's spine stiffened. Even if such a thing were possible, he still had no right to her private pain.

"Oh, I'm not condoning it," Viola said. "Though I confess I did it once myself, to my sorrow. The problem is our visions may or may not be complete. It's easy to misconstrue what we see. That's why I warned him against using his gift to spy on someone close to him."

Julianne traced the yellowed profile on the cameo. Could it contain imprints of things past? If so, what had the ornament shared with Jacob?

"If it's any consolation to you"—Viola ruffled the shock of hair that had fallen forward on Jacob's forehead—"he's paying for his curiosity quite handsomely now."

"What do you mean?"

"Whenever we use our gift, Jacob and I are stricken with blinding headaches. They can last for days." Viola sighed in sympathy with her cousin. "Quinn says it proves the old Spanish proverb. 'Take what you want, God said to Man, and pay for it.' I suppose it makes sense that there's a price to be paid for using an ability few possess."

Jacob groaned in his sleep and flopped a forearm over his closed eyes.

"This is as bad as I've ever seen him," Viola said.

"Something in my past did this to him?"

"No, *looking* at something in your past did this to him," Viola corrected. "This is not your fault. He knew full well what would happen. But please don't be angry with him. He must love you quite a lot if he's willing to subject himself to this sort of torture to learn more about you."

Love? Jacob had never said anything about love. If he had, she'd probably do what she usually did when a man tried to get too close—cut him loose.

It was what she should do in any case. If she didn't allow herself to need him, he couldn't hurt her, but something inside her couldn't bear the thought of separating from Jacob.

"I'd better join Quinn or he'll come looking for me," Viola said, stifling a yawn. "Jacob will probably sleep well enough now, but I hate to leave him alone after one of these episodes.

If you'd rather not sit with him, I can wake one of the servants."

"No, I'll stay for a while," Julianne heard herself saying. The words surprised her, but she wouldn't call them back. She knew she ought to withdraw to her own chamber, but when she'd discovered him on the floor of her room, the only thing he could say was "don't go." That simple plea wrapped itself around her heart and wouldn't turn her loose. She wouldn't abandon Jacob if there was a chance he might need her.

After Viola left, Julianne carried a straight-backed chair over next to the bed and sat down to watch him sleep. She ought to be angry with him for invading her past, but instead, tenderness bloomed in her chest.

No, she couldn't let herself care for him. Had she forgotten what had happened each time she opened her heart to someone? No matter what they promised, she had always ended up alone. It was better, safer not to have expectations of anything else.

She had to be strong.

Jacob stirred in his sleep, jerking his arm back down by his side. A muscle in his cheek ticked and his eyes scrunched more tightly for a few heartbeats. Then his face went slack in the relaxation of sleep again. After a few more moments, the pained expression returned and didn't abate this time.

Julianne padded over to the washstand and wet one of the small cloths. Then she wrung it out and folded it so it would fit neatly across Jacob's forehead.

He relaxed visibly under the cool touch. Julianne smoothed his hair back and his lips lifted in a quick half-smile, but his eyes didn't open.

"What in the world did you see in that old cameo, Jacob?" she whispered.

His eyelids twitched. "You." His lips formed the word without a sound. Then he gathered his strength and found his voice. "You and . . . Mary."

He opened his eyes and looked at the cameo she'd set on the bedside table, his gaze drawn to it as surely as a lodestone to true north. Julianne wondered if the piece was still giving him some sort of view into her past. Then his gaze wandered back and focused on her face.

"So. You know about me now." He licked his lips as if his throat were also dry. "Viola explained it to you?"

She nodded grimly at him.

"Be angry at me tomorrow if you like, but for now, get me a drink, will you?"

She poured another goblet of wine and helped him sit to drink it. "There's no laudanum."

"Just as well," he said, his lips white with pain. "After what I saw, I understand why you hate it. I won't ever take it again."

The wall of protection she'd so carefully constructed around her heart crumbled a bit. He was in obvious agony the wine couldn't begin to touch, but he'd bear it without opiates for her sake. She blinked back tears.

"How much did you see?" she asked.

He related the events of the last time she ever saw her sister with such clarity, such knife-sharp detail, there was no question in Julianne's mind that Jacob's gift of touch was real.

"I lost you when you ran away," he said, trying to sit up but failing. Jacob settled for propping himself slightly more upright on his pillows and caught her hand so she couldn't move away from him. "Did you ever find Mary?"

Her chin trembled. "No."

His mouth tightened into a hard line. "What happened?"

In halting tones, she told him. She'd wandered all night, looking for her sister and the man who'd taken her. She'd dodged shadows and kept out of sight of the riff-raff that prowled the narrow streets. When dawn broke, she curled up in an alley doorway and fell into exhausted sleep.

"It turned out to be the stage door of the Drury Lane theatre," she said. "About mid-morning, some of the stage crew arrived. It had started snowing so the costume mistress took pity on me and let me come in to get warm."

The theatre was like a magical world. The rabbit warren of small dressing rooms and property closets, of flying flats that soared upward for quick scene changes and scrims that lowered to bathe the stage in hazy light, the wardrobes filled with outlandish costumes—it was as if Julianne had stepped into another realm, a place where nothing was as it seemed and perhaps losing her sister was simply a bad dream. Her loss was temporarily assuaged as she took stock of that new undiscovered country.

No one had the time or the inclination to take full responsibility for a small child, but she was quiet and undemanding. And constantly on her best behavior, lest they send her back to the streets. Gradually, they became used to her presence. Julianne was little more than a pet to the backstage crew. She was better fed than the tabby they kept as a mouser, but not much more noticed.

Julianne had soon realized finding Mary was a lost cause, so she worked to make a place for herself among the ragtag troop of players. She painted flats, sewed costumes, and kept track of props—anything to make sure she wouldn't be tossed aside to fend for herself again.

There was no going back to her aunt, the woman who'd cared for her and Mary after their mother died. Aunt Nell had been kindness itself at first, before the opiates poisoned her soul. After she fell into that brown bottle, she wasn't the same woman. She'd sell Julianne for more laudanum if she got half a chance.

Mary had taught Julianne her letters, so she practiced them by copying scripts and reading the alternate parts to help the actors rehearse their lines.

"The director overheard me one day and decided to use me for some bit parts after that," she told him. "As I got older, the parts got bigger. I suppose you could say the theatre gave me a life."

It stole one from her as well. Over time, she lost all sense of what normal was like, what was real and what was pretend. The niggling sense of impermanence, of being one bad performance from the streets, kept her belly roiling with panic, but she learned to control and hide her fear.

Eventually, she turned that nervous energy into the driving force behind her performances and the effect was electrifying. Julianne slid into her character's skin with unmatched ease because her own life was such a cipher. She thrilled audiences with her portrayals. She became a lead player.

And someone whom she herself no longer recognized.

But when she imagined what had likely become of Mary, she considered she'd gotten the best of the trade.

She still looked for her sister, peeping out from behind the curtain each night, hoping to recognize her in the milling crowds before the show started.

"Once I became successful, I hired a runner to look for Mary, but nothing ever turned up. Algernon engaged an investigator to look into the matter, but he couldn't find anything either. She disappeared without a trace."

Julianne had harnessed her fear, but she'd never gotten over the guilt of not finding Mary.

Jacob squeezed her hand. "I'm sorry you were so alone."

He might as well have squeezed her heart. Even after she married Algernon, she was alone in many ways and still afraid she might be set aside.

"It's not knowing that's the worst," she said softly. "After all this time, I don't suppose I shall ever know what befell my sister."

Jacob winced and brought a hand to the bridge of his nose involuntarily. Julianne dipped the cloth and applied it to his forehead once again.

"Better?"

"Not really." He caught her hand and brought it to his lips. He brushed her knuckles with his mouth and then inhaled deeply. "You smell sweet."

"I don't feel particularly sweet," she said.

"I thought we agreed you'd be angry with me tomorrow."

"I believe you're the only one who agreed to that," she said tartly, but didn't try to take her hand from him. Judging from the hard set of his jaw, he was still in a good deal of pain. If simply holding her hand gave him a little relief, she wouldn't begrudge him. "You knew this would happen when you used your ability to invade my privacy, so why on earth did you do it?"

"Damned if I know," he said raggedly. "I just sensed you were afraid. Almost all the time. But you're so tight with your confidences, so unlikely to share anything of yourself with me, I decided this was the only way I'd learn anything about you that you didn't want me to know."

"Was it worth it?"

He looked at her, his gray eyes clouded by pain. "Yes."

She felt exposed under his intense gaze, as if she were suddenly soul-naked before him.

"You have nothing to reproach yourself for. There was nothing you could have done to save Mary. I don't want you to be afraid, Julie," he said.

"What makes you think—"

"I don't think you're afraid. I *know* you are, at no small cost to myself, I might add." He reached up to stroke her cheek. "But you're safe with me. I won't hurt you. I won't cast you aside."

He cupped the back of her head and gently tugged her down till their noses nearly met. "I care for you, woman. God help me, but I do."

His lips found hers and she didn't have the strength to pull away.

God help us both.

Chapter 13

His mouth was soft under hers, as giving a kiss as she could imagine. Then he deepened the kiss, demanding entrance and sweeping in to claim her with his tongue.

Her insides boiled. Of course, she wanted him. She could scarcely be in the same room with Jacob without every fiber of her body going on high alert.

But if the man wasn't above using a gift that was nothing short of magical to invade her past, could she trust him?

"What about the pain?" she whispered when he released her lips and started to kiss his way down her neck. "Viola said your headache could last for days."

"Sometimes it can, but for some reason, when I kiss you, it escapes my notice that I even have a head." He nuzzled her jawline and then brushed his lips over her skin till he nipped her earlobe.

He cares for me. The words played over in her head like a refrain.

Others had said the same thing, had even professed to love her—directors who wanted to use her body in exchange for advancement on the repertory roster or theatre patrons who thought they could make her their mistress for the price of a midnight supper. She'd been cautious about which offers she accepted, knowing the fine words were false. The time they'd actually spend with her would be short, but depending on her needs at the moment, it was sometimes a fair exchange.

She didn't want what she had with Jacob to be that sort of mercenary quid pro quo.

Then there were the ones who truly had cared about her—her mother, her sister, even Algernon. They hadn't meant to leave her, but they had all the same.

She straightened, pulling away from Jacob for a moment. Had she somehow doomed those who loved her?

"Julianne." Jacob said her name as if it were a prayer. Then he untied the belt at the waist of her wrapper. His fingertips nicked her skin through the fabric like little flicks of a whip, driving her body to respond with a deep ache. "I want you so badly, but not if you're still afraid."

He means it, her heart urged her to believe.

But she'd read about Jacob Preston even before she'd come to London. Of all the men to launch her soul on, why would she choose this one, a man with the reputation of a rogue and a debaucher of married women?

"Are you afraid of me, Julie?" His gray eyes darkened to gunmetal and she tumbled into them. Jacob was tumultuous as the North Sea, but somehow, she felt safe to ride out the storm with him.

He cares for me. She slid the wrapper from her shoulders and stood before him in just her thin nightshift.

"No, Jacob. I'm not afraid."

He ran a long finger up her arm. All the small hairs on her body leapt to attention. Then he pulled back the sheet, baring himself to the groin to invite her into the bed. His hard shaft rose like a tower between his legs, completely ready for her.

The way her body throbbed, she suspected she was just as

prepared to receive him. She bent over, grasped her hem and pulled off her nightshift in one smooth motion.

As his gaze swept over her, his smile was a wicked hallelujah. The pinched paleness brought on by his headache seemed to have passed completely.

Julianne climbed between the cool sheets with him, his body almost feverishly warm by comparison. Her skin glided against his skin. Her body molded to his. Even before joining completely, they fit together, her softness yielding to his hardness.

Would that the crooks and wrinkles in their souls blended as easily. If misshapen parts of their spirits somehow fit together as well as their bodies, it would be nothing short of a miracle.

"Do you remember when I told you about how I thought of you by night?" he said as he traced her collarbone and then dipped lower to tease the crease beneath her breast. "What I wanted to do with you?"

"You said you'd like to kiss me"—she paused to gulp—"everywhere."

"So you were listening. Good."

He rolled, taking her across the smooth linens, and stopped with her pinned beneath him. Her legs had parted enough for his hips to settle between them and she felt the tip of him against her opening.

She wiggled down a bit.

"Patience," he said before he ran his tongue around her nipple. "I know you like to take the lead, but this time, let me. Keep still now, love."

Love, he'd called her. She almost believed it.

Her nipple tightened into a hard pink button, aching for him to suckle it. He teased her with his mouth, brushing past the charged flesh, but not giving in to her need.

She made a soft growling noise in the back of her throat, but he only chuckled. When he scraped his teeth across her nipple, she cried out. He finally took her into his mouth and sucked.

A zing of desire arced from her breast to her womb. She ached so, the heavy longing between her legs was almost painful, the need to be filled unrelenting. If he rammed himself home in one hard thrust, she'd sing out in relief.

But Jacob was in no rush. He gave her other breast the same unhurried treatment before he kissed his way down her ribs. He dallied with her navel, his warm breath flooding over her belly and lower.

Everywhere. He's going to kiss me everywhere.

Anticipation and niggling worry vied for first place in her mind. Would he find her most private place fair? Would she be as much a feast for him as he was for her?

His mouth was a wonder, leaving delight shivering in its wake. Julianne felt her heartbeat between her legs, pounding with more intensity as he continued to move down her body.

The ache was fast becoming unbearable, a torment, yet she didn't want it to end. He was so close. Inches away from her tender folds.

Then he slid down, kissing her thigh and running his tongue around her knee.

Completely skipping over *everywhere.*

Disappointment hollowed her gut. Jacob threw the sheet back and a fresh whiff of her arousal filled the room. She was swollen and achy, wet with need.

She wanted his mouth on her, to feel his lips on her most sensitive parts. To be accepted and cherished entire.

But instead he was kissing her ankle and sliding his tongue between her first and big toes. It was a lovely sensation and desire sizzled up her leg, but it wasn't what she was hoping for.

What he'd promised.

Then he switched to her other foot and began to move back up.

"Relax, Julianne," he said as he eased her legs farther apart. "Your muscles are all tense."

Hope flared in her again as he moved past her knee. His stubbled jaw was rough on her inner thigh. She bit her lip as he moved closer. His breath warmed her and the curls at the juncture of her legs swayed with each exhalation.

Then his mouth claimed her. He nibbled each lip. He separated her delicate folds with his tongue. He found her most sensitive spot almost immediately.

She could have wept with gratitude.

Instead she fisted the sheets to keep from flying off the bed in sheer joy. Her body wept fresh dew for him. He kissed. He suckled. He swirled the tip of his tongue around her special spot and over it.

As if she were the most delicious thing he'd ever tasted. As if he couldn't get enough of her.

Julianne couldn't get enough of him either. She had known hunger in her life, but never this kind of hunger. She was empty, ravenous.

Jacob reduced her to quivering need.

Her insides tightened. She was on a journey, going someplace she hoped she'd reach, but was never quite sure she would. Jacob had taken her there before with far more ease than her other lovers, but that was no assurance he would again. Fear often sidetracked her body.

Fear of being abandoned again.

She'd ended her affairs when the men began to talk of love because she couldn't bear to involve more than her body. It would hurt even more if she allowed herself to need someone that way. Once her heart was in jeopardy, her body didn't respond the same way. It was as if she didn't dare let herself be vulnerable, be open enough to dance the full insanity of lust once her heart might be at risk.

Would it be different with Jacob now that he'd admitted he cared for her?

His tongue made love to her, seeking out her hidden places, lavishing her with soft caresses. She throbbed against his mouth. The internal spiral caught her and she descended to a hot dark place where everything was wet and slick and aching.

Julianne stopped fretting over whether she'd reach her desired end because this time the journey itself was unbridled pleasure. Like a drowning victim who stopped struggling and surrendered to the waves, she gave herself up to it.

But she didn't sink. Jacob buoyed her along, carrying her to fresh ecstasies. By the time her release came in shuddering contractions and blinding light, she was sobbing his name.

And on the last glorious spasm, he moved up her body and filled her, the heat of him like taking a banked fire inside her. She pulsed around him in welcome as he kissed her damp cheeks.

"Are you all right?" he whispered.

She smoothed her palms over his shoulders, then down his arms to lace her fingers with his. "I've never been so all right in my life."

He covered her mouth with his and began to move. Julianne thrust her hips up to meet him. Their clasped hands were spread out to the sides. Then, without breaking off their kiss, Jacob lifted them so her arms were pinioned above her head. Hands, mouth, and cock, he claimed her.

The world corkscrewed down to heat and friction and pounding need. Julianne crested again and Jacob came with her. He arched into her and she reveled in the deep pulses of his release as he buried himself in her. A feral sound of male triumph tore from his throat.

Then his body relaxed and she felt his full weight descend on her, settling deeper into the feather mattress. The linen molded around them as if it were a cocoon.

What transformation was taking place? What manner of being would they be when they emerged from this linen nest?

His breathing slowed and his heart stopped galloping against her breastbone. He lifted his weight on his elbows and searched her face.

"I'm sorry, Julie. That wasn't very gentlemanly of me," he said, his gray eyes darkening with concern. "I meant to pull out."

"I'm glad you didn't." She cupped his cheek. "I wanted to feel you inside me . . . for all of it."

He released the breath he'd been holding and laid his head beside hers on the pillow. "It was wonderful to stay with you to the end. I've never done that before."

"Never?"

"On my honor as a rogue," he said soberly.

Perhaps it was the way her body felt like a limp noodle. Perhaps it was that she felt so wonderful, she simply didn't give a damn, but the situation was suddenly too hilarious and Julianne laughed.

"What's so funny?" he asked.

She covered her mouth with her hand, to stifle her mirth. "Oh, how astounded the ton would be if they only knew. Jacob Preston, foremost debaucher of the wives of the Upper Ten Thousand, has actually had a new sensual experience. They'd never believe it."

"Perhaps you'll allow that my reputation as a Lothario is a trifle overblown."

"With your bed skills?" She giggled again. "I should think not. After tonight I've no doubt your fame as a rogue is well deserved."

"All right, I'll admit I've been in more beds than most men, but this wasn't just another bedding, Julie," he said. "Not to me."

Her laughter dried up and she met his intense gaze. She read truth in his eyes. This joining meant something to him. It wasn't just a mindless swive. Something real had passed between them.

"Not to me either," she said softly.

He rolled off her. She took it as the signal she should climb out of the bed and return to her chamber.

"No, Julie, don't go." He wrapped his arms about her and pulled her back, her spine pressed against his chest.

Don't go. It's what he'd said when she first found him collapsed on her floor. He needed her, and it warmed her to her toes.

"How is your head?"

"Fine," he said with a puzzled expression as he ran a hand across his forehead. "The pain is gone. You seem to be my own private brand of laudanum."

"Opiates are addictive, you know."

"I don't mind being addicted to you."

He cinched her tighter and she relaxed into him. His breathing fell into a steady rhythm and after a few moments, Julianne realized he'd drifted to sleep.

She ought to ease out of the bed and make her way back to her own. She was a guest in Lord and Lady Kilmaine's home. They might have expected her to spend the night in his room, sitting upright in a chair while Jacob slept away his debilitating headache, but they'd surely be shocked to find her naked between his sheets.

Even so, she couldn't bring herself to leave the warm circle of his arms.

It wasn't just another bedding for either of them. Something was different. She was different. And until she understood what that difference was, she couldn't bear to abandon this strange new development.

Or abandon him.

Chapter 14

Jacob slept a sleep without dreams till the sky outside his window began to lighten from black to pearl. It wasn't the faint rays fingering across his closed eyelids that woke him. It was the round feminine rump snuggled close to his groin.

Bare and warm, Julianne still spooned against him, her uncovered shoulder bathed in the growing light. His hand splayed possessively over one of her breasts. He thrummed her nipple and it tightened into a taut little peak. She stirred, but didn't wake, burrowing deeper into his embrace. Her hair tickled his chest and neck. As the sun brightened, the rosy shell of her ear was almost transparent.

He inhaled deeply and her breathing adjusted to match his. A faint whiff of camellias wafted from her skin.

The woman must bathe in the stuff, he thought with approval. The sweet scent was as much a part of Julianne as her wide dark amber eyes and kissable mouth. His body roused to her between one heartbeat and the next.

Even though he was feeling pleasurably male, he didn't rock his hips against her. He'd never wakened beside a woman before and surprisingly enough, he didn't want anything to end this quiet moment. With his previous lovers, he'd always slipped away from their trysts as soon as decently possible once the lovemaking was over. The possible imminent arrival of a jealous husband precluded any other course.

Which suited Jacob just fine.

He'd always thought it would be awkward to share a bed all night, that he'd never be able to truly descend into the relaxation of sleep in another's presence. It would be too revealing, too vulnerable.

But somehow his body had found deep rest with Julianne by his side. What's more, even though he'd used his gift last night, his head was clear and free of pain.

He began to wonder what it would be like to wake beside her every morning.

Alert the London Crier. *The rogue Jacob Preston has discovered yet another new sensual experience,* he thought with a wry grin. *Simply sleeping with a woman.*

He was loath for this sweet idyll to end, but if he wanted to spare Julianne embarrassment, she needed to return to her own room before the chambermaid arrived to sweep the hearths and stir up the fires for the day.

He eased out of bed and drew on his banyan. When he turned back to Julianne, she had propped herself on her elbows to watch him through narrowed eyes.

"Are you well enough to be up and about?" she asked.

He raked a hand through his hair. He felt entirely well, suspiciously well. He'd never had such a speedy recovery after using his gift. If someone told him Julianne was a witch and had hexed him with health and well-being, he'd have believed them.

"If I felt any better, it would be illegal," he said. "Or at least immoral."

"Given your reputation, I've no doubt of that." She slanted him a teasing look.

He leaned down and kissed her. She tasted so good it was all he could do not to tumble back into the rumpled sheets with her, but she wouldn't thank him for leading her into scandal, even if the Kilmaine servants were the only ones nattering about it. "It's dawn. Let's get you back to your chamber before the household wakes."

She wrapped the sheet around her and slid out of bed. "Turn around so I can dress."

"A little late to be shy, isn't it?" He chuckled as he complied with her request. *May as well act the gentleman.* After all, he'd already seen and touched and loved every inch of her glowing skin.

"A woman needs to maintain a bit of mystery," she said.

He heard the rustle of fabric sliding over her bare flesh and wished he hadn't agreed to turn around quite so quickly. Julianne in nothing but her skin was an eyeful to tempt a much better man than he.

"Believe me, madam, no matter how familiar I am with your exquisite body, there are enough mysteries rolling around in that lovely head of yours to keep me baffled for years to come."

"Good," she said. "And while we're on the subject of mysteries, have you given any more thought to the portion of my manuscript that's in a language you don't recognize?"

"I have a friend who might be able to read it. He's a member of the Royal College of Physicians and quite learned in a number of fields." He caught a shadowy reflection of Julianne in the window glass as she wiggled her nightshift on over her head. "I believe I mentioned him to you before, George Snowdon."

"Ah, would this be George of the wee beasties called germs?"

"That's the one." He heard the bed creak and figured she'd sat down to put on her slippers. "I thought we'd nip over and see if he can help us after breakfast."

"You're sure you can trust him?"

"As much as I trust anyone."

George was another one of the few who knew about Jacob's unusual ability and the havoc he suffered after using it. Snowdon had suggested that there might be a metal that would act as a buffer for him, in the same manner as the relatively harmless cowpox inoculations protected patients against the dreaded and often deadly smallpox. George had helped Jacob discover that platinum provided a sort of shield for him from the invasion of other metals.

But Julianne had given him far more relief than platinum. All her rosy flesh was more or less covered, but she didn't give him permission to turn around until she'd cinched up her wrapper too.

"May I say you look lovely by the light of the rising sun?" Jacob put his arms around her.

Her eyes flared as she realized how bright the sky was growing by the minute.

"I must go." Julianne pulled away from him and padded to the door. She opened it a crack and peered up and down the hall to make sure it was empty.

Jacob pushed the door closed and swept her back into his arms. "Not until you give me a kiss good-bye."

"It's not as if we're parting forever. We'll see each other at breakfast in short order."

"Does that mean you'll kiss me in the breakfast room with my cousin and her husband looking on?" He cocked his head at her, enjoying the embarrassed flush that crept up her neck as he teased her.

"No, I suppose not." She stood on tiptoe and pecked his cheek.

"Do I remind you of a doddering uncle?"

"No."

"Then don't kiss me like one."

She arched a brow at him. "Very well, but remember. You asked for it."

Julianne put a hand to both his cheeks and pulled his head down. Soft and pliant, her lips teased his. She nipped at his mouth. She suckled his lower lip. She slipped in her tongue and tormented him with it. By the time, she drew back, he was in danger of spilling his seed on the silk banyan just from the seductive play of her mouth on his.

"There," she said, running a fingertip across his lower lip. "Satisfied?"

He palmed her buttocks and lifted her, pressing her close to his hardness. "Not even close, you little minx."

She reached around to give his bum a playful swat. "Do not expect sympathy from me, sir. If you're in discomfort, it's your own fault."

Then the teasing light went out of her eyes and he saw desire, banked but glowing hotly, in their depths.

"If it's any consolation, I'm paying for that kiss too," she admitted, her tone breathy. "But I expect you to remedy matters later."

He kissed her again, passion-rough this time. "Depend on it."

After he released her, she slipped out his door and he watched till she disappeared without incident into her own chamber down the hall. Rubbing his stubbled jaw, Jacob rang for a valet and his morning shave.

Yes, waking up beside a well-swived woman was a sensual pleasure he'd missed until now. He wondered how often Julianne would allow him to sleep all night with her in the future.

Of course, there was one way to make sure it happened with regularity, he realized as the servant appeared with a straight razor and all the accoutrements for his shave.

I could marry the lady.

The thought surprised him. Jacob had always considered himself too wily to succumb to the parson's mousetrap. It was part of why he insisted on taking lovers who were already married. No danger of being leg-shackled by a conniving woman if she was already spoken for.

Of course, he'd already thrown that rule out the window for Julianne.

She'd told him early on that she wouldn't trade the freedom of widowhood for another marriage. Her adamant stance should have given him comfort, but instead, he felt stymied by her insistence on independence.

Now that he thought about it, he was the only one who'd admitted to any degree of caring last night. Julianne's touch was more loving than any he'd ever experienced, but she hadn't professed to any tender feelings for him at all.

He'd finally met a woman who took her pleasures as he'd always taken his.

The knowledge didn't sit well with him at all.

Jacob squired Julianne to George Snowdon's professional office, located on the ground floor of his town house near Lincoln Inn Field. It was only a few blocks from the College of Surgeons and the operating theatre where the leading practitioners gave their lectures and their students trained on cadavers and the occasional unlucky live patient.

"George operates his medical practice out of his home," Jacob explained as they pushed through the unlocked front door. Of course, George wasn't officially a doctor yet. While he had the requisite education to be called a physician, he was part of a growing group of medical professionals who aspired to combine traditional medicine with the skills of a surgeon to become a "General Practitioner," as adept with a prescription pad as with a bone saw.

But the nature of his private practice didn't require he be expert with either of them.

No servant met them, but Jacob knew George didn't have

any live-in help. It might intimidate his patients, he always said, who rightly valued their privacy.

"I thought surgeons worked at hospital."

"They do. This is George's other practice." The one that actually paid the bills, if his friend was to be believed.

Jacob led Julianne down a long corridor to the rear of the town house where chairs lined the hall. No patients were waiting, but he wasn't surprised. He and Julianne had raced over with the manuscript in tow as soon as they finished their breakfast of eggs and kippers. He raised his hand to knock on the heavy English oak door that led to George's examination room when a sound from inside stopped him.

A feminine moan.

"Starting early I see," he whispered.

The sound came again, followed by rapid and loud breathing.

"What in the world—"

Jacob clapped a hand over Julianne's mouth. "George has a very specialized practice."

"Yes, yes!" the woman chanted.

Julianne's brows arched. "My goodness. What's her problem?"

"George says all his patients suffer from hysteria, a disease of the womb," Jacob said with a smile. "She sounds a little hysterical, doesn't she?"

Julianne sat in one of the waiting chairs and Jacob settled beside her. "And the treatment for this condition is . . ."

"A rather intimate massage actually." Jacob took her hand and started a little massage of his own on the inside of her wrist. "All quite the done thing if you ask a medical professional, but George doesn't follow the rules exactly."

"Is it wise to deviate from standard practice?"

"George thinks so." Jacob leaned toward her, breathing in

her sweet scent clear to his toes. "According to his medical books, which he's lent me from time to time—they're excellent reading, by the way—"

"Correct me if I am wrong," she said, her tone breathy, "but does your raid on his library account for the fact that you know your way around a woman's body better than most?"

That and dedicated practice. He nodded and undid a few more of her glove buttons, the better to stroke her forearm. She smiled up at him and made no protest.

"In any case, the recommended treatment for hysteria is continuous pelvic massage until a state of . . . paroxysm is achieved, but that can take hours if the woman is . . . seriously hysterical. George gets better and quicker results with his own methods."

"Paroxysm," she repeated, a smile curving her lips. "Good word for it, though I'm not wild about the term *hysterical* as it's applied here."

George's patients might try to pretend the treatments he gave weren't sexual in nature, but Julianne's knowing look told Jacob she understood exactly what was happening behind the thick oak door.

"So what are George's methods?"

"First, he blindfolds his patient," Jacob explained.

"Why?"

"George says it releases the inhibitions which lead to hysteria, but I think it's because when one of our senses is hobbled the others become more acute."

"That sounds like the voice of experience talking," she said, with a sideways glance. "Have you permitted one of your lovers to blindfold you, Jacob?"

No, but he'd done his share of slipping silk over his bedmates' eyes. "I'm not talking about me. I'm trying to explain George's medical methods to you."

"Medical methods," she repeated. "Quite."

"Then he binds his patient's hands and feet so they are immobile."

"Heaven forefend that a woman should move." She rolled her eyes at him.

"It's not meant to hurt them," Jacob explained. "If they are bound, his patients are not responsible for any sensation that is forced upon them, you see. They are free to merely accept what happens as the natural course of treatment."

"How very convenient."

"Yes, quite," Jacob said. "I'm glad you understand the science of it."

"Science, my foot. I meant it's convenient for Dr. Snowdon," she said drolly. "His patients are unable to see what he's doing and if they are bound they can't stop him either. They have no control over the encounter whatsoever."

"Treatment, not encounter." Jacob raised a pointed finger in correction and wished he hadn't because Julianne took the opportunity to button up her glove again. "George assures me they do not mind. Especially once he administers warm oil and begins the massage."

The patient on the other side of the door emitted a few rhythmic yelps.

"It's a wonder he doesn't slip a gag in their mouths," she said, crossing her arms over her chest.

"He would if he thought it would help them." Jacob frowned, not sure why she'd drawn away from him. "George takes his Hippocratic oath seriously. He's dedicated to relieving suffering."

George's current patient made a piteous needy sound.

Julianne arched her brow. "Someone is certainly suffering by the sound of things."

"Sometimes George says a patient must be brought to the edge of madness before a cure can be affected. Of course, since hysteria is a chronic condition, most of his patients return weekly for another treatment. Some more often."

"Are you listening to the words coming out of your own mouth?"

"Yes, and I wish you and I were acting on them." He took one of her hands, brought it to his lips, and pressed a kiss on her palm. "I could be the wise physician and you the hapless hysterical sufferer in need of a paroxysm."

"Or I could be the doctor who'd cure your ills," she said archly, "and you the poor bewildered man who can't manage to figure out how his own body works."

Amazingly enough, Jacob's cock cheered this line of thinking just as heartily as his own little fantasy.

"If your friend truly wants to help his patients, why does he go through this farce?" Julianne asked.

The yelping grew louder.

"Honestly, there's nothing wrong with her that skillful sexual congress wouldn't fix," she said. "If she's unmarried, Dr. Snowdon would be doing her a favor if he took off her blindfold and showed her what to do to help herself."

Jacob's jaw dropped. A woman who took matters into her own hands, so to speak. He'd never heard the like, but his body warmed to the idea of watching Julianne try it.

"I believe he has a spinster or two who come for treatment, but most of George's clients are married."

"Do their husbands know about these treatments?" She balled her fingers into a fist, which Jacob tried unsuccessfully to smooth out.

"If they don't, they are as willfully blind as their wives, but to be honest, most men don't believe their wives capable of having such needs," he said. "Don't you see, Julianne? George's patients don't want to know the truth. As long as they believe they have a condition which requires treatment, they experience no guilt over the relief they feel."

The woman in the next room nearly howled as she reached her "paroxysm."

"Imagine if she had to confess to her priest that she let a stranger diddle her till she screamed," Jacob said. "This way, she has all her knots untied, with her husband's blessing. She's perfectly happy and without a shred of guilt. Believe me, George provides a much needed service."

"Rubbish." Julianne pulled her hand away from him. "A woman needs to take responsibility for herself. In every area."

"Much as I admire your forward thinking on this issue, I have to ask: Is that what you were doing in my bed last night? Just taking responsibility for yourself?"

"No, that was different. We were taking responsibility for each other," she said with a twitch of her lips that turned into a reluctant grin.

"Well, I guess we were at that." He leaned toward her and dropped a kiss on her forehead. "Wonder if you'd feel like taking responsibility for me again this evening."

"Why?" she asked with a mischievous wag of her brows. "Are you feeling hysterical?"

Yes, he almost admitted. He couldn't be near the woman without wanting to swive her silly, but something made him resist telling her how he was growing to need her. Jacob was spared a reply when the door of George's examination room creaked open.

"Be sure to take a long hot bath this evening," his friend told the woman who stepped into the hallway. "And wear loose fitting undergarments for the next two days."

"Then I suppose a chastity belt is out of the question," the woman said. "My husband suggested I resume wearing one since I've shown such marked improvement under your care."

"Absolutely not," the doctor said, taking a pad of paper from his pocket and scribbling a note on it. "Give this to your husband. It's my recommendation that you abstain from wearing that device in the future. In my experience, it greatly compounds the problem of hysteria."

"Thank you, Dr. Snowdon." She tucked the note into her reticule. "Same time next week then?"

"Yes, indeed. Even if you are feeling well, it's better to be safe than sorry," George said, his somber tone matching his words. "Skipping a treatment can only result in the increase of ill humors and could lead to a setback in your overall health."

The woman smiled. "We wouldn't want that, would we?"

"Not for worlds."

"Very well." She turned to go and then stopped. "Oh, I almost forgot. You mentioned once that a referral would be appreciated. I have a friend whom I suspect endures the same malady as I. Would you have time to see her tomorrow, say at two o'clock?"

George pulled the small notebook from his pocket again and consulted it. "Better make it two-thirty. Thank you for sharing the blessings of health and well-being with a fellow sufferer. As a token of my appreciation, the fee for your next treatment will be waived."

The woman smiled brightly, then noticed Jacob and Julianne for the first time. "Oh, sir, how thoughtful of you to escort your wife to her treatments. My husband is too busy for such things."

"I've never seen Dr. Snowdon for treatment," Julianne said, retreating a step.

"Don't fret. He'll have you right as rain in no time." The woman patted Julianne's shoulder, then turned to Jacob. "You've brought her to the right place. Dr. Snowdon works miracles."

Chapter 15

To Julianne's surprise, the examination room held all the usual accoutrements of a genuine physician's office—an examination table, a privacy screen for the patient to decently disrobe if necessary, and a set of sheets for modesty draping. The jar of leeches on the windowsill proclaimed Snowdon a proponent of traditional medicine while the collection of surgical implements displayed in a glass case proved he was combining the disciplines of a physician and a surgeon in pursuit of "General Practice."

"Well, Preston, it's good to see you again," George Snowdon said once he'd ushered them into his examination room and closed the door. While not handsome, the doctor was a lean, presentable fellow with pale blue eyes and a wide smile that displayed a good set of teeth. The warm oil he used on his patients evidently was scented with vanilla for the room was awash in the smell, though an undertone of a distinctly clinical stench lurked beneath it. "I'll hazard a guess that you have not brought this charming young woman here for a treatment."

Julianne narrowed her gaze at him. "And the charming young woman will thank you not to speak of her as if she's not even in the room."

Jacob introduced her to his friend, clearly hoping to forestall the riot she felt building behind her eyes.

Perhaps if Julianne had never read Mary Wollstonecraft she'd not have been so prickly when men treated her as if she were less than a rational being. But the writings of that somewhat scandalous feminine visionary only helped solidify Julianne's own sense that she should not be relegated to less than adult status. Her education might be inferior to that of the men in the room, but her mind was not.

"Actually, George, we were hoping you could help us with a different sort of problem." Jacob took the partial manuscript out of the carpetbag and laid it on the examination table. He thumbed through the pages carefully till he came to the part that was written in an ancient alphabet of unknown origin. "What do you make of this?"

Snowdon pulled a pair of spectacles from his pocket and peered down at the page. "Fascinating."

"Do you recognize the language?" Julia asked.

"Shh!" The doctor held up a hand to signal for quiet while he skimmed over the pages. He leafed back to the beginning of the manuscript and then forward to the puzzling part several times. His silent reading was punctuated with an occasional "hmm" and once with an "astounding," but he apparently didn't feel compelled to elaborate further.

With a sigh, Julianne looked around the room and realized she'd located the source of the medicinal smell. Jars filled with unlikely objects in formaldehyde were propped on a shelf ringing the small space—an eyeball with a couple inches of the optic nerve still intact, a baby pig, a star fish. When she came to one containing what appeared to be a severed human hand, she jerked her gaze back to the doctor and Jacob, who were still bent over the manuscript.

"What have you learned?" she asked.

Snowdon looked up suddenly and blinked at her twice as if he'd only just remembered she was in the room. Then he removed his spectacles and began cleaning them with a handkerchief from his pocket.

"This seems to be a tale of the dispersion of a set of six ceremonial daggers," the doctor said, putting his glasses back on and wrapping his fingers around his lapels in preparation for delivering a scholarly lecture. "There are some carefully worded clues as to the whereabouts of five of these blades—"

"My late husband has already discovered them," Julianne interrupted, impatient for him to tell her something she didn't know about the codex. "We are specifically hoping you can help us uncover information about the location of the remaining dagger."

"I see. Well. Nothing immediately apparent about that here."

Julianne's shoulders sagged. "Then you can't help us."

"I didn't say that. Now the first part of the manuscript is in Latin, and rather badly conjugated Latin at that. I suspect the Druids made a convert of a minor cleric, who penned this treatise. Or, and this is rather more likely, the monk was coerced into writing down their tale of the daggers. But even though he was no grammarian, the author was fiendishly clever," Snowdon said. "He fixed the Druids good and proper. You see, this last bit isn't in any known language at all."

"What!" Julianne exclaimed, crestfallen. If the rest of the manuscript was gibberish, even if she located the last half, she'd never find clues to the other dagger. "How can you be sure?"

"I am familiar with a goodly number of ancient tongues, milady. However, judging from the apparent age of this codex, it's highly unlikely the writer of the manuscript would have been acquainted with more than Latin. Possibly Greek, but if that portion of the text were in Greek, then even Preston could have rendered a translation."

"You damn my scholarship with faint praise," Jacob said dryly.

"Perhaps you'll allow that my memory of our days at Cambridge is accurate. You were never one for pegging the books that hard, my friend," Snowdon said, tapping his finger to his temple. "Nevertheless, the reason you can't read this portion is because it's in code."

"Diabolical fellow." Despite his words, the glint in Jacob's eyes showed he was more excited than daunted by yet another twist in the mystery. "How do we crack it?"

"It looks as if our unknown author has obligingly left us a key, or part of one at any rate. See here." George pointed to the penultimate line on the last page. "He switches back to Latin at this point, but I doubt many would notice this." His finger traced an imaginary line back to the start of the coded bit. "The words in that last section contain exactly the same number of characters as the part that seems to be incomprehensible."

Julianne peered around him to study the weathered parchment. "So one only needs to match up the letters in Latin to the corresponding symbols in the previous section and it should be readable."

"Exactly." George nudged Jacob. "Bright girl there, Preston."

Julianne still wished the doctor wouldn't speak as if she weren't present, but at least he gave her a compliment that made her proud.

"However, there is a problem," George said. "Since the manuscript is incomplete, so is the key. You wouldn't happen to have the rest of it, would you?"

"Not yet," Jacob said. "But we will shortly. Do what you can with this portion, will you, old chap?"

George smiled broadly. "Nothing I like better than untangling a puzzle for a friend." A timid rap on the door interrupted him. "Unless, of course, it's relieving a patient in need. That must be my eleven o'clock."

"Keep this business under your hat, would you?" Jacob said as Julianne and he moved toward the door. "And keep the manuscript under lock and key when you aren't working on it. There are other interested parties who might try to relieve you of it."

George Snowdon tapped the side of his nose in the time-honored gesture of collusion and secreted the document in a desk drawer, which he promptly locked.

"I should have something for you based on this bit by tomorrow morning," George promised.

"And with any luck at all," Jacob said, "we'll be in possession of the rest of the manuscript by tomorrow night."

Luck has nothing to do with it, Julianne decided. Surely Sir Malcolm had the other half of the Druid codex and she'd ferret it out when she attended her "initiation" into the Order within the Order. But Jacob's words reminded her that the invitation was for her alone, and he still spoke as if he meant to accompany her when Sir Malcolm's factor came for her tomorrow evening.

She'd deal with that later. Julianne turned to Jacob's friend and offered her hand in gratitude.

"Dr. Snowdon, I thank you for your expert assistance. You have helped me immeasurably," Julianne said as Jacob opened the door leading to the corridor.

A middle-aged matron with a worried frown fretted on the other side of the door, shifting her weight from one foot to the other. She brightened when she saw Julianne.

The woman squared her shoulders and breezed past them into the office. Then she pulled Julianne aside to whisper, "I wasn't sure about this hysteria treatment business, but if Dr. Snowdon helped you, surely he can help me, too."

The rest of the day passed peacefully enough. Jacob and Julianne made it a point to be seen strolling through Hyde Park at the fashionable hour and later supped at home with Viola and Quinn. They enjoyed a quiet evening with his cousin and her husband. Viola coaxed Jacob into playing her pianoforte and Julianne demonstrated that her singing voice was every bit as pleasant as her speaking one.

After their tranquil, almost domestic day, Jacob was once again plagued with thoughts of making his arrangement with Julianne permanent. It was an unwelcome idea for one as devoted to the delights of bachelorhood as he, but he couldn't seem to shake it.

Whether they were plotting over the manuscript with George, wandering among the upper crust, or engaged in the homely pursuits of a domesticated evening, he simply enjoyed being with her. He found himself wondering what she thought before she expressed her well-considered opinions. He caught himself watching her when she wasn't aware, simply for the pleasure of studying the play of light on her features.

When he retired for the night, instead of climbing into his bed, he paced his small chamber keeping one ear cocked for the sounds of the household retiring for the night. Julianne wouldn't thank him for causing a scandal by being caught sneaking into her chamber, so he'd take pains not to be.

Caught, that is. He had every intention of passing the night in her room.

He looked out the window to the street below. Movement drew his eye to a shadowy figure down by the corner. Too short for a man. It was probably Gil, the boy he'd tasked with following Julianne. Of all the street rats he employed on a regular basis, Gil showed the most promise, exceeding his assignments and showing more than a flash of untutored intellect. Jacob had caught sight of the lad tailing them discreetly a few times while he and Julianne made their way about the city.

The longcase clock downstairs chimed the hour. *Not much longer now, if there's a God in heaven.* He stepped away from the window and resumed pacing.

Jacob would have to give the boy an extra bonus for staying at his post so long. Perhaps a permanent position within his household wouldn't be out of reason for such a likely lad.

Permanent. There it was again.

He'd never considered such a thing before, but the thought of going back to his life before Julianne had entered it made his chest constrict smartly.

Granted, he was not considered much of a catch. His reputation was too wild. Marriage-minded matrons with debutantes to protect would not let him within a foot of their precious lambs, as if he'd be interested in a green girl.

Who'd want an insipid child when he could have a woman worthy of the name?

And what a woman! Beautiful, intelligent, courageous, Julianne was fast becoming his obsession. Of course, some women would be put off by his romantic history, but considering that Julianne's theatrical past smacked of unsavory associations and behavior, he was hopeful she'd be willing to overlook his checkered reputation.

Then there was his dubious gift. It was one thing for him to go through life dodging unnecessary contact with metals, another to expect Julianne to deal with it daily as well. Then too, the ability to glean information from touch and pay for the privilege in pain seemed to run in his family. Perhaps she wouldn't want to burden her future children with such an ill-omened legacy.

He snorted. Thinking about children meant he was really getting ahead of himself in the permanence department. Besides, there were plenty of other reasons for Julianne to reject him.

He had no title to offer her. She'd been a countess. That was important in the world's eyes. Would simple Mrs. Jacob Preston be enough for her?

Of course, he was sufficiently well off. He'd make sure she wanted for nothing and—

He dragged a hand over his face. What was he thinking? He was not the marrying type and he knew it. He'd known her less than a fortnight. They'd made love only twice during that period—well, two and a half times if he counted the second interlude in the coach when he'd been gentlemanly enough to give pleasure without expecting it to be returned. Even so, it was a record of restraint for his relationships.

Perhaps that was why he was even considering something as rash as proposing matrimony. He was still in the white-hot heat of initial lust. If he found his way into the lady's bed with more frequency, maybe this affair would burn out as quickly as his others had.

He was more than willing to find out.

Silent as a wraith, Jacob slipped out of his room, down the corridor, and into Julianne's chamber.

CHAPTER 16

"Jacob, what is it?" Julianne whispered. She hadn't found sleep yet, so she wasn't startled when he slipped into her room, but she wished he hadn't come. They'd dodged discovery the night before. They might not be so lucky again. She rose from her bed and donned her wrapper. "What's wrong?"

His hands found her waist and he tugged her close. The deeper pull of his body made her melt into him, fitting together so snugly it was as if they'd been designed to click like magnets.

"Why does something have to be wrong?" he asked with a sensual lift of a dark brow. "I've been thinking about being alone with you all day."

Having Jacob all to herself had crossed her mind more than once or twice too, but she couldn't admit it to him. It would only make what she had to do harder. She pushed against his chest, fighting against her natural attraction to him. Jacob might be the finest thing she'd ever seen, but if she didn't have independent means, a woman had to care what the world thought of her. Welcoming Jacob to her bed meant she risked losing Lady Kilmaine's good opinion.

"We can't do this," she whispered. "You're in my bedchamber when you have no business here."

"You were in mine last night," he reminded her.

"That was different. You were ill." She tried to wiggle away from him, but his warmth and strength radiated through the thin layers of his banyan and her bedclothes. She stopped struggling against the undeniable draw. His body put hers on high alert, sending tingles of awareness fluttering through her. "I had a legitimate reason to stay in your room. You needed someone to sit with you."

"No, I needed someone to sleep with me." His smile was sin incarnate. "Once we wore each other out, of course."

He bent and nuzzled her neck, his mouth wet and warm. If she didn't get some space between them soon, she wouldn't have the strength to.

"Jacob, please." She ducked and slipped out of his embrace. "What will your cousin think?"

"She'll think it's about bloody time I found someone to care about."

"Lower your voice," she hissed. She couldn't be swayed by his protestation of affection. Men spoke easily of such things when it suited their purpose. "If you truly cared about me, you wouldn't be trying to put me in a compromising position and embarrass me before your family."

The only light in the room came from the yellowish street lamp that filtered in her window, but it was bright enough for her to see his dark frown.

"Now just a minute," he said. "Correct me if I am wrong, but while we were waiting outside George's examination room this morning, didn't you tell me you expected me to deal with your *hysteria* tonight?"

Her belly jittered enough to qualify as that mysterious feminine ailment. "No, I think you're the one who suggested that."

"Well, either way, it's a damn good idea."

His hair was disheveled; his banyan loosely belted enough

to bare his muscular chest to the waist. A quick glance downward showed a satisfying bulge beneath the silk. His gaze seared into her, a promise of pleasure. Jacob Preston was enough to tempt a much stronger woman than she.

He must have seen surrender in her eyes because he advanced on her again. She stopped him with a shaky hand to his chest.

"Not in your cousin's house." Her body clamored against her will, but Lady Kilmaine had been so gracious, so welcoming, Julianne couldn't tread on her hospitality by acting like a common strumpet in her guest room. It was bad enough that she'd spent the previous night in Jacob's chamber. Only dumb luck had kept them from discovery. She couldn't tempt fate twice.

The roguish light left his eyes. "What if I were to ask you to come to my house?"

"That's no better. Then the whole world will know we are lovers."

"Not as my lover," he said. "As my wife."

The word hung in the silence that followed for the space of several heartbeats. He couldn't mean it. Not Jacob Preston, the ruination of so many society matrons even the *London Crier* had lost count.

"You don't want to marry me," she said softly. "You just want me in your bed."

"What if I want both?" He ran a hand over his hair in exasperation. "How the bloody hell do you know what I want or don't want?"

"I don't," she said. "And that's my point exactly. We've been thrown together by chance and this business with the dagger. Then poor judgment led us to tumble into bed with each other, but I really don't know you at all. And you don't know me either."

"I know you better than you think."

Before she could stop him, he swooped her into his arms and claimed her mouth in a kiss tinged with desperation. His longing turned her knees to water. Her muscles unclenched and she sagged into him as his kiss drained her will to resist. Moist warmth pooled between her thighs. She ached to welcome him, to take him inside her so they could rut each other till she screamed his name and damn the consequences.

"Now, tell me I don't know what you like, Julianne," he said when he finally released her mouth to deliver a string of nipping kisses along her jawline that ended with her earlobe. He suckled that needy little bit of skin. Pleasure sparked over her. "Tell me I can't make you happy."

His maleness pressed against her belly. She throbbed in response, but she couldn't give in. "Can you tell me you love me, Jacob?"

"I already did." He cocked his head at her. "Twice now I've admitted I care about you."

"That's not the same. I care about a good many things." *And a good many people.*

The girls at Mrs. Osgood's school were depending on her. If she couldn't find the last dagger and sell the set, she realized the only way she'd be able to continue to support the school was if she interested Lady Kilmaine and other women of the ton in donating to the cause of orphaned girls who would be cast on the streets otherwise. For the sake of those children, she dared not alienate Viola Preston by behaving foolishly with Jacob while under her roof.

"Caring is not all there is to loving," Julianne said. "And just because we bed each other well, it doesn't signify that we are suited for a more permanent relationship."

His face went stony. "Then your answer is no."

She nodded, because he couldn't possibly be serious about the question. She was no green girl. A man intent on bedding a woman would say anything he thought she wanted to hear.

Of course an experienced seducer would assume an unattached woman wanted an offer of marriage. "Please Jacob, it's late and I don't want to argue with you."

"Then don't." His voice was brittle. If she didn't know better, she'd swear he was hurt.

"I must ask you to return to your room." She eased out of his embrace and was grateful he didn't try to force her to stay. "We both need to get some sleep. Dr. Snowdon is expecting us first thing in the morning and I've no doubt what he learns will be useful when I attend the initiation ceremony tomorrow."

"You're probably right." Even though he agreed with her, his features were screwed into a frown. "It may be a long night with the Druids and we'll need all our wits about us."

At the risk of upsetting him further, she had to disabuse him of the notion that he'd accompany her to the secret meeting of Sir Malcolm's sect within the Order. "There will be no 'us.' I was the only one invited. Therefore, I must go alone. This may be my only chance to find the other half of the manuscript, and I can't risk losing the opportunity by failing to follow Sir Malcolm's instructions for my initiation."

"No," he said, forgetting to lower his voice. "I can't allow it."

Julianne straightened to her full, if inconsiderable, height. "One of the lovely things about being a widow is making my own choices. Since you are not my husband, you have no say about this."

"The hell I don't."

"Keep your voice down."

"You aren't going alone and that's final," he said even louder.

"You'll wake your cousin."

"I'd wake the queen if I thought it would make you see reason," he shouted.

Footsteps pattered down the hall. A soft rap came at the door. Julianne's belly spiraled downward. They'd been well and truly caught.

"Is everything all right?" Viola's voice seeped through the keyhole.

"Yes," Julianne answered.

"No," Jacob said at the same time and strode over to open the door to admit his cousin and her yawning husband. "Tell her she needs to use some sense."

Julianne wished she could sink into the floor. "I'm sorry we woke you. Jacob and I were having a difference of opinion on how to proceed in the matter of . . . the business dealings with which he's assisting me," she said through clenched teeth. How dare he expose her to scandal like this! She glared at Jacob. "I don't think Lord and Lady Kilmaine would be interested in how I conduct my business." Then she turned back to her hosts, her cheeks burning. "I apologize for the disruption. Jacob was just leaving."

"Damn right I am." He pushed past Viola and Quinn, then stopped in the corridor and shot a defiant glower back at Julianne. "When you're ready to use your head for something other than a place to hang your bonnet, Lady Cambourne, you know where I live."

He stomped down the hall. Viola sent her husband an urgent silent message and, grumbling only a little, Quinn followed Jacob.

"My cousin isn't used to being thwarted by the women in his life," Viola said. "You'll have to forgive him for being such an ass."

No, I don't. Julianne was too furious with Jacob to forgive. "Perhaps a little thwarting is just what Mr. Preston needs."

Viola laughed. "No doubt."

"Since Mr. Preston is leaving your home, I ought to as well." Sir Malcolm had said she'd be contacted at Lord Kilmaine's town house, but she didn't see how she could remain in residence after this embarrassing debacle. Jacob was probably counting on that outcome when he stomped off. *Drat the man.* "However, if it's not too much trouble, may I stay the night and return to my hotel in the morning?"

"Out of the question." Viola shook her head. "We don't want you going anywhere. You don't need to leave just because the two of you have had a lover's spat."

"Lover's spat? It's not like that—"

"It's exactly like that. I recognize the signs even if the two of you don't," Viola said, her hazel eyes twinkling. "And I wouldn't miss a ringside seat when Jacob crawls back on his hands and knees to apologize to you for all the jewels in the Gorgeous East. Quinn and I would love for you to stay with us as long as you like. Please say you will."

Viola gave her an unexpected hug. Amazingly enough, Lady Kilmaine was on her side. Tears pressed against the back of Julianne's eyes. She'd expected censure from a member of the ton, but instead she found acceptance.

Whatever else happened while she sought the last dagger, she'd finally found a real friend in Viola Preston.

But despite that, her chest still ached. Her irritation at Jacob dissolved as she realized he was abandoning her. No matter how many friends she drew around her, they'd never make up for that loss.

"Whatever you do, Quinn, do not let her leave with Ravenwood's factor tomorrow evening," Jacob said as he shrugged into his jacket. He'd send Fenwick over in a day or two to pack up the rest of his things. For now, he had to get as far away from Julianne as possible. If she'd been a man, he'd have punched out her lights for such willful stupidity. But because she was a woman, he was more likely to disgrace himself by begging her to marry him again. "It's not safe for her to go alone."

"Agreed," Quinn said. Once Jacob had explained about the Order within the Order, his cousin-in-law understood and was completely on his side. "Though I may have to tie her up to keep her here if she's as stubborn as you say."

"Just don't tell Viola if you do."

"Of course not. Women tend to gang up on a man," Quinn said. "What my lovely wife doesn't know won't hurt me." He put a hand on Jacob's shoulder. "Julianne won't leave with anyone tomorrow evening under my watch."

Jacob nodded his thanks and tromped out of the town house. Maybe Julianne would listen to Quinn, but he doubted it. A hackney cab rattled past, but he wasn't tempted to hail it. He was counting on the long walk home to cool his ire.

How could she be so mulish? Didn't she realize he was only concerned for her safety?

And how could she swat down his proposal of marriage as if it were no more than a pesky fly?

They didn't know each other, she'd said. *Like hell.* They knew each other in all the ways that counted. She obviously just didn't want him. Not for very long, at any rate. Or in any manner other than her own choosing.

When he reached the corner, he slowed. His boy, Gil, was there, leaning against the lamppost.

"Got yerself a tail, guv," the lad said softly.

Jacob gave a barely perceptible nod and kept walking. Sure enough, he heard footsteps behind him, trying to match his stride. A shadowy presence was betrayed by the slap of leather on cobbles every few steps. He chided himself for not paying attention before. As long as this business with the dagger was in play, he needed to stay focused on the game. Considering the way Julianne's husband had died, it was clear the other side was playing for keeps.

He'd been as stubbornly blind as she, ignoring the dangers and pressing ahead.

When he came to the alley he usually cut down, he pressed himself into the shadows as soon as he rounded the corner. Jacob held his breath lest a puff of vapor in the cold night reveal his location.

The footsteps behind him quickened.

Jacob's muscles tensed, ready to pounce. After the argument with Julianne, he almost welcomed the chance to throttle someone. His shadow rounded the corner.

It was another boy, smaller than Gil.

"What do you think you're up to, lad?" he asked.

The boy startled and tried to run, but Jacob grabbed him by his grubby collar and held him fast. Despite his small size, he kicked like a Thoroughbred with a burr under his saddle and wasn't above biting if Jacob gave him half a chance.

"Stop that or I'll tan your backside for you," Jacob ordered.

Gil came jogging up to them. "Let me have a whack at him, sir. I'll knock some sense into his noggin."

The boy stopped struggling then, as if sensing that while Jacob might not strike him, the older lad had no such compunction.

Jacob loosened his grip, but didn't release the boy completely. "Now, who are you and why are you following me?"

"Me name's Pete." The boy scratched his head vigorously and then shoved his hands into his pockets. "I was told to keep an eye on ye."

"By whom?"

Pete studied the hole in his left shoe where a broken-nailed toe protruded. "I can't say."

"Can't or won't?"

"I don't rightly know his name, see? And every time I ask

someone what lives near him, they gives me this." The boy's fingers curled into the sign against evil. "And then they tells me I should keep my nose out of that beehive if I knows what's good for me. But he pays, so I does what he tells me. A bloke's got to eat, don't he?"

"Let me guess at your employer," Jacob said, releasing the boy completely since he seemed to have settled. "He's a big chap, about my height, with blond hair. And he always wears black."

The boy's eyes grew round and he made the sign again.

"Sir Malcolm Ravenwood," Jacob said to Gil. The older lad let out a low whistle. Evidently, he too was aware of Sir Malcolm's reputation.

"What sort of thing do you tell him about me?" Jacob asked.

"Where ye go. Who ye see. Like that."

"And he pays you for this?"

The boy named the insultingly low amount.

"Well, Pete, I have a proposition for you," Jacob said. "I'll pay you four times as much for you to report on Sir Malcolm to me."

"Oh, I couldn't do that, sir." The boy bobbed his head like a nervous sparrow. "He'd catch me at it sure."

Jacob tapped his temple in thought. "Not if he thought you were hanging about in hopes that he'd hire you again."

"Ye mean to get me sacked?" Pete said, clearly distraught.

"Exactly. It's the only way you'll be able to watch him safely." Jacob fished some coins from his pocket and held them out to Pete. "Will you do it?"

"Aye, sir. I'll be yer eyes on Sir Malcolm."

"My distant eyes." Jacob dropped the blunt into the boy's outstretched hand. "I don't want you caught and I'd be obliged if you didn't return to him for your last report."

"No, sir."

"Now off with you and mind how you go."

The boy scampered away clutching his newfound wealth.

Jacob turned to Gil, who was frowning after Pete. Clearly, he thought the boy had been rewarded overmuch for changing employers.

"I have an assignment for you that's beyond your usual scope," Jacob said. "It'll mean a permanent place in my household, if you accept it."

Gil straightened. "I accept."

"Wait till you hear what it is. It's not without risk," Jacob warned. "I want you to go to Sir Malcolm and tell him you caught Pete skulking after me. Since you work for me, you felt obliged to protect me by beating the truth out of him. Then tell him you saw an opportunity. You know a lot more about me than Pete ever could and you're willing to share what you know for the right price."

"While I'm still workin' for you?"

"Yes. He's the sort who'll appreciate the subtlety of a turncoat and think he's stolen the march on us. In reality, you'll be in a position to feed him only the information I want him to have," Jacob said. "But look sharp, lad. The man is dangerous."

One corner of the boy's mouth turned up. "So is sleeping on the street."

"Well, then, it looks as if we have an accord," Jacob said. At least one thing had gone well this night. "Mrs. Trott will fix you a pallet in the kitchen for tonight and by tomorrow I'll have figured out what I want you to tell Sir Malcolm at your first meeting."

Chapter 17

Sir Malcolm eyed the boy who'd come calling shortly after daybreak. His name was Gilbert Stout. With his spotty cheeks and stringy hair, he didn't look much like a Judas, but he offered to play the role. Malcolm judged Gil to be about fourteen, though his deep-set eyes seemed much older. Like most street urchins, poor food and constant scrambling had left him undersized for his age.

"And so, after I sent your lad Pete packing with a black eye for dogging my employer," Gil said with a little swagger, "I says to meself, that Sir Malcolm Ravenwood's like to be needing another bloke to help him, since Pete's no good at all. I figure ye need someone what can get more information than a boy what just follows a body around is likely to hear. So here I am."

When Malcolm merely sat in silence, the new boy cleared his throat and went on. "For example, I figured you'd want to know Mr. Preston broke it off with the lady he's been squirin' about."

Malcolm knew this already. Since the countess had started spending so much time with Preston, his gazing ball had been cloudy whenever he tried to observe her. Last night, the magical orb was clear as a cold midnight sky and Preston was nowhere to be seen near the lady. "And you know this how?"

"He left the countess at Lord Kilmaine's last night and nipped back to his own place," Gil said. "I was in his kitchen eating a bite this morning—his housekeeper's got a kind heart, ye see—and I hear Mr. Preston's valet tell her as Himself wouldn't be stirring from his bed till noon and didn't want to be disturbed. Usually him and Lady Cambourne are out larkin' about long before the rest of the upper crust, so it stands to reason he's not dancin' attendance on Lady C. no more. He don't usually waste time on women once he leaves 'em. Though to hear Mr. Fenwick tell it, he's taken to his bed over the lady. I expect he'll be looking to meet up with her again in the future."

"Hmph! Much as I appreciate the information, I have to wonder why you offer it," Malcolm said. "You eat in the man's kitchen and take his coin and yet you're willing to turn on him?"

The boy frowned. "I can see where that might look bad, but think on it from my point, sir. A fellow like me has to shift for himself. Won't no one else shift for me. I ask ye. Who's a better employer for a likely lad looking for the main chance—a man who's only got the chinks thanks to his brother the earl or a knight of the realm in his own right?"

The boy sketched a clumsy bow.

Malcolm recognized flattery when it reared its frilly head, but it pleased him all the same. "Yet what you're actually proposing is to take payment from both of us?"

Gil gave him a crooked smile. "Well, ye've the right of it there, I expect, but then I'd have to, wouldn't I? If Mr. Preston still thinks I'm his lad, he'll keep me close and tell me the things ye'll be wanting to hear."

"But if you have to choose between your two employers, where would your loyalty lie?"

"Why, with ye, sir," Gil said quickly.

A little too quickly. *Time to give the boy a lesson in what it means to be in the employ of a Grand Master.*

Malcolm stood, retrieved a candlestick from the mantle and placed it on the desk before the boy. Calling fire was the most elemental of all magicks. Malcolm could do it as easily as breathing. When he passed his hand over the wick, flame leaped to life.

The boy startled like a spooked colt and might have bolted, but Malcolm clapped a hand on his shoulder. Then he grasped the boy's delicate wrist. The small bones grated together in his firm grasp.

"Unclench your fingers," he ordered and Gil Stout complied, his breathing unsteady. "Good. The first thing you must learn is obedience, Master Stout. What I tell you to do, you must do without question. I need to know how well you can hold your tongue."

He pulled the boy's hand forward until it was positioned above the flame. Then he forced his palm down till the fire licked at his skin. Gil Stout trembled and bit his lower lip, but he didn't cry out.

A small blister formed and Malcolm heard the boy's back teeth grind together. When he released him, the lad yanked his hand back and cradled it against his chest. All color drained from his face and his eyes were over-bright with unshed tears, but his white lips were firmly clamped. He refused to give voice to his agony.

Giving pain held a special fascination for Malcolm. Unusual tolerance for it never failed to impress him.

"Very well," he said. "I believe you'll do. Let me know if Preston contacts Lady Cambourne again and anything else you find that's pertinent as it touches the two of them."

He pulled a few coppers from his pocket and laid them on the desk. Gil reached for them with his uninjured hand.

"No." Malcolm slapped his palm over the meager amount. "Use the other."

With obvious difficulty, Gil made the fingers of his burned hand work long enough to pick up the coins and pocket them.

"That'll be all, Gil."

The boy walked unsteadily toward the door.

"Oh, by the way, there is something specific I want you to find out for me," Malcolm said. There had to be a reason he couldn't view the countess in his gazing ball when Preston was near. "You saw me take fire from the air, so you know I have some unusual abilities. Mr. Preston does too, or I'm much mistaken. Find out what it is that's out of the ordinary about him. Or don't come back."

The boy nodded mutely and kept walking.

"But if you don't come back," Malcolm called after him and Gil stopped in mid-step, "I'll want to know why you didn't. So I will find you. And I'll make learning why you didn't return to me very unpleasant. For you, at least. Do we understand each other?"

"Yes, sir."

"Good lad. Off you go," Malcolm said with as much cheer as if he'd been taking tea with the boy.

Once, Malcolm's conscience might have bothered him over giving the lad that painful lesson. Now he realized it was really a kindness. Better Gil Stout should know the way of things from the outset. Less chance of him going astray later and requiring Malcolm to take sterner measures with his new acolyte.

With the boy gone, Malcolm positioned his gazing ball to take advantage of the wan morning light stabbing through the shutters in long thin shafts. There was no point in having special abilities if one wasn't willing to use them to bring about the greater good.

Once Malcolm reunited all the daggers, he'd be in a position to affect so much—turning the minds of princes without their knowledge and silently directing events to rid the world of inequities. It made no sense for some to bask in wealth and others to suffer in squalor. Everyone should be equal.

Almost everyone. It was only right Malcolm should claim more than most. And decide who else among his closest associates would benefit from a double portion of wealth.

Of course, there was also the promise of immortality for the one who wielded the reunited power of the daggers. But that was really no more than his due once he set the world to rights, wasn't it? People were sheep. If the shepherd sheared them once in a while, it was for their own good.

Bands of illumination struck the gazing ball. The interior of the orb glowed and a vaporous mass began to swirl. Then the mass coalesced into a recognizable shape.

"Ah! Lady Cambourne," Malcolm said softly, as if he feared she might hear him. "There you are."

Even though Jacob hadn't returned to his cousin's town house to accompany Julianne that morning, she still needed to learn what Dr. Snowdon had gleaned from the manuscript they'd left with him. When she alighted from Lord Kilmaine's carriage, her insides jumped with nervousness. She wasn't sure whether it was because of the way Jacob had deserted her or because she was calling on a doctor who specialized in hysteria patients.

Fortunately, there were no sufferers waiting in the corridor. After putting her ear to the examination room door for a few moments, she decided none were being treated that early in the morning either.

She rapped on the thick oak.

When there was no answer, she knocked again.

"Come in, come in, confound it. Can't a man study in peace?"

Julianne pushed open the door and found Dr. Snowdon hunched over the manuscript, scribbling notes on a separate paper. He glanced up with annoyance, but then a smile lit his face when he recognized her.

"Ah! Of course, I should have expected it was you, countess." He shoved his spectacles up onto his creased forehead, giving him the disconcerting appearance of having four eyes, the top two scrunched tightly closed. "My apologies for being so surly, Lady Cambourne, but when I'm deep into a mystery, I loathe interruption. Fascinating stuff, this is. Positively riveting."

She held out her gloved hand for his slight obeisance and noticed his notes scrawled over several pages, covered with ink blots and scratched out portions. "It looks as if you've made splendid progress. What have you learned?"

"I decoded everything I could, but there are some disturbing blanks since the key is incomplete," Snowdon said. "Then because the text is in Latin, I've been working on a translation."

"Good show, old chap," came a voice from behind her. Jacob leaned against the doorjamb with his hands in his pockets, looking cool and unflappable, as if their "wake the household" argument had never happened.

Julianne stiffened at his unexpected intrusion. If he meant to abandon her, he ought to at least do her the courtesy of staying gone. She'd wept over his departure last night, once all the lights in the Kilmaines' home went dark. Balling her fist in her mouth to muffle her sobs, she hadn't imagined there were that many tears in her. When the sun rose this morning, she resolved not to let herself care what Jacob Preston did.

It was all she could think to do to protect her heart. Though the way it throbbed now, she knew her resolve was utterly useless. Jacob had marked her and there was no escaping.

Blithely unaware how his presence unsettled her, Jacob

sauntered in and peered down at Dr. Snowdon's work. "Wouldn't want an academic lightweight like me trying to translate it, after all."

"My thoughts exactly," Snowdon said with a grin. "Here's what I have so far. Please forgive the crudity of the rhyme, but I was trying to capture the spirit of the original."

Julianne picked up the topmost piece of foolscap, grateful for the distraction from Jacob's nearness, and read:

"Beware the blades from Merlin's Staff
The final dagger's final laugh.
A mage's curse on he who finds
A double curse on he who binds.
Sons of forest brave halls of stone
To leave one lying ne'er alone
'Neath—"

Then there was a section of squiggles and lines Julianne couldn't make sense of.

Dr. Snowdon shrugged. "As I said, incomplete. If you find the other part of the manuscript, I ought to be able to decipher the rest for you with no trouble."

She turned back to the page.

"Once and future king of kings
Powers tremble, riches brings
At the source the end is hidden
Meet at grave and ring and midden."

More squiggles and scratched out sections followed. Even if they had a full translation, the meaning of the text was pretty obtuse. Her respect for her late husband's mind ticked up sharply. Working by himself, Algernon had untangled five similar riddles and located the daggers associated with them.

Surely with the assistance of Dr. Snowdon, she'd be able to do the same. She resisted looking in Jacob's direction. If he continued to insist she not go alone to the Druids' gathering this evening, he'd be more of a hindrance than a help.

"Merlin's staff, curses galore, graves and kings and all that rot. Cracking good stuff, what?" Snowdon's eyes sparked with enthusiasm. "Wherever did your husband acquire this manuscript in the first place, milady?"

"He was known to be a collector of oddities. A troop of gypsies came through Cambourne one spring and offered it to him for what he said was a ridiculously low sum. They told him he was meant to have it and they dared not ask for more," she said. "The earl always said it was the most significant find of his life."

And yet it had led to his death. "A mage's curse on he who finds," she repeated. "Do you suppose that's why my husband died?"

"Now we're treading on lunatic ice. There is no such thing as a curse." Jacob gathered up all Dr. Snowdon's notes and the manuscript. "It's just an old book about some old daggers, but all the same, not something to trumpet about. Right, George?"

Snowdon nodded his understanding and Julianne suspected the two of them had collaborated on a number of unusual "mysteries" in the past.

"You'll be back when you've found the rest of the manuscript, won't you?" Snowdon said.

"Of course." Julianne favored him with a glowing smile and thanked him for his help.

Jacob hustled her out of the examination room with the determination of a sheep dog rounding up a wayward lamb. She couldn't protest without causing another scene and after last night, she was tired of fighting with Jacob Preston. But once they were back in the corridor, her smile faded.

"I'll thank you to return my property."

He handed the manuscript and sheaves of notes to her without comment. She squirreled them away in her carpetbag and started down the hall. Jacob fell into step beside her.

"Before you whisked me out of his office," she said, studiously not looking at him, "did it occur to you that I might have more questions to ask the doctor?"

"Did it occur to you that revealing more about this whole mess might put him in danger?" he countered. "The fellow who rifled through your hotel room is still out there. George is my friend. I don't want to see him hurt because he helped us."

Julianne worried her bottom lip. She hadn't considered that.

They stepped through Dr. Snowdon's front door and onto the street. Clouds obscured a cold, late autumn sun and a light patter of rain fell. Jacob helped her into the waiting hansom, gave the driver instructions, and climbed in behind her.

She was still upset with him, but being confined in a small space with him might weaken her resolve to stay upset. She hoped never to spend another night weeping over a man. Especially this one. "I didn't invite you to join me."

"No, you didn't," he said agreeably as he rapped on the ceiling of the coach to signal the driver they were ready to go. "Are you still so angry with me you begrudge me a ride home in the rain?"

She clamped her lips tight. At least he'd taken the opposite squab so she didn't have to feel his thigh and shoulder snug against hers. Unfortunately, it meant she couldn't help looking at him unless she turned her head to watch rainy London plod by in a blur through the isinglass windows.

"There seems to be a good bit of Arthurian lore in the manuscript," he said in an obvious attempt to fill the silence that stretched between them.

It wasn't an apology, but his tone was more conciliatory than she'd ever heard him. "Yes, I caught that too. What do you suppose this Merlin's Staff business is about? I don't recall any mention of it in *Le Morte d'Arthur.*"

"Nor I," he said. "The manuscript seemed to suggest the daggers came from the staff. I have some books on the Arthurian legend in my library if you'd care to take a look."

It was an olive branch. He still wanted to help her. When she met his gaze, his gray eyes darkened. Everything would be so much simpler if her blood didn't heat every time she looked at the man. Why couldn't Jacob Preston have been a bespectacled academic like his friend Dr. Snowdon?

"Yes, Jacob. I'd like to take a look. I mean"—flustered, she went on—"Maybe we'll find something in your collection about this mysterious staff."

He reached forward and took one of her hands.

"Regardless of what you may think, I do care about you, Julianne, and you can't fault me for trying to protect you," he said softly. "But if you're still intent on going alone tonight, I will not try to stop you."

His thumb swept over her knuckles in light touches.

Her insides melted and she felt petty and mean for being angry with him. Jacob meant extremely well. She'd have to give him credit for that. And as for showing up in her room last night, part of her had wished he would.

She smiled at him and he nodded in satisfaction. The coach rattled to a stop before Jacob's front door. He climbed out and asked the driver to return in a couple hours to take Julianne back to Lord Kilmaine's town house. She appreciated his gentlemanly forethought.

The rain whipped itself into a steady torrent, but there was no help for it. They dashed together into Jacob's home. In those few short steps, Julianne was drenched clear through to her frilly all-in-one.

Dripping on the oak foyer, Julianne removed her soggy bonnet. The wood floor triggered another thought. "*Sons of the forest* obviously refers to the Druids themselves. What do you suppose they'd consider halls of stone?"

"A city, perhaps?" Jacob helped her remove her coat, calling for Fenwick, but his gentleman's gentleman didn't immediately appear.

"Algernon always said Londinium was considered a large city even in the seventh century. There was something in the manuscript about leaving a blade 'never alone.' One is never truly alone in London," she said, then gasped. "Do you suppose the dagger is here, perhaps hidden in plain sight?"

"It's certainly possible," Jacob said as he draped both their coats over the side table next to the longcase clock. "The question is . . . where? Fenwick!"

"Oh, sir. I'm ever so sorry, sir, but we've a bit of a situation in the kitchen, you see." Fenwick came down the long hall at a dogtrot. "Here, milady. Allow me to take your satchel."

Julianne handed over the carpetbag with the precious manuscript and translations inside.

"What's amiss in the kitchen?" Jacob asked. "Surely nothing Mrs. Trott can't handle."

"Well, I'd lay odds on that, to be sure, but since it concerns one of your lads, I was thinking you might wish to see about it, while I escort the countess to the parlor. There's a fire laid there and she can dry off nice like."

"Which boy?" Jacob asked.

"Gilbert Stout, sir."

Jacob pushed past Fenwick and bolted down the hall.

"If you'd be so good as to follow me, milady," Fenwick said.

"Not on your life," Julianne said and tailed Jacob back to the kitchen. He was usually so imperturbable. Even though she was drenched and chilled enough to set her teeth chattering, she had to see what had lit such a fire under him.

A lank-haired boy was seated on a tall stool near the counter. The lad's clothing was ragged and Julianne would wager he'd not had a bath since spring. She reckoned he must be one of the homeless urchins Jacob hired to be his eyes around the city. The boy grinned at them, a biscuit in one hand and the other soaking in a shallow bowl of milk. He lifted the milky hand to wave to Jacob, but the housekeeper swatted him on the shoulder and he resubmerged his fingers.

"Just you keep that where it is, young man. Milk will draw the fire out," Mrs. Trott said briskly.

"What happened, Gil?" Jacob demanded.

The boy had missed his calling as a bard and the tale of Sir Malcolm's cruelty lost nothing in the telling. Finally, he shot a darting glance at Mrs. Trott and decided he dared remove his hand from the milk bath long enough to illustrate his story. His palm was blistered and angry. No amount of milk could disguise the livid red ooze on the boy's flesh.

Julianne's gut roiled. What kind of monster could do that to a child?

"And then when I didn't cry out, Sir Malcolm seemed satisfied and agreed to take me on." Gil's voice broke unevenly in the manner of a boy who was on his way to becoming a man.

"I shouldn't have sent you." Jacob frowned. "I knew he was dangerous, but I didn't expect him to be sadistic. You're not to go back to him."

The lad's brows drew together. "But I have to. If I don't go back with the information he wants me to find out about you, he promised to find me. And next time, he says he's not like to be so . . . pleasant."

Julianne pressed her lips together. Jacob had sent this youngster to spy on Sir Malcolm, to beard the lion in his own den, but he still didn't think she should attend an initiation ceremony on her own. On the other hand, when she considered Gil's injured palm, she began to think better of her plans as well.

What if Sir Malcolm was more sadistic with adults than he was with young boys?

"He didn't want you to follow the countess?" Jacob asked.

Gil shook his head. "No, he was more interested in you, sir." The boy glanced toward Julianne. "Beggin' your pardon, milady. I'd much rather keep an eye on you, I'm sure."

"It's not as if I hide in a hole," Jacob said. "What could Ravenwood want to know about me?"

"Well, this is the strange thing, and I don't know if you'll believe me. I don't rightly think I'd believe it myself if I hadn't seen him do it, but Sir Malcolm has what you might call magical powers." Gil told how he'd lit the candle merely by passing his hand over the wick. "It weren't no parlor trick. As God is my witness, he pulled fire clean from the air. And he thinks as you can do it too, or something else magical like."

Jacob flinched in surprise. "Me? No, Gil, I assure you. When I light a candle, I use a match, same as the next fellow."

Jacob shot Julianne a quick glance and she knew they were thinking the same thing. When he touched metal, the vision he received from it was a sort of magic. But how could Sir Malcolm know Jacob had an unusual gift? He guarded that secret as tightly as Julianne guarded her freedom.

Gil sighed, clearly disappointed. "He was sure you had special abilities, he called 'em. I'm supposed to find what's beyond the common about you and report back to him." The boy's face lit in an enthusiastic smile. "I know. I could tell him you can fly. If I had my pick of things fantastic, that's what I'd choose. If he thinks you can fly, it'll make him ashamed of his piddling trick with fire."

In a friendly kitchen with a fresh biscuit in his hand, the boy was feeling brave, but his voice cracked again on the word "fire." Julianne's chest ached for him. She knew what it was to be a child who had to make his own way in the world.

Jacob laid a hand on Gil's shoulder. "I want you to stay in this house until I tell you otherwise. No larking about, no running off. You'll make yourself useful to Mrs. Trott as soon as you're able. Is that understood?"

The boy nodded.

Gil had been harmed in Jacob's service, so one might argue he was only doing his duty by his employee. But the rough edge on Jacob's voice belied a fondness for the lad as well. Julianne thought he might understand why she was so adamant about supporting Mrs. Osgood's girls, after all.

"Now everyone clear out of my kitchen so's I can bandage young Master Gil up proper after I give him a thorough scrubbing," the housekeeper said, her nose wrinkling at the dusty smell of boy-sweat emanating from the lad. Then her sharp eyes fell on the puddles forming around the circumference of Julianne's broad skirt. "Oh, gracious sakes, your ladyship! You're dripping all over my kitch—I mean, you're soaked. Chilled to the bone, too, like as not. You, too, . . . sir." She shot a glare toward Jacob, adding the "sir" as an afterthought.

He merely smiled at her like the naughty boy he was.

"Fenwick, don't just stand there like a mutton-head." Mrs. Trott barked orders with more authority than a line sergeant. "Go draw the countess a bath in the guest room so her clothes can dry by the fire. I'll be along with linens and things in a trice, milady."

She sent a long-suffering look in Jacob's direction. "I suppose you'll be wanting a bath too, sir, but you'll just have to wait until we see to the lady."

As Julianne climbed the stairs behind Fenwick, she decided she liked Mrs. Trott very much.

When Waitstill Trott took charge of a matter, things happened with the efficiency of well-oiled clockwork. In no time,

Julianne had reveled in a delicious hot bath and afterward slipped into a soft, thick wrapper of unknown origins. She knew Jacob had female guests from time to time, but she decided to pass over that observation without rancor because the wrapper was as comforting as a warm hug.

Rain still lashed the windows, making the room seem all the more cozy and welcoming. All her wet things were draped near the fire. The room smelled comfortingly of damp wool and rising steam and the crackling blaze. A pot of tea chased the last bit of chill from her bones.

She'd just settled into the tufted chaise longue when someone rapped on the door.

"Come," she called out.

Jacob entered, dressed in a fresh suit of clothing with a small stack of books under one arm. "My Arthurian collection. Shall we see if we can discover something about Merlin's Staff while your things dry?"

"Oh, yes." After she poured a cup of tea for Jacob and sweetened it with one lump, she selected one of his books and began leafing through it.

Jacob settled into the wing chair and did the same, concentration gouging a line between his dark brows.

The book she was reading focused more on the acts of Arthur and his knights than the doings of the High King's resident wizard. Since she wasn't finding the information she sought from the book, it was hard to stay focused on it.

Julianne glanced up at Jacob from time to time. She was naked under the wrapper. They were alone in his guest room. Usually, a situation like this would be like waving a red flag before a bull. By rights, Jacob ought to be trying to seduce her into the bed tucked into the corner alcove.

Instead he was behaving like a perfect gentleman and scowling at the book in his lap.

Then Julianne realized the book was upside down. He wasn't really reading it at all. She rose and walked over to stand beside him.

His gaze darted up at her, then went back to his book.

"Perhaps this will help," she said and flipped the volume right side up.

He snorted. "Well, how can you expect a man to concentrate on reading when you're . . . oh God, Julianne."

He shoved the book onto the floor and pulled her down onto his lap.

Since becoming a widow, Julianne had tried to keep her world quiet and unassuming. Continuing her dalliance with Jacob Preston would complicate her life beyond knowing. But when he looked at her with his soul shining in his eyes, suddenly everything seemed very simple.

Chapter 18

He reached a tentative hand toward her face, but halted shy of her satiny skin.

"Why did you stop?" she asked.

He wasn't exactly sure. He'd never been the sort to ask permission of his lovers. It had never seemed necessary. He took what he wanted and made sure they enjoyed the taking. But then, none of them had ever thrown him out of her chamber.

Or turned down his proposal of marriage.

"I don't want to go beyond where you'll welcome me," he admitted. For the first time in his life, he wanted more than a bedding from a woman. He wanted her to accept him, all of him. And he wanted to accept her back.

She cupped his hand with hers and brought it to her cheek. Then she turned her head and pressed her lips on his palm.

Jacob wished he could feel her soft mouth on his hand like that for about a week. But she turned to face him again, still nestling her cheek against his palm.

"Where would you like to be welcome?" she asked.

Her sultry tone plucked at his gut and made his balls tense.

"I'd like to touch your face," he lied. He wanted to touch her everywhere. He wanted to stroke her heart. He wanted to caress her soul. Instead, he skimmed his fingertips around the oval of her face, exploring the hollow beneath her cheekbones, the indentation at her temples and her little pointed chin. "Then I'd like to touch your neck."

She nodded and smiled at him.

Her skin was smooth and unbearably soft. He stroked her lightly, as if she'd break, but in reality it was because he didn't think he could stand more direct contact. Just those feathery touches made his cock iron-hard.

She sighed with pleasure, and he stopped asking for permission.

He savored every bit of her, smoothing his palms along her shoulders, pushing the wrapper aside and down her arms because he couldn't help himself. He lingered in the crease of her elbow. He tickled along her ribs. He gazed at her exposed breasts, but didn't touch them. Her nipples were drawn tight and her breath unsteady.

"I never know where I am with you," he said, his voice husky with need. "Why do you let me love you sometimes and not others?"

"Men take their pleasure with impunity. A woman has to protect her reputation. We're not likely to be discovered by your cousin here in your home, are we?" she said. "This is safe."

In the silence that followed, all he heard was the steady patter of rain, the crackle of the fire, and the determined beating of his own heart. Didn't she think he could keep her safe, that he'd never see her shamed?

"Viola is no threat to you. She's not that sort." Jacob trailed his fingers along the crease beneath her breast and watched her nipple bunch even tighter. "No, it's more than that."

She made a small helpless noise in the back of her throat.

"It's about control," he realized. "You came to me this time. You started this. You want to be in charge."

"Is that so bad?"

"Not in some things," Jacob said, circling her nipples with his knuckles. "But not now. Not with me. You don't have to be in control. Neither of us does. This is about giving."

She swallowed hard. "Most men want to take from me."

"I'm not most men." He covered her mouth with his and kissed her. She kissed him back.

Fragile. Hopeful. Trusting.

He rose with her in his arms and carried her to the waiting bed, still kissing her.

He was inside her mouth, all wet and slippery, hidden from the world. His tongue loved hers; then he kissed the corner of her mouth, spreading the moisture there.

He laid her out on the bed, parting the wrapper to bare her completely, breasts, belly, hips, long legs. The lovely dark curls over her sex glistened with dampness.

He climbed into the cool linens with her, determined to taste every bit of her. Julianne arched her back like a cat stretching, thrusting her breasts toward him. She raised her arms in welcome.

It was as good a place to start as any.

His lips were wet and soft on her breast, nuzzling and sweet, at first. She thought it was like a glimpse of heaven. Then he tugged at her nipples, sucking fiercely. That was even better.

With only his mouth, he was taking her to that tumultuous place she wanted to be. She shifted under him, unable to keep still.

He moved down her body, pleasure dribbling down with him like raindrops streaking a window. He settled between her splayed legs. His breath was warm on her, his freshly shaved cheek smooth on her inner thigh. She nudged herself into his mouth, accepting without question the bliss he offered. When he put his lips against her sensitive spot, she almost ceased to exist. Blood pounded between her legs.

Body, heart, body, soul, body, mind.

Whose body, whose heart, whose soul and mind, she wasn't sure. She and Jacob were getting all tangled together, tighter than a Gordian knot. Whose sigh? Whose quickened breath? Whose exquisite touch? They moved as one, petting and soothing, tormenting and fondling. The distinction between them blurred and blended. Where did one end and the other begin?

He brought her to the ragged edge and stopped. She moaned, but then he raised himself and lay prone over her. They coupled without effort, without thought, sliding together with a sense of rightness that set her blood singing, pounding around their joining, bathing him in her salty sea.

"I won't leave you, Julianne," he promised, the heat and friction making his words come in short bursts. "You'll have to drive me away."

She was beyond speech. She couldn't get enough of him. She gripped his buttocks and tilted herself into him, taking him all the way in. She wrapped her legs around his waist and hooked her ankles at the small of his back. The way he pounded into her, she knew he was bruising her but she didn't care. Jacob's face was taut with the joy of their coming together.

Julianne closed her eyes and from a dark corner of her mind, other faces rose up to taunt her. The men who'd used her. The ones she'd used. Need and shame washed over her in equal measure. She wished they'd all go away.

All but Jacob. Only him.

Harder. Yes. She needed Jacob to drive out the others, to swive away the ones who'd only taken from her, to forgive her for the ones she'd hurt, till only he was left.

He quickened their pace.

Was he driving away the women from his past with each bone-jarring thrust?

"Look at me, love," he urged.

She opened her eyes and saw only him. And only herself, reflected in his gray gaze.

She glowed inside, as if lightning curled and tightened between her legs. Then when she felt him come in hard pulses, the bolt unleashed itself. She coiled around him in rings of pleasure. Bliss spread outward in concentric waves, bathing her entire body in joy.

She half-expected light to shoot from her fingers and toes.

A thunderous boom shook the town house and rain washed the windows. She realized vaguely that the downpour was still going on outside. The storm in the bed was subsiding.

And so was the storm in her heart.

Eventually the rain battering the panes slackened to a gentle patter. Julianne didn't know how long they lay together, tangled on the sweat-damp sheets. She knew only that she was perfectly content not to move.

Jacob started to speak, but she put her fingers to his lips.

"Let's not talk," she said. "We might ruin it."

"I don't think that's possible." His smile was wide as the Thames.

She cocked a brow at him. "Given our history, do you want to rethink that? We argue with regularity."

"I suppose you're right." He lay on his back, one hand behind his head, the other arm wrapped around her. "We should make a pact. No serious discussions after lovemaking."

"I'm amenable to that."

"Now all I have to do is see that we engage in this most pleasurable activity as often as possible." He tickled her ribs and she rolled away from him with a laugh.

"I'm amenable to that as well, but no tickling."

"There's a challenge no man can resist. Where else are you ticklish?" He dove toward her and soon had her pinned down so he could torture her into peals of laughter.

A knock on the door interrupted their play.

Julianne snatched the sheets and pulled them to her chin. "What is it?"

"The hansom, milady. The driver has returned as Mr. Preston requested," Fenwick said through the door. "It's waiting for you below. Would you like me to send Mrs. Trott up to assist you?"

"No, I'll manage. Thank you." She didn't move till she heard Fenwick's footsteps retreating down the stairs. Amazingly enough, she felt no embarrassment over being caught in bed with Jacob by his servant. It felt as if she belonged there and Fenwick had accepted her presence as a matter of course. "You'll help me, won't you?"

"I knew it would come to this," Jacob said ruefully. "I'm destined to end my days as a lady's maid."

"That remains to be seen," she said as she scampered out of bed in nothing but her skin. "Do you think you can perform the duties of one well enough to contemplate making it a permanent position?"

His gaze sizzled over her. "Probably not. My mind is not at all on dressing you at the moment."

"Nevertheless, I expect your help," she said as she wiggled into her all-in-one and sat down to slip on her stockings. She tied the garters above her knees and fit her corset into place. "If you'd be so kind as to tie my laces, sir."

He proved very competent when it came to women's undergarments, cinching her snugly, but not so tight she couldn't breathe.

"Are you still set on going alone to the Druids' gathering this evening?" he asked.

Her shoulders tensed. "I sense a serious discussion in the making."

Jacob turned her around to face him and pulled her close. "I need to know."

"I don't see as I have any other option." She eased out of his embrace and stepped into her crinoline. "I'm not happy about the idea, especially after seeing the cruelty Sir Malcolm is capable of, but if we want access to this gathering of the inner Druid circle, it behooves me to follow instructions."

"I was afraid you'd say that." He held up her skirt so she could slip it over her head. The yards of fabric billowed over the crinoline.

"Please don't try to talk me out of it." Julianne shrugged into her jacket and fastened the silver frogs that closed the bodice. "I'll use extreme caution and if I find I'm uncomfortable in my surroundings, I promise I'll leave. I'm still a countess, after all. It's not as if they can hold me captive."

"Oh, I'm pretty sure they can," Jacob said. "The only question is whether they will."

A shiver trembled over her, but she gave herself a stern mental shake. "I've tried to hit upon another way around this."

"Good. You're open to another idea, which I happen to have," Jacob said. "I intend to follow you."

She shook her head. "Isn't that the same as going with me? If you're seen by the Druids, they may not allow me in, and we'll lose the chance to find the other half of the manuscript."

"First, we don't know for sure they even have the other half." His tone grew testier by the moment. "And second, no one will see me."

"Does that mean you have the ability to become invisible? You should tell Gil. The boy so wants you to have a magical power. Invisibility is almost as good as being able to fly." She raked her fingers through her hair, trying to arrange it in some semblance of a dignified style and failing miserably. Then she turned toward Jacob with a frown. "Somehow, Sir Malcolm knows you do possess an extraordinary gift. How do you suppose that happened?"

"I don't know," Jacob admitted. "Even my own brother hasn't a clue about me and metals. Jerome knows only that I had a lot of headaches when we were growing up. It's not something I talk about freely to many people."

She stood on tiptoe to kiss his cheek. "Your secret is safe with me," she said lightly.

"And yours are safe with me," Jacob said in all seriousness. "I care about you too much to let you come to harm. Don't fault me for trying to protect you."

"I care about you too," she admitted, letting a small bit of the shield she'd built around her heart fall away. "I suppose you think I won't know you're following me tonight either."

"You won't. Unless you need me."

"If you ruin this for me, Jacob—"

"Will you let it ruin us?" He looked down at her, earnest and intent.

Us. We. Oneness. They had certainly been joined that afternoon, but now she felt entirely separate again. Surprisingly enough, it wasn't a good feeling.

This was normally the point in her amorous adventures when she'd call a halt to the relationship. Jacob's question implied a future, or at least a continuance, for them. Needing someone had always brought her to grief.

She reveled in the independence of widowhood. She delighted in making her own choices, but now that she'd tasted that delicious *us* with Jacob, her solitary *me* didn't seem nearly so appealing.

"It won't ruin us." She walked toward the door, stopping to look back at him when her gloved hand touched the knob. "But try very hard not to be seen."

Chapter 19

Julianne was welcomed back to Lord Kilmaine's home by his butler, who promptly fetched a silver tray laden with several envelopes.

"Madam has received some correspondence while she was out," the stiffly correct fellow said. "If she wishes to respond, she will find writing necessities in the parlor escritoire."

Julianne thanked him and wandered into the parlor to read her letters. One was from Mr. Farthingale, director of the Drury Lane theatre, with the urgent request that she contemplate a return to the stage as his Desdemona. She laid that one aside, considering it a course of last resort.

Another had been redirected to her from the Golden Cockerel. It was from her stepson, demanding she return to Cornwall forthwith and agree to marry his friend. He repeated his promise to cut off her funds if she didn't return before Christmas. Algernon's heir had always resented her and meant to humble her by insisting she accept his choice of a husband for her. He knew she found his friend the baron odious. It was probably why he forced the issue. She ripped the note in two and tossed it into the fire. It was most satisfying to watch the threatening missive flare up and then curl into gray ash.

Unfortunately, disposing of the note didn't dispose of the threat.

Surprisingly enough, one of the other letters was from a Lady Sotheby, who introduced herself as a friend of Lady Kilmaine's. She'd be pleased if Julianne would call at her home on Thursday next at four o'clock for tea. Lady Sotheby had a reputation for glittering parties and tasteful soirées. She was known to support artists and poets and musicians. Perhaps Julianne's theatre background had prompted this invitation.

No matter the reason, the closed door of the ton had inched open for her a bit. Unfortunately, Julianne didn't know if she'd be able to accept. It was only a guess that the last dagger was in London. If they retrieved the other half of the manuscript and Dr. Snowdon was able to decipher and translate the rest, she and Jacob might be off to who knew where looking for the final dagger by Thursday next.

The last item was a small package that contained a black domino mask and an envelope sealed with red wax into which an image of a tree had been pressed. Undoubtedly from a Druid. She ripped it open and read:

> *At midnight a carriage will pass through the alley behind Lord Kilmaine's home. Meet it at the garden gate promptly. Wear the mask. Come alone or forever abandon the evergreen path.*

The note was unsigned, but it bore the same sharp juniper scent she associated with Sir Malcolm.

No one would call to collect her at her host's front door that evening. No one would know when or where she'd gone. Jacob intended to shadow her, but he was expecting a coach to arrive in a conspicuous manner. If she slipped out the back at midnight, she'd be alone.

She settled at the escritoire to write Jacob a note about this new development. Then she remembered the way she'd been followed and watched since she'd arrived in London. If a runner departed from Lord Kilmaine's town house and delivered her note to Jacob, someone would probably be aware of it. She might ruin her chance at finding the rest of the manuscript before she began.

She replaced the inkwell and closed the desk. Somehow, when her mysterious ride came for her at midnight, she'd have to get by as she'd done all her life.

On her own.

Jacob shifted uncomfortably in the shadows at the corner of the block. The rain had stopped. Every pothole and chink in the cobbles was filled with liquid silver shimmering in the lamplight. The infernal stink of the city had been washed away for a bit, but the wind was raw and chill and touched with enough damp to flay any exposed skin. He promised himself to double the pay of his pint-sized watchers in the future simply for putting up with the damned London elements.

He glanced up at the moon, now on its descent across the dark sky. Even though he'd sent a note to Quinn, telling him it was all right to allow Julianne to leave that evening after all, no one had called at Lord Kilmaine's town house. One by one, the homes on the Mayfair street went dark. The only sound was the occasional bark of a stray dog and the plodding clop of horses' hooves. Since he saw no carriage, he figured the conveyance was traveling on a neighboring block and the sound had echoed down the manmade canyons of four-storey town houses.

He was almost ready to give up, assuming Sir Malcolm had

changed his mind, when the new lad, Pete, came running toward him and skidded to a halt.

"I been watching at the other end of the block, like ye told me, guv," Pete said between gasping breaths. "A coach just turned down the back alley behind the house where the lady's stayin'."

"Good lad." That had to be Julianne's ride. Jacob gave the boy an extra coin. "Time to seek your bed."

The little blighter took to his heels, disappearing into the night without another word. Jacob stole across the street and walked around to peer down the alley. A brougham was stopped behind his cousin's home. He caught sight of a billowing skirt disappearing into the equipage along with the glimpse of a slim ankle he thought he recognized.

Julianne was on her way. He ducked back against the brick exterior of the end town house when the driver chirruped softly to his horse. As the brougham rattled by, Jacob noticed Julianne wasn't alone in the conveyance. At least two men and another woman were with her, all wearing masks.

Before the driver turned out of the alley and onto the main street, Jacob leaped onto the boot and grasped the luggage rail. The driver whipped the horse into a trot and Jacob hung on as they clattered over the cobbles.

They left the rarified air of the fashionable neighborhoods and rattled along the Strand, past Temple Bar heading toward Ludgate. The brougham finally stopped before an unprepossessing tenement on Ivy Lane hunkered in the shadow of St. Paul's.

The coach door opened and one of the men alighted first in order to hand the two women out. Then the other fellow climbed down from the brougham, muttering under his breath.

The house they were stopped before was narrow and a single candle burned in the one ground floor window. Faint light shot out under the door. There was a crack big enough to allow any sort of vermin in.

Fitting, Jacob thought.

"I say, this don't look like much. The way Chelmsford went on, I certainly expected more," the last man said to his friend. "You, there. Driver, are you sure this is the right place?"

"It's the right place. Door's unlocked," the driver said with gravel in his tone. "Don't go in if you don't want to, guv."

Then he slapped the reins over his horse's back and the brougham lurched forward. Jacob pressed himself flat against the back of the coach, figuring the darkness would hide him.

He needn't have worried. The four initiates headed toward the door without a second glance at the retreating coach. He waited until the last man disappeared through it before he dropped from the rear of the equipage and headed back to the door.

It didn't appear to be guarded, but he inched it open slowly in any case. He heard the retreating footsteps of the foursome and stole in behind them, trying to follow the sound since the solitary candle in the entryway was the only source of illumination. One of the men complained loudly of the dark and confounded tawdriness of the place until his companion ordered him to shut it or leave. Neither of the women said a word as they disappeared into a chamber off the long corridor.

Jacob put his ear to the crack in the door and heard a creaky scraping sound. A blast of air rush past him tinged with a stale, moldering odor. Then the scraping came again and the foul breeze stopped as suddenly as it had begun. The sound of footsteps was gone. There was no more complaining voice for him to follow.

He rushed forward into an empty room.

* * *

Julianne was uneasy about the darkness in the house on Ivy Lane, but she didn't have long to fret. Once the other woman, who turned out to be their guide, opened a secret door behind a bookcase, a narrow tunnel yawned before them, lit at intervals with smoky torches. Julianne marched along behind their guide. The two gentlemen followed in single file.

The space smelled of damp earth and burning pitch, but the floor of the tunnel was relatively level. The walls and ceiling along the secret pathway were braced with blackened beams. Julianne wondered what sorts of wriggling creatures might thrive in the packed earth and pulled her skirts as close to her legs as she could.

After one of the men beaned his noggin on a low hanging beam, the men learned to duck their heads. Julianne and their guide were able to walk upright.

"Damnation, there's another spider's web. I don't know what the rest of you were expecting, but this is not my idea of a good time," said the man who'd been doing all the complaining. "This is all a bunch of rot, I tell you."

Their guide turned back to glare at him, her eyes glittering in the slits of her domino. "Do not let the Grand Master hear you speak such blasphemies. Not if you value your tongue."

No more complaints were forthcoming.

Finally the tunnel opened into a small antechamber. Their guide stopped.

"As I am, so shall you be." She waved a hand toward a row of pegs on which black robes hung. "Don a robe and shed your old life."

Julianne and the two men put on their robes. While it was easy to still tell she was a woman, since she was much shorter and her skirts billowed the robe out, the flowing black fabric rendered the two men virtually indistinguishable from one another.

"Come," the guide said and led them through another door into a large vaulted chamber lit by a massive chandelier dangling from the apex of the ceiling. The room was circular, but at intervals, three arched open doorways led off into darkened corridors.

There was no longer packed earth beneath Julianne's feet. A mosaic of obvious antiquity stretched across the space, the tiles tiny and their colors muted. A few patches of tiles were missing, but Julianne could clearly make out a group of hunters chasing a stag around the central dais. The room was ringed with other robed people who, at the sound of a low gong, began to walk toward the center of the room, crowding around a lit censer on the dais.

Julianne moved cautiously forward, peering around taller people. Aromatic smoke rose in gray curls to reform into thin clouds along the curved ceiling. The pleasing scent encouraged her to breathe deeply, but the incense caught in her throat and made her cough. Her vision grew hazy in the increasingly smoky air.

The group began chanting a slow, repetitive phrase in no language Julianne had ever heard. But the syllables sank into her brain, and she felt certain she ought to understand them. The meaning was there, clinging to the edge of her mind, waiting for her to discover it, if only she could listen hard enough.

The chant grew louder, faster and more guttural. The group broke into two and the chant became an antiphonal call and reply. Thrust and response, give and take, it was like sexual congress with sound.

A long drinking horn was passed around. Her guide drank from it and then forced it into Julianne's hands. She raised it to her lips. The aroma of the drink was sweeter than mulled wine. Julianne went through the motions of a swallow, but didn't take any liquid into her mouth. When she lowered the horn and passed it to the next person, her lips tingled, then went numb from the mere touch of the liquid.

Even if she knew what to say, she doubted she could speak coherently.

A loud thud sounded behind her and she glanced back to see that the door to the anteroom was firmly shut. Julianne's heart shot to her toes.

Even if he'd been dogging her up to this point, there was no way Jacob could follow her now.

Chapter 20

Four people could not simply disappear into thin air. Jacob circled the small room for the third time, but saw no other point of egress other than the door he'd come through. Not even an open window. He made his way back to the main entrance and retrieved the candle. As he returned to make another circuit of the room, the candle guttered when he passed by the bookcase. A current of air wafted from behind it.

He felt around the edges of the case until his fingers found the mechanism to open a secret passage. He dove through the entrance and made his way along the low-ceilinged underground corridor, careful not to betray his presence with the slightest noise.

When he came to an anteroom, he slipped on one of the black robes hanging there, figuring it was standard issue for initiates to the Order. Though he had no domino, the robe had a hood that effectively shadowed his face. It wasn't ideal, but it would have to do.

It was also less than ideal that he was unarmed. One of the worst things about his sensitivity to metals was that Jacob had been never become proficient with firearms. It was a damned shame, because a loaded Beaumont-Adams in his pocket would have eased his mind considerably.

He wished he could have brought his walking stick with its slim foil hidden inside. He'd have felt better knowing he had a blade he could wield close to hand.

But the platinum head on the walking stick was too unique, too well known. Someone within the Order might recognize it.

And him.

A low hum of rhythmic chanting rose from the next room. He tried the door. Panic rising, he realized it was locked from the inside.

And no one was likely to let him in.

The robed group swayed in time with the chanting as the room filled with ever more potent incense. Julianne's skin prickled. Each time her skirts brushed her legs, it was like a lover's touch. She could feel the tickling threads of the lace at the top of her all-in-one. A low ache started between her legs, empty and needy. She wished for Jacob as she shifted her weight, rubbed her thighs together and stifled the urge to touch herself.

Then as suddenly as it began, the chanting stopped and the group stood like statues. A bead of perspiration tickled hotly down Julianne's spine and slipped into the crevice of her buttocks.

A man emerged from one of the arched openings and the group turned as one to face him, parting to make way for his approach. He was dressed in red, from the crimson hood of his robe to the scarlet of his boots. His face was hidden by a golden domino. A shimmering torc, an emblem of obvious power, adorned his neck. He bore a gilded whip in his red-gloved hand.

Julianne couldn't tear her eyes from him as he mounted the central dais and lifted the censer skyward as if in offering to some unnamed deity. Shrouded in incense smoke, he was magnificent and terrible all at once.

"Welcome, Sons and Daughters of the Wood. May you find the power you seek. But know this. Real power is not for those the world deems high and mighty." His voice reverberated around the hall, deep and otherworldly. "It is for those strong enough to claim it. You are the power, my friends. You bear it in your bodies. Release your power. Revel in your strength. I free you to do as you will."

A wall of sound rose from the group at this proclamation, a feral cry. From somewhere a drum started beating and several people began dancing to the primitive rhythm, shedding their robes to reveal they wore nothing beneath them. By common consent, only their black dominoes hid their identities. These were obviously regular members of the Order within the Order since they were so well prepared to fling themselves into the wanton rite. Male and female, they writhed to the ancient cadence, touching, stroking and groping each other with complete abandon.

One of the men who'd ridden in the brougham with Julianne threw off his robe and began shucking out of his street clothes, baring his fish-belly white shanks.

"Now this is more like it," she heard him say.

She inched backward till her spine pressed against the curved outer wall. Part of her wanted to join in the carnival, to throw off her restrictive clothing and let her pores revel in the intoxication of the incense. But she still had enough presence of mind to realize the sweet fumes were dulling her inhibitions. The drink in the cow's horn was probably another aphrodisiac. A powerful one, judging from the way her lips still prickled.

Much as her body clamored for release, she wasn't there to join an orgy. Her mind was hazy as a foggy day at sea, but she knew she hadn't come here for sexual congress. She was looking for . . . something else. No matter how her body ached and urged her to embrace her own needs, she was almost sure of it.

She eased along the outer wall till she came to the arched opening from which the man in red had appeared. She ducked through it and found herself in another narrow tunnel like the one that had brought her here. The incense fumes hadn't penetrated this corridor. The air was cold and damp and musty smelling.

It cleared her head in a few breaths. Then she remembered. She was looking for the other half of the manuscript and though this tunnel wasn't well lit, there was a faint glow in the distance. Hands outstretched before her, she started walking forward.

Jacob wasted several precious minutes working on the metal doorknob. All it earned him was the iron claw of a headache. Then he realized he'd have more luck knocking the pins out of the hinges. Fortunately, the chanting coming from the next room was so loud, no one would hear him striking the pin heads with a stone.

He was forced to stop when silence descended on the company behind the door for a bit, but then a massive shout went up and a drum began sounding. Jacob timed his strikes to match the drumbeats.

When the last pin came free, he wedged the door open enough for him to slip through.

He'd been concerned that someone might notice his invasion. He needn't have worried. There was a full-scale orgy in progress and no one seemed aware of anything but the abundance of sweaty, naked, willing flesh in every direction.

Jaw clenched, Jacob scanned the room, looking for Julianne. To his relief, she wasn't involved in any of the multiple couplings around the chamber, some standing and balancing precariously, some writhing on the floor amid piles of discarded robes.

Thank God. He might have committed murder if he'd caught some fellow swiving her. Yet part of him would have sympathized with the poor blighter. Between the drum and the hazy smoke and the flashes of bare bodies, no man could remain unaffected. Still, he tried to tamp down his body's reaction to what he was seeing and feeling. He had to find Julianne.

The incense smoke curled around him. The drummer shifted to a set of triple beats. "Ju-li-anne, Ju-li-anne," it repeated in Jacob's brain. His cock rose in an iron-hard stand and no amount of willing it away could ease the throbbing ache.

A man dressed in red was tying a naked woman, spread eagle, to a pair of stakes driven into one curved wall. She struggled and kicked at him, but he subdued and gagged her. Then he brought out his whip.

Jacob looked away, suppressing the urge to help her. He had no way to know if the woman's protests weren't part of some sexual theatre being acted out before the assembly. Besides, he was there to find Julianne. The bound woman's hair was pale blond, not Julianne's rich dark hue. If she wasn't in the vaulted chamber, she must have gone through one of the three arched doorways. He slipped through the nearest one.

There were no doors leading off to side rooms, but there was a dim light in the distance. He pressed toward it, ducking to keep from bashing his forehead on the low beams.

When he reached the end of the tunnel, light filtered through a grill near the packed dirt floor. There was obviously a room on the other side of the wall, but he could find no door. He knelt down to peer through the man-sized grate and saw . . . Lord Nelson's sarcophagus.

"I'll be damned," he whispered. "The crypt of St. Paul."

The resting place of one of his nation's best-loved heroes was on the other side of the grill. Jacob grasped the iron bars and gave them a hard yank. Shards of pain lanced his brain from the cold metal, but the grate moved. Another good tug and he'd have it out.

But it didn't seem likely Julianne had come that way. She was seeking the other half of her codex. There was nothing in the crypt but old bones. The vibrant drumbeat of the living called to him. So he turned to retrace his steps back to the vaulted chamber.

The light at the end of Julianne's tunnel emanated from behind a partially closed door. She peered around it and found the floor was decorated with another ancient mosaic, this time with a male figure wearing a two-horned headdress and a female bent over at the waist, prepared to receive his third "horn." An oil lamp sat on the edge of a well-appointed desk, stocked with all the necessary writing equipment. Despite the salacious mosaic, it was a surprisingly cozy room. A bookshelf was crammed along the back wall, full to bursting with leather-bound volumes.

The source of the musty smell. Old books.

She lifted the lamp so she could read some of the titles from the spines. *Wizards of the Wonder Years*, *Shadows of Power or Relics and their Uses*, *Standing Stones and other Ancient Marvels*—each book celebrated a topic more arcane than the next, but she didn't find the other half of her manuscript on the shelves.

"Well, of course not," she said, shaking her head. The incense was obviously still affecting her ability to think clearly. She had no doubt now that Sir Malcolm was the man in red and this private enclave was his. Even if he hadn't deciphered the clues to the location of the last dagger, he'd appreciate how valuable the manuscript was and would keep it under lock and key.

She made a thorough search of the desk and came up empty, though there was one locked drawer she was unable to jimmy.

She plopped into the desk chair, wondering what she could use to pry open the final drawer. Even if she managed it, there was every chance she might find nothing but mouse droppings and shredded parchment. In despair, she laid her head on the desk and let herself weep.

"The incense affects some people like that, Lady Cambourne." The masculine voice made her jerk upright. The man in red filled the doorway. "It releases whatever we normally repress. Let your tears flow. Undoubtedly, you have earned them."

"Sir Malcolm, I presume," she said, wiping her eyes. Even under the influence of drugging smoke, she was not going to let the man watch her cry.

He threw back his hood and removed his gold domino, revealing that she was right. "Usually I keep on my mask for our solemnities, but that's for the masses. The time for subterfuge between you and me is past, I think."

"Solemnities? Is that what you call the debauch in the next room?" Julianne said, rising from the chair, but still keeping the desk between them. She curled her lip with disdain. He was not a man who'd be moved by weakness. "I'd expect more class from an evening in a brothel."

A wicked smile lifted his mouth. "I give my followers what they want. And they give me what I want."

His gaze seared over her, leaving no doubt in her mind what he wanted from her. She fancied he could see through the black robe and her layers of clothing and sense her body was still aching and needy from the effects of that aphrodisiac incense. No matter how badly she'd been drugged, she bloody well didn't need him.

"I came expecting mysteries. I thought you were seeking knowledge," she said when he took a step toward her.

"Knowledge is only a stepping-stone. Power is the goal." He parted his robes, revealing that unlike his followers, he was not naked beneath them. He reached into his pocket and pulled out a key on a slender ribbon. "You didn't come for mysteries. You came to find something to unravel them with. And you are in dire need of this."

Before she thought better of it, she glanced at the unopened desk drawer. When her gaze darted back to him, his pale brow arched in triumph.

"It's in there," he said, dangling the key before her.

How did he know what she was looking for?

"All you have to do is remove your clothing and give yourself to me freely. Without reservation." He pulled a length of red silk from his other pocket. "Of course, I will require you to be bound. It is necessary in order to make you a worthy vessel, but I won't insist it be in the temple with the others this time. You can make your offering to me right here on the desk."

"Like hell she will." Jacob burst through the door behind him.

Sir Malcolm whirled on him, but wasn't quick enough to dodge Jacob's fist. It connected with his jaw and sent him reeling. Sir Malcolm punched back, splitting Jacob's lip with a solid jab. Jacob feinted left, then followed with a hard right to Malcolm's temple. The Grand Master Druid dropped like a felled oak.

Julianne skittered around the desk and into Jacob's arms, nearly knocking him over.

"You came for me," she said, a sob in her voice. "However did you manage it?"

"Part bloodhound, I guess. You didn't leave much of a trail." He ran a bruised-knuckled hand over her head and pressed a kiss to her temple. "There's no time to lose. He won't be out long. Let's get out of here."

"Not until we find what we came for. We need the key." She knelt and found it in the dirt next to Sir Malcolm's inert body. Then she scooped up the red silk. "Tie him up."

"Wish this was sturdier stuff," Jacob complained as he jerked Sir Malcolm's hands behind him. "Did you find the manuscript?"

"I think so." She shoved the key into the locked drawer and gave it a quick turn. Then she yanked open the drawer with enough force to pull the whole thing from the desk. Nestled in its oak cradle, there was an illuminated codex missing its front cover. The same sort of writhing beasts drawn in the margins of her half danced along the edges of these sheaves.

She removed the codex from the drawer and spread it carefully on top of the desk to inspect it. The bindings, frayed at the edges, were identical to her portion of the work. The same florid hand had lettered the pages.

"Yes," she said with a nod. "This is definitely it."

"Give me your stockings," Jacob demanded.

"What?" Her head jerked up in surprise. In her elation over her discovery she'd almost forgotten everything else.

"We need something to gag Ravenwood so he can't call for help right away and I want to bind his feet as well," Jacob said. "It may take us longer than we'd like to escape this place. We need all the time we can get."

She toed off her slippers and unrolled her stockings without another word. In a few moments, she and Jacob were stealing back down the dark tunnel toward the large vaulted chamber. She pulled both her arms inside her robe to clutch the manuscript tight to her chest, hiding it from any eyes that might not be glazed with the drugging smoke.

The cloying incense had fingered its way down the corridor.

Jacob cinched her close and kissed her before they passed through the arched doorway. His kiss was rough, demanding, and he pulled away from her with a growling curse. His kisses were usually kinder, though no less stirring than this primitive one. He was as affected by the incense as she.

"Stay close," he ordered. "Don't stop. And everything will be fine."

Fine? How on earth could everything be fine?

They had to slip unnoticed through the riotous Order without succumbing to the incense fumes, escape through the antechamber and long tunnel, and back through the dark house on Ivy Lane before Sir Malcolm raised an alarm. Then somehow, if they managed that astounding feat, they still had to make their way back to Lord Kilmaine's house before anyone discovered she was missing.

Fine was as unlikely an outcome as finding a virgin in the next room.

CHAPTER 21

Malcolm swam through the blackness, straining toward consciousness. Once he escaped the sucking darkness, he found himself bound and gagged, lying across the mosaic that celebrated the Horned One.

This was not part of his plan.

He'd intended to make Lady Cambourne his newest consort, to bend her to his will in all things, the better to monitor her progress in finding the last dagger.

Where the hell had Preston come from?

When Malcolm observed the lady in his gazing ball prior to sending the coach to collect her, he hadn't seen Jacob Preston anywhere near her all evening. Obviously, the man had some power than enabled him to evade Malcolm's notice.

He worked at the silk binding his hands and finally managed to free himself. Malcolm spat out the gag and cursed Preston to the ninth circle of Hell as he untied his feet. He'd have to destroy the red silk since it had been used to subdue him, but he decided to pocket Lady Cambourne's stockings. They could come in handy. Who knew when a rite might call for a token, a thing belonging to the one he wished to influence?

He glanced at his desk and realized the codex was gone. It was just as well. He'd meant for her to have it in any case. He simply wanted more in exchange for it than a lop-sided bout of fisticuffs.

Malcolm rubbed his temple and winced at the painful lump forming. It grated his pride that Preston had laid him low, but in the long view of things, it was an acceptable trade. What was a blow or two compared to reviving the land of Albion, the ancient Celtic world that had disintegrated into Victoria's England? In the reborn Albion, the Druid who wielded the Staff of Merlin would rule in secret, turning the hearts of princes as easily as a man diverts the flow of water from a tap. Wealth and robust health, and preternatural long life to enjoy them both, would be his.

Yes, a bruised temple was a fair swap.

He didn't think Preston and Lady Cambourne had been gone very long. If he raised an alarm now, his followers would probably catch them.

Which wouldn't do at all.

He stooped to pull a book from the bottom shelf of his bookcase and checked inside the false cover. Within the innocuous-sounding *Maypoles and Other Phallic Symbology*, the precious volume that explained the mysteries of the Staff of Merlin was still hidden there. If Lady Cambourne had nicked that one, he would have sent his hounds after her immediately.

"He who binds cannot be he who finds," Malcolm quoted. If he hoped to wield the staff of power, he couldn't be the one who located the scattered daggers. He must only receive them from the finder's hand or their magic would be nullified.

Malcolm was ever conscious of an entity, a Watchful Eye was how he thought of it, which was trained on him with vigilance which did not sleep. The Eye made sure he did everything according to plan. The powers that governed the daggers' unique properties would not be mocked. According to the text of the *Staff of Merlin* volume, the binder might aid the finder obliquely, but couldn't make the task so easy it was obvious he was controlling events.

The powers were difficult to predict. It was best not to irk them.

He'd intended to give Lady C. the damaged codex after he humbled her by taking her roughly and in every imaginable way. But in retrospect, it was probably fortuitous that Lady C. had stolen the manuscript instead. That way, the powers would reckon he was definitely not part of the "finding."

He'd give Lady C. and Preston another few minutes to get away. Then he'd reappear in the vaulted temple and send his minions flying after them. May as well let Lady Cambourne, and the watchful powers, believe she acted independently and wasn't actually doing Malcolm's bidding unaware.

It would make the binding all the sweeter once he possessed the daggers. He'd refashion them into the staff using the prescribed method, amassing all its power for himself.

And then to seal his covenant with the Watchful Eye, he'd bathe the newly formed magic rod in the finder's blood.

Ancient tradition, Malcolm mused, *was a lovely thing indeed.*

The incense was even stronger now. With each breath, Jacob lost the will to press forward. Why were they there? Who were all these naked people? And most importantly, why was Julianne still clothed?

His hand on the small of her back sent a riot of sensations rippling up his arm. Even through the layers of her robe and clothing, the dip of her waist called to him. The rounded mound of her belly, the curve of her bum, the soft, secret folds between her legs—all her delights flashed through his mind. He ached to rip off the crude fabric hiding her beauties and worship every bit of her with his body.

Everywhere he looked, couples were locked in poses of the

"two-backed beast." They strained against each other in search of the oblivion only mindless rutting gives.

He and Julianne should be doing the same. Jacob swung her around and pinned her to the curved outer wall. He devoured her mouth with fierce hunger and she answered his kiss with her own nips and groans. When he pressed his hard groin against her, she melted into him with little "oh's" and "yes, there" and "now, please, now."

He parted her robe and reached in to claim one of her breasts. She arched into his hand, lifting her lithe arms to drape them around his shoulders. Something dropped between them and landed on his boot. He almost kicked it aside, but he made the mistake of looking down at it. His brain refused to make sense of it at first. Then its significance burst in his mind like a sunrise.

The manuscript.

"Don't stop," Julianne urged.

She pressed fevered kisses on his neck and suckled his earlobe. His eyes rolled back in his head for a blink or two. Then with supreme effort he pushed himself away from her and bent to pick up the codex.

"It's the incense," he said hoarsely. "We can't tarry here."

"Don't you want me?" She sidled close and rocked her pelvis against him. "Oh, Jacob. I need . . . I want you so. Just let me kiss you and . . ." She dropped to her knees before him and parted his robe. Her blessed hands worked the buttons at his waist and caressed his erect length through his flannel trousers.

To be so accepted, so desired . . . not only did his body respond with an intensity he'd never known, his heart constricted with a flood of emotions that threatened to swamp him. Love and lust and longing tangled into a pulsing knot that lodged in his chest.

He'd never thought a man could die of a cockstand, but he

was tempted to revise that opinion. He was primed and ready and if she so much as touched him with her bare hand, let alone her mouth, he'd spill his seed.

And even if she didn't, he might come anyway simply on the strength of imagining her sweet lips and tongue wrapped around his cock.

Or he might go mad.

The incense wove a song of lust in his head. A song of taking, of animal heat and single-minded selfishness. In another few heartbeats, he'd lose his humanity completely and become a rutting beast. He had to get them out of there while he was still himself.

"I want you too." *God, what an understatement!* "But not here." He yanked her to her feet and grasped her elbow to propel her along the outer wall. She made incoherent little sounds of protest, but he ignored her.

A bellow like a bull being butchered alive made him stop. He glanced over his shoulder to see Sir Malcolm emerge from his enclave, fire all but sparking from the slits of his golden domino.

"Intruders have invaded Albion! A man and a woman," he thundered as he pointed toward the exit door directly across the circular space from him. "They can't have gone far, my friends. After them."

The door was still a quarter of the way around the circular room from Jacob and Julianne. There was no chance for them to leave the way they'd come.

"Time to go," Jacob said and dragged Julianne down the nearest archway and into the dark corridor he'd wandered earlier. Stooped low, he pulled Julianne along. He heard a chorus of shouts behind them, punctuated with the sound of ripping cloth as the members of the order struggled back into their robes. The slap of countless feet on ancient tiles thundered in the room behind them.

Fortunately, no one followed them down the dark tunnel, but Jacob couldn't trust that happy state would continue. Another shout and series of curses revealed someone had discovered how he'd nearly dismantled the door by removing its hinge pins. Until they unlocked it and let it fall from the jamb, the stampede of people trying to catch him and Julianne would have to slip into the anteroom one body at a time.

Which meant someone might decide to give up on the obvious escape route and try the tunnel they were actually in.

"Where are we going?" Julianne's voice was a piteous bleat, like a lost child.

Jacob covered her mouth with his palm. "We are going to church," he whispered, "so you must be very quiet."

He felt her nod and they moved forward toward the faint light at the end of the tunnel. With each step, the air grew less tinged with incense and more touched with the moldering damp of the crypt.

It was a trade Jacob was willing to make. His body settled and his mind cleared with every breath.

Julianne had found the other half of the manuscript. He'd found Julianne. Now he only had to keep them both safe.

When they reached the end of the tunnel, he knelt and gave the grate a hard yank, ignoring the pain from the touch of cold iron that shot up both his arms and clawed the base of his brain. The crumbling mortar around the grill gave way and Jacob pulled it free to open a hole into the crypt.

"Take off your crinoline and the robe," he said as he shrugged out of his black fabric. She'd never wiggle through the opening with those hoops and they might as well dispose of the costumes that marked them as attendees of Sir Malcolm's unholy rites.

She complied without complaint and shimmied through the hole in the wall, her long skirts dragging behind her. Jacob shoved the manuscript after her, then followed, barely able to squeeze his shoulders through.

When he stood on the other side, Julianne was dusting off the manuscript with her handkerchief, ignoring the fact that her clothes were covered with dirt. Most women would be frantic over the bedraggled state of their ensemble. Julianne's attention was focused on the ancient text she'd come for.

She was a wonder.

"How many countesses could do what you just did?" he asked in admiration.

"How many would have to, you mean?" Her eyes flashed at him. "Or how many would? Jacob, I ask your pardon. I behaved abominably in there. Cheaply."

Her voice echoed around the crypt, bouncing off the lime-washed walls.

"No, you didn't," he whispered, "but let's talk about it someplace else. Sound carries in these underground spaces. We don't want anyone following our voices this way."

They mounted the curving staircase that led to the sanctuary above. Though the crypt had been lit by a single gas lamp, banks of lit candles were scattered around the cross-shaped cathedral, little islands of light in a silent sea of darkness. They heard no footsteps in the cavernous space but their own.

"St. Paul's is unlocked," she whispered. "We should be able to slip through the church yard unremarked."

"In a bit." Jacob settled into a pew and pulled her down beside him. "Sir Malcolm's hordes may have made it to the street by now and Ivy Lane isn't far. We should wait here for a while and let them disperse."

She laid the manuscript across her lap, gripping it as if it were a shield.

"You didn't behave abominably. Or cheaply," Jacob said. "In fact, in another place and time, I would totally applaud your behavior."

She slanted a tight-lipped look at him. "That doesn't help. The fact remains if you hadn't insisted we leave, I wouldn't have had the strength to."

"We were both affected by that incense, but beyond that, I don't see why you're unhappy. We've tumbled into bed often enough that there's no denying we want each other, whether we're under the influence of an aphrodisiac or not."

"But I should have been able to control myself and, well, this is not the place to discuss it," she said, glancing primly around the empty cathedral. In the silence that followed, the shush of air currents and the sense of an unseen Presence made it seem much less empty.

"Do you really think the Almighty is surprised by the urges of His creatures?" Jacob asked.

"Jacob!" She must have spoken louder than she'd intended because she clamped a hand over her mouth to hush herself.

"The thing is, I believe we passed something of a test this night," Jacob said. "We wanted each other pretty badly in that vaulted chamber, but I also knew you wanted the manuscript. So I put what you wanted first."

"If it was a test, you may have passed, but I didn't," she said softly. "I forgot all about the manuscript and the dagger and everything. Sir Malcolm said the incense releases what we normally repress. Jacob, I would have done . . . anything for you, if you hadn't stopped me."

"Then I wish you'd stop repressing," he said with a chuckle. Letting those happy possibilities roll around in his head lessened the residual pain from his contact with the iron grate. Then he caught up her hand. "In all seriousness, I love you, Julianne. And I think you care for me, which accounts for why you wanted to do those things for me. You didn't have the urge to do anything for those other blokes, did you?"

She shook her head. "I didn't even think about the other people there. It was as if they weren't real. That's what bothers me most, I think. Not that I'd have happily rendered you a lover's service, but that I'd have done something private and special before strangers. Even if Queen Victoria herself had been standing by taking notes, an audience wouldn't have stopped me."

Jacob grinned. "You do have a history on the stage, you know. An audience generally encourages theatre types."

"That's not what I meant."

"And what a memorable entry that would have made for our Sovereign's journal. She's said to be quite good with watercolors. I wonder if she'd have been moved to capture the moment in more than words."

Julianne swatted his shoulder. "I'm serious, Jacob. How could I so forget myself?"

"Forgetting yourself is what love is about. We were both trying to put each other first. I thought you wanted that manuscript more than anything. And you must have been reading my mind because you knew exactly what would please me. Maybe"—he brought her hand to his mouth and brushed a kiss across her knuckles—"you love me. More than you know."

She laid her head on his shoulder and released a little sigh. "Maybe I do."

Chapter 22

"I can't work with you hovering about like a vulture waiting for the carcass to stop jerking." Dr. Snowdon propped his spectacles on his forehead and sent a gargoyle's frown toward Jacob. "If you leave the manuscript with me, I'm sure I'll be able to have something for you by tonight. Tomorrow at the latest."

"I'm sorry, doctor, but we dare not leave the manuscript here. It might not be safe for you to be in possession of it and we value you too highly," Julianne said soothingly. "But he's right, Jacob. Come sit down. You'll wear a groove in the floor with all that pacing."

Jacob plopped into the chair beside her. They'd spent the night in St. Paul's, snatching what sleep they could and ducking down in the pew when the sexton made his rounds through the dark space. Once dawn broke, they slipped out and hailed a hansom. Jacob ordered the driver to take them to his home, where they stayed just long enough to liberate the first half of the manuscript from his safe. Then, ignoring Mrs. Trott's pleas that they take time to break their fast and tidy up a bit, they came directly to Dr. Snowdon's office.

Julianne probably should have insisted they return to Lord and Lady Kilmaine's town house, but the odds of her being able to reenter the home without being discovered were exceedingly thin. If her reputation was already ruined in the eyes of her hosts, another few hours would not make it worse.

Ordinarily, Julianne would be frantic over the scandal that was sure to ensue when she finally dragged herself back over their threshold. Especially looking as disheveled as she was. She'd left her pelisse in the Druid's antechamber and her crinoline in the tunnel leading to St. Paul's crypt. Her long skirts hung limply. Clinging to her legs and bunching under her feet, they threatened to trip her with each step. Her hair was a fright, she was sure.

But every time Jacob looked at her, she felt like a queen. He loved her. And even more astoundingly, there was every possibility she loved him back.

She'd avoided love as if it was smallpox. Love made women too pliant, too weak. It robbed them of the ability to choose their own path. Marriage might be a necessary evil, but love was a disease to be shunned at all costs.

And yet she'd been infected with it anyway.

Julianne wasn't ready to think about what that meant for her plans. But when she slanted a glance at Jacob, her chest nearly burst with tenderness. She was willing to shove questions about the future aside and concentrate on the sweetness of now.

"Hmm. Fascinating," Snowdon murmured and Jacob leaped to his feet.

"What?"

"Patience, old boy. I deciphered this section but haven't translated it satisfactorily yet. Celts were souls of poetry, you know, and I want to stay true to the spirit of the original." George removed his spectacles and scrubbed them with his handkerchief. "But iambic pentameter doesn't exactly flow from my pen this early in the morning and—"

"Hang the poetry, George," Jacob interrupted. "What does it say?"

"Something about a dagger in Merlin's Cave."

"What about it?"

"Well, it's a bit odd, since I always assumed the cave associated with Arthurian lore would be in Cornwall, near Tintagel, you know," George said. "Or maybe in the Forest Sauvage where Arthur was fostered."

Jacob crowded close to peer over George's shoulder at his squiggly Latin notes. "I see it mentions Penton."

"Good show, old chap. Guess you haven't forgotten everything you tried not to learn at Cambridge. That's what it seems to say, though I'm at a loss to explain it," George admitted. "It's beyond strange to think that Merlin's Cave might be right here in London, beneath Penton Rise, if my assumptions are correct."

"Oh, I think you'd be surprised to learn what lurks beneath the streets of London," Julianne said. *Or beneath St. Paul's cathedral, for that matter.*

"Penton Rise," Jacob repeated under his breath. "I always assumed that was a natural hill. Do you suppose it's actually an ancient mound of some sort with a hollow space inside?"

"Anything's possible," Julianne said, believing those words for the first time in her life. Love, or even the chance of it, was giving her a far rosier outlook than usual. "Does the manuscript say anything about where to find an entrance to the mound?"

"Well, there's a bit here about seeking the dwelling place of spirits beneath the spirits. Odd, that." George scratched his head. "Don't know what to make of it. Not exactly an X marking the spot, what?"

"It's more than we had before we arrived here," Jacob said. "Thanks, George. We'll be out of your way now."

He gathered up the manuscript and his friend's notes.

"Wait," Dr. Snowdon said. His face fell in dismay, the sad expression reminding Julianne of a disappointed bloodhound. "There's much more for me to do with the manuscript."

"And we'll be happy to let you do it," Julianne said, checking her silver pendant watch. Half the morning was gone and facing her hosts wasn't going to become any easier as more time passed. "But we don't want to disrupt your practice and we can only chase down one clue at a time."

"Come by my place this evening," Jacob said. "I'll let you tinker with syntax to your heart's content."

He held open the door for Julianne. She stepped into the corridor, where she nearly stumbled into the neatly dressed woman waiting there.

Probably one of Dr. Snowdon's hysteria patients.

The woman ran a disapproving gaze over Julianne's disheveled ensemble and then sent Jacob a censorious look. "You waited far too long, sir. I'll warrant your wife has the worst case of hysteria Dr. Snowdon's ever seen."

Then she smiled kindly at Julianne and patted her forearm. "Keep your appointments with the doctor regularly, dear. He'll put you to rights in no time."

"It's not as if you're about to face a dragon," Jacob said as the hansom bore them closer to Lord and Lady Kilmaine's home. "It's only my cousin Viola, for pity's sake."

Julianne sighed. Men had no idea what sort of dragons lurked beneath muslin and lace. An enraged hostess who felt her hospitality betrayed by the improper behavior of a guest could be every bit as formidable as a fire-breathing lizard.

And far more vindictive.

There was nothing else for it. Julianne had sown the wind. It was time to face the whirlwind.

Once Jacob handed her out of the cab, she squared her shoulders and marched up to the front door of the Kilmaines' home. When the door swung open, she and Jacob were ushered inside. While they waited for the butler to fetch his mistress, she mentally rehearsed her apology for the umpteenth time.

But she never had opportunity to speak it. At the announcement of their arrival, Viola came flying down the hall toward the parlor where they waited. Julianne was engulfed in a hug before she could sputter a word.

"Mercy, I was so worried about you. Nearly called the constable to start a search but Quinn wouldn't let me," she said as she released Julianne and then gave Jacob the same bear-hug of welcome. "Of course, once we sent to your home and found out you were missing too, Jacob, we figured everything was all right." A puzzled frown drew her brows together. "But you haven't had time to go to Gretna Green and back. What did you do, you sly-boots? Get a ship's captain to cast off in the Thames and say the words over you? Jacob, you never said a word about procuring a special license and—"

Then she stopped gushing, taking in Julianne's missing hoops and grubby gown. Jacob was minus his collar studs and the knees of his trousers were black with grime.

"Oh, dear! I fear I've made a mistake. You didn't elope, did you?" Viola said slowly.

"No," Jacob said. "Though it's an idea with merit. God save any sane Englishman from the folderol of a formal wedding."

Julianne flinched. Did that mean he wanted to elope with her or was the abstract idea of it only slightly less repugnant than a church rite? He'd asked her to wed him once, though at the time she'd been certain it was only because he wanted to bed her and thought a proposal would ease his way. Now that they'd spent the night together, even if it was only huddled chastely in a church pew, society would expect them to wed to hush up any hint of scandal.

Jacob hadn't broached the subject and Julianne wasn't sure

what she'd say if he did. Marriage still meant surrendering her freedom to a man's whim. Even if the man was Jacob, it was a risk.

"Better get Quinn," Jacob said to his cousin. "We owe you both an explanation of what's going on and I'd rather only go through it once."

"I'm sorry to have worried you, Viola," Julianne began, but Jacob's cousin cut her off.

"Never mind. I'm sure you had a perfectly sound reason for slipping out of the house last night. At least, you used the back door. I've been known to go through a window or two myself," she said with a wink. "Let me get Quinn before I burst with curiosity."

Viola bustled off and Julianne released a pent-up sigh.

"What did I tell you?" Jacob said.

"You were right. She's wonderful." Julianne smiled after Viola's retreating form, then turned to give Jacob a hug. "I love your family."

"Don't be too hasty," he said, running a hand down her spine and pressing her close against him. "You haven't met them all yet. I'm saving the lunatic aunt and the second cousin languishing in Fleet Prison for later."

"How much later?"

He dropped a kiss on her forehead. "I figure I'd better wait till you're firmly in love with me."

"Oh," she said as Viola and Quinn's footsteps clicked down the hall toward them. She stood on tiptoe to brush his lips with hers. "You may not have long to wait."

Jacob told Viola and Quinn everything. He explained about the final dagger and their search for it, about George Snowdon's part in deciphering the ancient codex and the secret society of Druids.

Julianne shared their sleepless night in the shadowy sanctuary of St. Paul's after they made good their escape from the underground temple. She added her hope that somehow during their search they could prove her late husband had not taken his own life. And she was entirely frank about her anonymous buyer for the full set of daggers, what the sale would mean to her and those who were depending on her.

"But if we aren't successful in finding the remaining dagger, I hope I can interest you and some of your friends in supporting Mrs. Osgood's school," Julianne said. "There's no place else for these poor girls and I can't let them be cast back onto the street."

"Of course not," Viola said. "Even if you do find the dagger, I hope you'll allow me the pleasure of helping the school as well. The world is a difficult place for a woman without the protection of a good man." She smiled at her husband and a not-so-secret message of love and trust passed between them. "It must be even worse for a young girl without family or a benefactor."

Julianne blinked back tears. Viola understood how important the school was to her. No one had provided a safe haven for her and her sister Mary when they were young. In some small way, providing one for others filled up a hole in her heart and eased her guilt over not finding her sister.

"Viola and I haven't had an adventure for, oh, a week or two at least." Quinn rubbed his palms together in anticipation. "What can we do to help you find this mysterious dagger?"

"Well, if you happen to know a way to burrow under Penton Rise to find Merlin's Cave or where a fellow might 'seek the dwelling place of spirits beneath the spirits,' I'd bless your name," Jacob said with a yawn. "For now, a bath, breakfast, and a bed for a few hours are at the top of my list. In no particular order, actually."

The conundrum of how to find the dagger hidden in London swirled around Julianne's brain, but she too felt the call of soft linen to her tired body.

"I'd appreciate being able to stay with you for a while longer," Julianne said. "At least, until we uncover the final dagger."

"Of course, you can stay. That goes without saying," Viola said. "We want you to know we're willing to help in any way we can. My word, a search for a Druid dagger is much more exciting than the first story you told me about some dry old business partnership between you and Jacob. Of course, I didn't believe that sorry tale for a minute. Come." She held out her hand to Julianne. "Jacob may prefer his comforts in no particular order, but I'll wager you'd like something to eat while your bath is being drawn. Then I'll have Maggie turn down your bed."

Julianne linked elbows with her hostess and let herself be led to the breakfast room for a quick repast. Viola hadn't recriminated her, hadn't turned a hair, even though Julianne and Jacob had spent the night together in an unwed state.

She reveled in the sure knowledge that she had more than a friend in Viola Preston. She had found a kindred spirit. Almost . . . a sister.

Julianne would probably never know what had happened to Mary. But the love she'd received from her sibling was now echoed in this unconditional acceptance from Jacob's cousin.

Jacob loved her. His family welcomed her with warmth she'd never known. If only she had all six daggers in her possession, she'd be perfectly content.

"Julianne, wake up."

She forced one eyelid open. The shades had been drawn to darken the bedchamber, but a thin strip of light stole through a slit in the curtains. The last rays of daylight still burned outside. Judging from the grittiness Julianne felt around her eyes, she hadn't slept the clock around. She reasoned it must be late afternoon of the same day.

A soft rap sounded on the door, and Viola's voice came again.

"May I come in?"

Julianne rose and donned a wrapper to cover the corset and all-in-one she'd dropped off to sleep in, as she crossed to admit her friend.

"I'm sorry to wake you, but I simply can't hold it in a moment longer," Viola said as she breezed into the room and plopped onto the foot of the bed. "Quinn and I may have found something."

"Oh?"

"You need to get dressed. Nothing too fancy." Viola hopped up and opened the wardrobe. She pulled out one of Julianne's less fashionable half-mourning ensembles, a pale skirt and matching jacket in sturdy bombazine. "This will do." After draping it over the dressing screen in the corner, she turned back to Julianne, her hazel eyes dancing with excitement. "It may be nothing, of course, but Quinn thinks it's worth exploring. Oh, this is so exciting!"

Julianne disappeared behind the screen. "What on earth have you found?"

"Not on earth. *Under* it. Well, maybe," Viola admitted. "Once you and Jacob found your beds, Quinn and I drove to Penton Rise to have a peek around with fresh eyes. Believe me, things look entirely different when you're imagining what may lie beneath them."

"I daresay they do." Julianne wiggled into her narrowest crinoline and slid the skirt over her head. She stepped from behind the screen as she put on the jacket and fastened the mother-of-pearl buttons down the bodice. "Are you going to tell me what you found or am I to guess?"

"Guess if you like, but I'm not going to tell," Viola said impishly. "I'd rather you see it for yourself."

Viola continued to resist Julianne's efforts to draw out her secret and soon the women were joined by the men in Lord Kilmaine's coach. Traffic clogged the narrow streets, but the coach was much preferable to walking or riding since the November wind whipping through the man-made canyons was raw and tinged with the breath of winter.

When the coach came to a halt, Quinn rolled up the isinglass so they could see out clearly. They were stopped before an unremarkable tavern on a side street at the base of Penton Rise. Then Julianne read the swinging sign over the door and gasped.

The placard proclaimed the name of the place was Merlin's Cave.

"Seek the dwelling place of spirits beneath the spirits," Julianne repeated Dr. Snowdon's rough translation of the codex. "Could it really be that simple?" she wondered.

"Trust me," Jacob said with a grimace as he alighted from the coach and handed the women down. "Nothing is ever that simple."

Chapter 23

Merlin's Cave was a working man's tavern, with rough benches and tables worn slick from hundreds of years of pints sliding across the venerable oak. Even though Jacob and the others had dressed down, they still stuck out as "quality" in this salt-of-the-earth haunt.

Unlike the proprietor of the King's Arms, the ale-keep behind the bar of Merlin's Cave showed no sign of fawning on them in hopes of drawing in more custom from among their class. The same sort of earthenware mugs the other patrons quaffed from were plopped down before each of them, along with a basket of crusty bread, a dish of clotted cream and bowls of thick stew, featuring mostly potatoes, leeks and rutabaga with very little meat. Jacob eyed each stringy bit of what was supposed to be beef with a healthy dollop of suspicion.

Nothing else seemed to be on the menu.

When the serving girl returned with a fresh round of ale for all, Quinn demanded, "What's a man have to do to get whisky here?"

"Ask," she said simply.

"Good," Quinn said, slapping a sovereign on the table.

"Bring your oldest bottle. And four glasses. Clean ones, for choice."

Jacob watched the girl disappear through a door in the back of the common room that seemed to lead to a descending staircase. "They have a wine cellar," he said.

Julianne's gaze flicked to the door. "I wonder if there's anything beneath it. Spirits under the spirits, you know."

Viola shivered. "Spirits. Makes it sound as if the place is haunted."

When the girl reappeared, a low whooshing sound followed her until she closed the door behind her.

"Haunted indeed," Quinn said.

Jacob shook his head. "We've all heard a chimney moan on a windy day. That sound could simply mean there's an outlet leading from the cellar, possibly a larger void where air currents build up."

He resisted being more definite. All they had was conjecture. The hopeful expression on Julianne's face made him cringe. If he was wrong, she'd be sorely disappointed.

"How do we find out for sure?" she asked.

He looked around. The ale-keep was busy pulling pints. A rough-looking group of dock workers had just lumbered in and the serving girl slipped into the alcove where the stew pot bubbled to dish up helpings for them. Jacob turned to Quinn.

"If I'm not back in an hour or two, I'll expect you to come after me."

"You mean if we're not back," Julianne corrected, lifting her chin slightly.

There was no point in arguing. If he tried to leave her behind, she'd simply follow him. Strangely, he didn't seem to mind. Even though he had no idea what they might blunder into in the cellar beneath the tavern, he couldn't imagine blundering into it without her.

"If we're not back," he amended with a nod. "We'll need a diversion here if we're to slip into the cellar unseen."

"Leave that to me," Quinn said. He rose and called to the ale-keep, hefting the bottle of whisky in his direction. "I say, my good man, drinks all around!"

This pronouncement was greeted with cheers and a flurry of activity from the proprietor and the serving girl, who scrambled to find enough shot glasses, clean or otherwise, to go around. Quinn stood and moved about the room splashing whisky into upraised glasses and accepting hearty wishes for his continued good health, laughing and talking with everyone.

And drawing all eyes to him.

"Now's the time," Viola said.

Jacob and Julianne moved as quickly as possible to the door at the rear of the common room. They slipped through it and, leaving the world of light behind, descended a set of uneven stone stairs to the wine cellar. At the base of the steps, a kerosene lamp hung on a hook embedded in the rock face.

"Now's when a fire trick like your friend Sir Malcolm can pull off would come in handy." Jacob dug a packet of matches from his pocket and lit the wick.

"He's not my friend," Julianne said as she peered around him, taking in the dust-laden bottles and ancient kegs. "And I doubt it's a trick. If you see visions when you touch metal, and I'm certain you do, I'm willing to entertain the possibility that Sir Malcolm can pull fire from thin air."

The lamp guttered. "His is a damn sight better trick to have at the moment," Jacob said with a snort.

He trimmed the wick, a task made more difficult by his gloves, but he didn't want to hear the lantern's tinny voice. Then he relit it and lowered the flue to protect the flame.

"Stay close," he ordered and Julia fell into step behind him with her hand resting on his shoulder. They explored the length and breadth of the cellar, but found nothing but rows of bottles lying on their sides and a stack of kegs along the farthest wall.

"There's nothing here." Julia's shoulders sagged.

"I'm here." Jacob set down the lantern and put his arms around her, but she didn't relax into his embrace as he hoped. Instead, she trembled. "Easy, girl. There's nothing to fear in this cellar but getting your skirts dusty."

"I'm not afraid," she said testily. "I'm upset. I know it's stupid, but I was so certain we'd find something."

"What if we never do?" Jacob asked, tipping her chin up so she'd face him squarely. "You need to start thinking about your alternatives in case we don't uncover the last dagger."

"I don't know why I should think about them. They haven't changed. I can marry my stepson's toad-eating friend, return to the stage, or become a courtesan," she said, ticking off the possibilities on her gloved fingers with bitterness. "Not much of a choice, is it?"

"You're forgetting one." He wanted to be her main alternative.

But before Julianne could respond, the whooshing sound they'd heard in the tavern above came again. It was louder, closer and even more like the mournful groan of a disembodied soul.

"There's our mysterious spirit again. It's coming from behind those kegs," Julianne said, pulling away from Jacob to inspect them more closely. The tendrils of hair that escaped her neat coiffure wavered a bit as she drew near. "There's a definite air current coming from behind them."

She fairly danced in excitement, like a mare sidestepping and straining at the bit before a race. Her pleasure was a palpable thing, like a rush of lust to his groin. He'd do anything to keep her eyes glittering like that.

"Here." Jacob handed her the lantern and began clearing

away the kegs. After he'd moved half a dozen or so, they discovered a crack starting near the ceiling beams. It widened as it meandered down the stone wall. He quickly muscled the rest of the kegs out of the way.

By the time the cleft in the rock reached the level of Jacob's waist, the gap was wide enough for a man's shoulders to fit through. Jacob squatted before the opening and raised the lantern. Light shot into the darkness. "It looks like a tight squeeze, but it seems to open into a larger chamber in a few feet."

"If we could crawl through that grate into St. Paul's crypt, we can certainly get through there," Julianne said, starting toward the gap in the wall.

"Not so fast. Usually I'm a 'ladies first' sort of fellow, but not this time. You stay behind me or you stay here," he said with sternness. "Is that understood?"

She tossed him a saucy smile and raised an eyebrow. "I remember you demonstrating that 'ladies first' philosophy quite well. But since we aren't in a coach or your bed, I'll be happy to follow you now."

He nearly choked on his surprise. Her pupils had grown so her eyes appeared nearly black. A flush of color heated her cheeks. He'd heard some women found danger stimulating, that the threat of discovery added spice to a liaison. Even without drugging incense, Julianne was obviously stimulated by mystery, by the chase, by the unknown. He'd have to make sure this woman had her share of adventures in the future if he wanted to keep her happy.

And he wanted that more than anything, he realized. It was the only way he'd ever be happy.

He pulled her close and kissed her, willing her to feel what was threatening to burst out of his heart. She was his mystery, his adventure. Unriddling this woman would take him a lifetime and he was prepared to devote himself to the task.

If she'd let him.

She gave his lip a playful nip as their mouths parted. "Now, let's go find that dagger."

"Right," he said as he turned and bent double to squeeze through the narrow gap in the stone. "After me, then."

The low hum began as soon as he entered the cleft. The walls of rock were laced with metals. He felt them on the edges of his mind trying to press their way in as he brushed against the sides of the low tunnel. There was the shrill cry of tin, the drone of iron, splashes of nickel and zinc, a sprinkle of gold and silver, their laughing voices a whisper almost too faint to be heard.

He sighed with relief when the fissure in the rock opened into a high-ceilinged chamber. He was able to step far enough from the metal in the walls to make their voices fade. He lifted the lantern and surveyed the chamber as Julianne emerged behind him.

Striations of color streaked the rock face. Pockets of crystal dotted the cave walls, catching the lantern light and sending it dancing over the space in myriad prisms. The air was dry and cool, but Jacob heard the occasional patter of water.

Stalactites dripped from the vault overhead and stalagmites rose to meet them. Against the opposite wall a series of the formations had joined, looking like a rank of eerie, slick organ pipes. A pool glistened, dark and oily, in the center of the chamber.

"Careful," he said softly. "There may be fissures underfoot as big as the one we came through, so stay close."

She nodded and grasped his arm. "It doesn't look as if anyone has been here for a long time."

Or ever, he thought but didn't want to say. *No point in dashing her hopes immediately*. But there was no evidence any human had ever set foot in the cave. The floor was rocky and uneven. There was not even enough dust to capture a footprint. No stones had been gathered into a fire ring. No sign of soot stained the walls.

Jacob made his way over the uneven floor, stopping to help Julianne over the upraised stones that littered the space. "Careful," he warned. "Don't want you to turn an ankle or—"

He stopped dead as a low-pitched sound reached inside him and shuffled his innards.

"Do you hear that?" he asked.

"Hear what?"

He took another step and the sound grew louder, deeper. "There's something here."

It was similar to the voice of the dagger Julianne had first shown him, but only in the way that a lion in his prime is similar to a house cat. The song of this blade shimmered in the air around him and sank a claw into the base of his brain. He fought to remain upright as it sliced through him.

Jacob hadn't even laid eyes on the infernal thing yet. He didn't want to think what it could do once he actually touched it.

"Where is it?" Julianne whispered. Her voice echoed around the chamber in retreating sibilance.

Jacob closed his eyes to concentrate for a few breaths. The agony in his head subsided to a dull ache as he grew accustomed to the unwelcome presence of the dagger's voice. Then he raised a hand toward the formation that resembled a pipe organ. Power shot into his extended fingers and jolted up his arm.

He swallowed hard. In all his life, he'd never felt such intense energy emanating from a metal. "It's behind there."

Julianne took the lantern from him and scrambled toward the formation, untroubled by the nearness of the metal, oblivious to its soul-sucking drone.

"Yes, there's room to walk behind them," she called out and

slipped behind the tubular structure. Then, much more softly, he heard her say. "Oh, no."

Only the dismay in her voice moved Jacob toward the source of that diabolical sound. He hurried to her side and found her staring up at a wall covered with daggers hanging from lime-encrusted hooks.

"'Sons of forest brave halls of stone to leave one lying ne'er alone,'" she quoted from the manuscript. "There are hundreds of daggers. And they're identical. We can't take them all. How shall we ever tell which is the one?"

Chapter 24

Julianne reached up to touch one of the lowest hanging daggers.

"No!" Jacob grabbed her forearm. The droning voice thrummed in his chest now, melding with his heartbeat and making it gallop. Julianne didn't seem to hear a thing, but that didn't mean she was not in danger. Her late husband probably had never heard the dagger's song either. Until it was too late. "Don't. I can tell which is the right one, but first I'll have your promise that you won't lay a hand on it. Not now. Not ever. No one touches it but me."

"Why?"

Because it's evil, he wanted to say, but the words stuck in his mouth. "After what happened to your husband, do you have to ask?"

"Very well, I promise." Julianne lifted the lantern to throw more light on the wall of blades. Then she laid a slim hand on his shoulder. "Be careful, Jacob. I don't want anything to happen to you either."

"That makes two of us." He forced a grin and turned back toward the daggers. Somehow, her touch on his shoulder lessened the effect of the blade's song. He covered her hand with his for a moment, willing her to keep it there. Then he stretched his arm over his head.

The life force of the blade slammed into him, but he locked his knees, refusing to buckle. He followed the energy trail, now visible to him as well as audible. Its power sparkled in the air like flecks of gold leaf.

"There," Jacob said through clenched teeth. He grasped the real Druid dagger's hilt from among its many look-alikes, and the cave dissolved around him.

The dagger turned end over end before his eyes, leading him along a corridor of pulsing light.

Then suddenly Jacob stood at the edge of the smoking crater he'd seen before, looking down at the mass of metal the sky had hurled to earth. It was discovered by a band of Celtic hunters and carted back to their forge. With the clang of hammers and the song of poets, it was fashioned into a single gleaming sword.

Caliburn, he heard the men call it when the weapon was claimed by one named Arturus.

Not the sword in the stone, Jacob realized. *The sword from the stone.*

Battlefields and building fortresses, fire-scarred fields and golden grain ripe for harvest—years of hope and banished darkness scrolled before him. None could stand before the king who wielded Caliburn.

Only treachery would lay him low.

Perhaps that too was the metal's plan.

With the death of Arturus at his bastard son's hand, the sword was unmade and the sky-ore refashioned into a staff of power.

But that proved too strong for any one man to wield. At an order from a counsel of bards, the staff was divided, its magic dispersed.

The dagger in his hand wept for its lost mates. Its grief reached into Jacob's chest and twisted his heart.

Rejoin us, join us, join us, the dagger sang to him. *We will be yours and you will be ours and together no one can gainsay us in whatever we put our hand to. Nothing compares to the glory of oneness we will bring you.*

"No," Jacob said, resisting the pull of the metal with all his might.

Riches we will bring you and power and long life.

Jacob had dismissed such promises as hokum when Julianne first came to him about the dagger. They didn't seem so far-fetched now that he'd felt the smallest part of the blade's energy.

But the dagger wasn't for him. He'd found it for Julianne. He couldn't claim it for himself. He shook his head.

The dagger's voice curled around him again, this time seductive as a siren's song, the voice feminine and alluring. "We know what you want."

The blade sent a flurry of flashing images of Julianne—head bent to study a book, biting her lip in concentration, eyes flaring, ready to start an argument, flushed and rosy and waiting for him in a nest of tangled linens, lying beside him in perfect peace.

"We can make her yours for as long as you wish," the dagger promised.

He wished for her forever.

"Say the word and it is done." The offer wove around his heart, curled over his soul. He hardly felt the hooklike tendrils taking root. "She is ours to give."

"Now I know you lie," Jacob said. Julianne, more than any other woman he'd ever known, belonged to herself. He wanted her, but only by her free choice. "And I will do all I can to see you are never rejoined to the others. You will remain unmade."

The dagger roared, an unearthly, shattering wall of sound. Light pulsed around him and he was propelled back through a long tunnel, the blade's despair howling in his ears.

"Easy," the familiar voice said at his side. "Don't let him fall, Quinn. Fenwick! Come help us."

Jacob raised his head. His eyelids scraped across his eyes as if they were made of sandpaper. One of his arms was draped over Quinn's shoulder as they stumbled through Jacob's front door. In his other hand, he clutched the dagger, but he held it by the leather scabbard now, not the hilt.

Julianne called for Fenwick again. Both he and Gil came running down the hall toward them.

"Parlor," Jacob managed to croak out. Was there a vise clamped to his temples?

Between the two men and the boy, they carried Jacob up the stairs with Julianne and Viola following. He didn't fight them on the steps, but he twisted free when they tried to settle him into a comfortable chair.

Forcing one foot before the other, he trudged toward the fireplace. While the dagger cursed him in the language of demons, he opened the safe and thrust it inside with the other blade and the two halves of the manuscript. Only once he sealed and locked the platinum-lined vault did the malevolent voice cease.

Jacob sagged against the mantel and drew a deep breath. "There, that's done."

"Now you only need travel to Cornwall to retrieve the other four blades and then Julianne can sell them," Viola said.

"No." Julianne came up beside him and positioned herself under his arm. "We aren't going to Cornwall. I'm done with the daggers."

Jacob had no memory of walking back out of the cave or climbing the stone steps from the wine cellar to the tavern. The coach ride home felt as if it was something he'd dreamed. But now blood flooded back into his brain and hope came with it.

"You have the whole set, but now you say you're done with them?" He pulled her close, trying very hard not to lean on her. The reason she needed them hadn't changed. "Why, Julie?"

"Because I can't bear what they do to you." Tears shimmered in her dark eyes. "Help me get him to bed, Fenwick. And bring a tonic."

"No laudanum," Jacob said.

Her chin quivered and he bent to kiss her, not caring that there were four sets of eyes looking on. The softness of her lips eased his pain better than any amount of opiate.

"I'll be fine," he said.

She might accept his judgment about the laudanum, but she wouldn't be swayed against putting him to bed. He gave up and allowed Fenwick and Gil to shepherd him to his room.

Gil should have followed Fenwick down the servant's stairs to the kitchen once they saw to Mr. Preston's comfort, but he hung back in the corridor. He'd seen strange doings this day and couldn't rightly make sense of them. Ear to the keyhole, he strained to listen as the quality folk talked over his now sleeping employer.

"This is far worse than the last time he used his gift," Lady Cambourne said.

Gift? That meant something beyond the common, didn't it? Gil pressed his ear closer to the keyhole. This might have something to do with the special power Sir Malcolm suspected Mr. Preston could call up.

"Yes," Lady Kilmaine agreed. "There's something different about that dagger. I've never seen metal affect him quite so deeply."

Metal? How could metal knock a man off his pins unless it was in the form of a club? Since Gil had helped Fenwick put Mr. Preston to bed, he knew his employer hadn't been stabbed with the dagger. Gil reckoned Mr. Preston was simply deep in his cups. Quality folk was always drunk as lords simply because they could afford to be.

"When Jacob first touched the dagger, he went still as stone," Lady C. said, her voice quivering. "I thought it had killed him. Then he started talking . . . to the dagger."

Generally folk didn't talk to things what couldn't rightly talk back. Maybe Mr. Preston had hit a bottle or two without the lady's notice.

"Then he seemed to come back to himself and all the time we walked back through the cave to the tavern, he recounted the vision the metal had sent him. It was . . . unnerving," the countess said. "Especially since Jacob wouldn't respond to my questions. Didn't even seem to know I was there. He just kept repeating what he'd seen. Even now, I don't think he realizes he did it."

"Jacob's gift of touch is difficult to live with," Lord Kilmaine said. "His visions sound as vivid as yours, Viola."

"More so, I fear," his wife said. "And it sounds as if the information he shared with you was important."

"It was," Lady Cambourne said. "That's why I've decided not to try to sell the set of daggers after seeing what this one did to Jacob. His vision was proof positive that no one should be in possession of all six of them."

So, Mr. Preston had visions, did he? And it seemed to Gil that touching something metal was what set the visions off. As special powers went, it weren't quite as good as being able to fly, but it damn sure beat being a human matchstick all to pieces.

Gil was mortally tired of hanging about Mr. Preston's house all the time, never feeling the sun on his face or being able to swipe an apple when the cartman weren't lookin' or playin' a game of hoops with his friends. And Mrs. Trott! While he admired her cooking with heartfelt devotion, the meddling woman insisted he keep himself so clean he squeaked. Gil's life wasn't his own anymore.

He could go back to Sir Malcolm with the news about Mr. Preston's visions. It would put paid to Ravenwood's threat to come looking for him. Gil would have his freedom back. He'd be able to roam the city as he pleased and Sir Malcolm would be ashamed of his piddling ability once he heard about Mr. P.'s fantastical gift.

Then too, if Gil told Sir Malcolm that Mr. Preston and Lady Cambourne were all done chasing about after a set of daggers, and the countess wasn't going to part with them in any case, maybe it would kill Ravenwood's interest in his employer altogether.

All in all, it was a good idea. Mr. P. was always talking about how important it was for a fellow to "take the initiative." He'd thank Gil for acting on this matter once his head cleared.

The voices in the next room were louder, closer to the door.

"I'll sit with him till I'm sure he's all right." Lady Cambourne was saying. "Then I'll return to your home."

"We'll send the coach back for you," Lord Kilmaine said.

The sound of approaching footsteps made Gil abandon the keyhole. Lord and Lady Kilmaine were taking their leave of Lady Cambourne, so Gil nipped down the back staircase before Kilmaine and his lady could catch him eavesdropping. Fenwick hurried to the front door to see the quality folk out. Then when Mrs. Trott's back was turned, Gil slipped out the back door. He headed down the alley and set off for Sir Malcolm's home on Penton Rise at a mile-eating dogtrot.

Chapter 25

Jacob wandered the stone labyrinth with the remembered strains of the dagger's song pounding in his head. He didn't know where he was exactly, but he knew he had to reach the center of the maze, had to find the heart of the puzzle.

He'd find Julianne there.

She called his name from someplace up ahead and he started running toward the sound. The path ended in a pile of scree.

The dagger laughed.

Stone ground against stone and a fissure opened at his right to show Julianne on the other side of the rock wall. She was naked, bound hand and foot with red silk, her arms and legs spread like da Vinci's Vitruvian Man. Jacob realized suddenly that he was unclothed too.

God help him, his body roused to her.

"You see, we do know what you want," the dagger taunted.

"No, not like that. Not if she has no choice." But his aching cockstand didn't abate.

"You damn yourself for a liar. She is too stubborn to bend. She'll never be yours by her own free choice," the blade said and Jacob was hard-pressed to argue with its logic. He'd never met a woman more determined to maintain her independence. "Take her. We give her to you."

His body wanted her any way he could have her, but his heart tugged him in a different direction, threatening to split him in two.

If Julianne didn't choose him because she loved him, if she only picked him as the least noxious of her possibilities, there'd be no joy in their joining.

"You can make her love you," the dagger suggested. "You have the skills. Enslave her with pleasure."

Jacob didn't remember ordering his body to step through the opening in the rock, but he suddenly found himself on the other side approaching her. Julianne lifted her head and met his gaze, her eyes widening like a startled doe.

He could gentle her, then pleasure her. A bound woman could be brought to untold delights. She'd be grateful.

He bent his head to kiss her, but her lips were like stone.

"Take her. Make her yours," the dagger encouraged.

He kissed her harder, bruising her mouth, forcing a response. She moaned down his throat, desperate and needy. She kissed him back, her passion dark-edged. When he drew away, he tasted blood on his lips.

The iron in the droplets whispered her fear.

Not of him. Even bound, she'd match him for sensuality.

Julianne was afraid of losing herself, of surrendering her hard-won freedom.

He grabbed the dagger and used it to cut the red silk to free her. The blade screamed at him and the ground opened beneath his feet. He tumbled, weightless, into an abyss. Julianne fell beside him, her eyes showing white all around, her mouth stretched in a rictus of fear. He stretched out his hands as far as he could, but he couldn't reach her.

The bottom of the void rose to meet them. They'd be dashed on the cruel rocks. Another few heartbeats and—

Jacob jerked himself to wakefulness. His heart thundered, but his breathing was steady. Julianne was sitting by his bedside, focused on the rhythmic rise and fall of his chest. Her face was taut and drawn. Then her concerned gaze wandered to his face.

"Oh, you're awake."

"And glad to be so." His head still throbbed, but it was bearable. The heavy coverlet was balled at the foot of the bed and the sheets were twisted at his waist.

Julianne smoothed the linens, tucking them up to his chin. Then she laid a cool palm on his forehead.

"Guess I've been restless," he said, trying to chase away the disturbing remnants of his dream.

"You only stopped thrashing a moment ago," she said. "But then you went so still, it was more unsettling than your flailing about."

He'd made a spectacle of himself without knowing it. His brows drew together in a fresh wave of pain.

"I wish I could bear some of the pain for you," Julianne said. "Or make it better somehow."

She ruffled his hair and the pounding in his temple diminished.

"You do make it better," he said. "Simply by being here. Will you stay?"

Forever, he added silently. *Will you help me keep my sanity when the metal screams in my mind? Will you love me in spite of myself?*

He couldn't bring himself to speak the words. They sounded too needy, too coercive. If she stayed with him, it had to be her choice.

"I'll stay awhile." She smiled at him. "Viola and Quinn expect me back this evening."

"May as well make the most of the time we have then." Jacob lifted the sheet up to invite her into the bed with him. "Join me. I want to hold you."

Her gaze flicked over his rampant cock and her sweet mouth twitched in a suppressed smile. "My clothes are grubby from the cellar."

He grinned at her. "Take them off."

She beamed back. "I guess this proves you're feeling better."

Julianne unbuttoned her jacket, the fabric falling away to reveal her lacy undergarments and the swell of her breasts above them. His mouth went dry.

She unfastened her skirt and lifted it over her head. The crinoline was like a cage, keeping all her secrets safe, while giving him peeping glances at her shapely legs between the wires. She wiggled out of it, leaving the contraption propped against the chair. Then she climbed into bed with him in her corset and all-in-one.

Julianne lay on her side facing away from him. He doubted she was being shy. Not after all they'd been through together. She was simply teasing him.

Jacob rolled toward her, pulling her close so her bum snugged against his groin. He buried his nose in her hair and inhaled deeply.

"Mmmm," he groaned.

It was not a groan of pain. It was pure need. She burrowed deeper into his embrace.

"Fenwick could have sat with me. Julie, why didn't you leave with Viola and Quinn?" he asked, trying to get her to admit she wanted him. That she *chose* him.

"It's my fault you're in discomfort. I'm trying to make you feel better," she said, rocking her hips. His appreciation of her nearness grew by several orders of magnitude. "At least, part of you seems pleased."

"All of me is pleased," he said. But if she was only with him because she thought his pain was her fault, he was little more than a duty to her.

He'd have to change that.

He kissed her nape. The delectable skin was soft and sweet

and gooseflesh bloomed where his lips had touched. She shivered with delight.

She rolled toward him and searched his face. The concerned set of her mouth melted away and the frown line between her brows disappeared.

"Your head doesn't hurt?"

"Maybe a little, but you're a wonderful distraction." He bent to nuzzle her neck and kissed his way down to the channel between her breasts. Then he stopped, his big frame shuddering. It suddenly felt as if someone were driving a spike through his left eye.

"Jacob?" Panic pitched her voice up half an octave.

"My head." He rolled onto his back and the pounding spike stopped. "I need to lie this way for a bit." His breath came in shallow pants. Damn, he hated this weakness.

"I should go."

"No, stay." He pulled her close. She settled her head in the crook of his shoulder and pressed herself against the length of his body. The pain lessened. "That's better."

"Isn't there something I can do?"

"You can talk to me."

"Very well." She raised herself up and looked down at him, a wicked expression on her angelic face. "I think of you by night, Jacob. Alone in my bed, I imagine what I'd like to do with you."

He closed his eyes and groaned inwardly. Well, he couldn't rightly complain since he'd done this to her once. He'd known full well how his words were affecting her that day in the carriage. He'd seduced her with just the sound of his voice. Now she was giving as good as she got.

But if he couldn't act on the need her fantasy would generate, it would be pure torture to listen to her speak. Of course, he also burned with curiosity to learn what her fantasy entailed.

"Tell me," he said.

"First I'd undress you slowly," she said, her voice sultry and low. "But I'd take care not to touch you more than necessary, just the slightest of glancing caresses. Of course, you want me to do more—"

"Sounds like me."

"But I make you wait." She kissed his closed eyelids and the spike in his head dissolved. "Then I tell you to lie down on the bed—"

"Whose bed?"

"My bed in the dowager's house in Cornwall," she said. "It's not very fancy, but it's a sturdy four-poster and—but that's not important. I want you to lie down so I can look at you. Sort of like this."

She flipped back the sheets, baring him completely. His eyes popped open so he could watch her. Starting at his feet, she studied all his parts, a secret smile lifting the corners of her mouth. When she reached his groin, his ballocks drew up into a tight bunch under her scrutiny and his cock lifted toward her of its own accord.

Her smile widened.

But her gaze traveled on, searing over his belly and grazing his nipples. She inspected his hands, his forearms and on up to his shoulders as if she were cataloguing a collection of all the bits of him. When she met his eyes, he noticed her face was flushed.

"Then what?" he asked. The fact that she obviously liked what she saw made his body tighten with need.

"I'd touch you."

Starting with his head, she rubbed his crown, tracing the midline of his skull with her thumbs. It felt so good, he almost stopped her when she moved down to his neck and shoulders. She varied her touches, first hard, almost rough, then so soft he wondered if he had only imagined her fingertips brushing against him. His nipples drew tight as she circled them. His gut clenched when she explored his navel.

She ran her hands around his groin, teasing the small hairs in slow circles, but though she drew close, she didn't touch his cock or balls. He nearly bellowed when she skipped over them completely to run her palms down his thighs and calves, but he clamped his lips shut.

He would not beg. Either she'd choose him, all of him, or not.

"It's a pity you're not a Scotsman," she said. "You have the legs for a kilt."

"And you have the tongue of a temptress."

Her eyes glittered. "You read my mind. That's the next part. I'm about to kiss you . . . everywhere."

She settled herself on her knees between his legs and bent to kiss his thighs. Her tongue flicked out, leaving little wet runnels in its wake. As she drew near his straining cock her breasts brushed his legs, her nipples button-hard even through the muslin.

She cupped his balls and he nearly lost control. When she kissed him and ran her tongue along the dividing line between his testicles, he prayed for strength to make this heaven last. Her hair fell on either side of her face, a dark tent covering them both. The silken strands were like thousands of loving fingers on his skin. She slicked her tongue over his entire length.

Oh, God, she's going to—

She took him in.

He hadn't asked. She chose to, wanted to. If the little sounds she made were any indication, loving him this way gave her pleasure too. She lavished him with kisses. She licked. She sucked.

He buried his fingers in her hair. Pressure rose in his shaft. He started doing calculations from his brother's ledgers in his mind to keep from coming.

Then he realized suddenly that his head felt perfectly normal. Julianne drove out the metal barbs. She was a more potent shield than platinum.

His body tightened for release, but he fought against it. He wasn't ready for this to end. Jacob sat up and reached under her arms to lift her up. He kissed her mouth, that soft wet cavern that had so sweetly accepted him.

"Why did you stop me?" she asked when he pulled back.

"You know my motto. Ladies first."

Chapter 26

Jacob rolled over her and she welcomed his weight on her. Julianne loved the solid, comforting way he covered her completely. His hands found her fingers and laced his with them, stretching her arms out. His lips sealed her mouth, their breaths joined.

She was so wet and ready, he slid inside her in one slow thrust. Her insides expanded, greeting him with an involuntary squeeze.

He made a low noise of pleasure and her entire body sparked in empathy. She experienced the same shivering joy as when she'd taken him into her mouth. His bliss was hers. His need echoed in her bones. It was as if they were halves of the same whole, bonded with each other in all things. She didn't doubt he felt her deep ache with the same intense throb.

The line between taking and giving blurred. They both did each at once. They stroked, they kissed, they moved together with carnal grace. With each lunge, they were greedy and generous, selfish and serving.

But she sensed there was something missing, something else he wanted.

She felt it in the driving rhythm, the quickening pace. He reached between them to stroke her tender spot. His shaft pulsed once, but his body tightened with the effort of resisting the inevitable. He was waiting for her.

Tight as she was wound, she still couldn't seem to let go. She kissed him with fierceness, nipping his lips.

"Don't wait for me, Jacob," she pleaded. "I love you so."

A strangled cry tore from his throat and his release pounded inside her. Tears gathered at the corners of her eyes as she realized he'd been waiting to hear her admit she loved him. Why had she denied it so long?

His pulses pushed her over the edge and her whole body shuddered with him. They fairly glowed with their combined bliss. After a little while, or it might have been hours later—the way time expanded and contracted around them, Julianne couldn't tell for certain—she stopped trembling and kissed his neck.

"I love you," Julianne repeated, daring finally to believe the words that poured from her throat. Early in her life, she'd learned that love was pain. Love was loss. She knew better than to hazard her heart, but she couldn't help herself. Come heartache, come ruin, she loved the man whose strong body still covered hers. "I love you, Jacob."

"Careful, my heart." He raised his head from the pillow and looked down at her, his soul shining in his eyes. "I'm going to hold you to that."

Lady Cambourne didn't return to Lord and Lady Kilmaine's home that night. When she gave no sign of leaving, Fenwick finally sent the viscount's coach back with word that the countess was staying to make sure Mr. Preston was fully recovered from his ill spell.

Fully recovered. Sounds like what the upper crust would call it, Fenwick reasoned with a shrug.

Among his class, it was simply a good old game of "hide the sausage." Still, he went to his bed happy for his employer and the countess. It was about bloody time they stopped dancing about the issue, quit fiddling around during the day, and simply tumbled into bed with each other by night like normal folk. When a body got right down to it, there wasn't tuppence worth of difference between the wellborn and the salt of the earth when it came to the real stuff of life.

The next morning, Dr. Snowdon arrived quite early, rousting a yawning Fenwick from his bed. He rapped discreetly on Mr. Preston's door and amazingly enough, his employer appeared almost immediately, looking more rested than Fenwick had ever seen him.

Without waiting for his shave or breakfast, Mr. Preston disappeared with Dr. Snowdon into the parlor to pore over the combined manuscripts that were stored in his safe. Before Fenwick could slip back to the kitchen to wheedle a cup of tea from Mrs. Trott, Lady Cambourne emerged from Mr. Preston's chamber, with a decidedly rosy glow about her. After she prevailed on Fenwick to hail a hansom, she departed for Lord Kilmaine's home without taking leave of Mr. Preston.

Probably been more than enough taking last night, Fenwick thought with a wicked grin.

Then Fenwick made his way back to the kitchen to fetch a light breakfast for the quality folk in the parlor. And hopefully snag some for himself before his day started in earnest.

Mrs. Trott met him at the kitchen door.

"Have you seen that little rapscallion?" she demanded. "Wait till I get my hands on him. I'll skin him proper, see if I don't."

"Who?" Fenwick asked, mildly alarmed for the rapscallion in question and heartily relieved he wasn't the one who'd bunched Mrs. Trott's knickers in a knot.

"Gilbert Stout, o' course." She twisted her apron in her gnarled hands. Fenwick had seen her this distraught only once before when her Christmas pudding, which she'd worked on for weeks, unaccountably failed to set. "The boy disappeared in the confusion last night after Mr. Preston took ill. I didn't say anything at the time because I figured Gil would sneak back in after he had his fill of larkin' about, but his pallet hasn't been slept in. Where do you suppose he could be?"

"The lad's at home on the streets. I have no idea where he's got off to. He'll come back when he's hungry." Fenwick sniffed the air, hoping to scent something in the oven, but not even the kettle was heating. "What's a fellow got to do to get something to eat around here?"

Mrs. Trott snorted in disgust. "How can you think about your stomach at a time like this? The boy might be anywhere, getting into Lord knows what kind of trouble."

Despite her words, she handed him a knife and a loaf of day old bread, for which he was properly grateful. Her stale baked goods were better than what came piping fresh from most cook's ovens.

"There's clotted cream in the cooler. But after you eat, you have to *do* something, Fenwick. Something terrible's happened. I feel it in my bones."

When Mrs. Trott's bones felt anything, there was no peace in the house till she was satisfied. Breakfast was a help yourself affair. Luncheon would undoubtedly be cold, and tea nonexistent. If Gil wasn't found by the time supper came around, Fenwick figured the household would reach the "Root, hog, or die" stage.

Fenwick ate quickly and fixed a tray of sliced bread with a selection of preserves for Mr. Preston and his friend. Then he trudged up the back stairs to do the only thing he could do.

Tell Mr. Preston about Gil's disappearance. And hope for the sake of all their bellies his employer could do something to settle Mrs. Trott's bones.

* * *

The milk and egg man was still making his rounds in the back alleys of the elegant Mayfair street when Julianne arrived at the Kilmaines' home. Only the cook, the butler, and the maid whose job it was to sweep the hearths were stirring.

Still, Julianne was not the first person to arrive on the viscount's front doorstep that day.

"This message arrived for you shortly before dawn, milady," the butler said as he offered her an envelope on an ornate salver. His stiffly correct carriage betrayed nothing of what he thought of such an unusually early morning caller.

She turned the envelope over. No distinctive crest marked the glob of sealing wax on the back, but the handwriting on the front seemed familiar. "Did the messenger stay to wait for a response?"

"No, madam. He said . . ." The butler frowned and cleared his throat. "I ask your pardon, countess, but he said his master expected action, not a written response."

"Indeed?" She arched a brow at the cheekiness of the sender. If this was another threat from her stepson, he would wait a long time for action from her. She wasn't returning to Cornwall any time soon and would never marry his friend. He could cut off her allowance if he wished. It wouldn't make a particle of difference.

She didn't know what the future held for her and Jacob, but at the moment, it didn't matter. She still basked in the rosy glow of their night of loving. They'd declared their hearts to each other. It was enough.

If he asked her to marry him again, this time she'd say yes. If he didn't, she'd simply live with him in sin, devil take the hindermost. She didn't care what the world thought of her any more so long as she had Jacob.

As far as Mrs. Osgood's school, she could still keep her obligation to the children by selling all her jewelry and setting up a trust with a man of business to keep the girls safely funded. Lady Kilmaine could be counted upon to help as well, so she'd stopped fearing for her orphans. That plan left no safety cushion for her, but she was prepared to take each day as it came so long as Jacob was with her.

She was done with the daggers. Perhaps she would donate the two in Jacob's safe to the British Museum as curiosities of a dark and distant time in their land's history. No one would ever find the other four where she'd hidden them, so there was no danger of the entire set falling into the wrong hands.

Her way ahead was still murky, but one thing was clear. Jacob stood at the center of her future. Her heart hadn't been this hopeful, this light since . . . well, she couldn't remember a happier time.

She wandered into the parlor, perched on the settee, and tore open the note.

It was a good thing she was sitting, because an object fell from the envelope that made all the blood drain from her face. Then she read the missive, and the joy she'd felt only moments ago had completely disappeared. She was still sitting there, her heart like stone, when Jacob arrived a half hour later.

"Oh, thank God," he said when he saw her. "She's here, George."

Dr. Snowdon followed him into the parlor. "Clearly, I must have misconstrued the text when it indicated that the finder's curse would fall on the one who'd been in contact with all six daggers. She seems fine."

"No, she's not." Jacob took her by the shoulders and forced her to look at him. "What's happened?"

She couldn't bear to speak. She handed him the note, which Jacob read aloud.

"My dear Lady Cambourne— It has come to my attention that you are now in possession of all six daggers, but have, for some unaccountable reason, decided not to sell them. This is unacceptable. We had an agreement. But since you have altered your part of our bargain, I feel justified in altering mine.

"I hereby rescind my generous offer for the daggers in exchange for one which I feel certain you will be inclined to accept. You will deliver the set of daggers to me no later than December fifteenth and in return you will receive one Gilbert Stout, alive and unharmed."

Jacob stopped reading and raked his hair with his hand in frustration. "So that's what happened to him. Damn the little blighter. Why did he have to run off?"

"Gil is really gone? I'd hoped . . ." Julianne's belly turned a back flip. When Jacob nodded, the last chance that the letter was a wicked hoax died. "Read the rest."

Jacob frowned down at the letter. "Enclosed you will find a talisman which I believe you will recognize. I expect you to wear it without respite and shall know if you do not. Failure to comply will greatly increase Master Stout's discomfort in his confinement.

"Failure to deliver the daggers on time will result in his untimely demise. Any effort to discover his whereabouts and effect a rescue will lead to the same outcome, as will a misguided attempt to substitute the real blades with copies. The fools of the Ancient Order might be taken in by your look-alikes, but rest assured, Madam, I will not.

"You will receive further instruction as soon as you have retrieved the other four blades from their hiding place in Cornwall. I advise extreme caution in handling them. Wait at the Dowager House at Cambourne for my summons."

"It's unsigned," Dr. Snowdon said, peering over Jacob's shoulder. "Any idea who could have done this?"

"Sir Malcolm Ravenwood," Julianne and Jacob said in unison. She knew it to be from him because of the faint scent of juniper wafting from the envelope. Since she doubted Jacob would have noticed another man's favored fragrance, she assumed he simply had a good nose for skullduggery.

"What's this talisman he mentions?" Jacob asked.

Julianne held out her hand. A circle of iron, heavily ornamented with Celtic gripping beasts, filled her palm. When Jacob reached toward it, she drew it back. "Don't touch it. I already know all I need to about it without your using your gift."

"You've seen its like before?"

"Once. Algernon received an identical iron circlet just like this the week before he died." She swallowed hard. "There was no note, no indication of who sent it, but he was fascinated by the Celtic imagery. He considered it a luck charm."

"Was he wearing it the day he died?" Jacob asked.

"I don't know." She shrugged. From the moment the earl had been found dead, she'd been shuffled to the side and her stepson had taken charge of all the arrangements. "Maybe."

"If he had that amulet around his neck, then we know how your late husband was murdered and by whom," Jacob said darkly. "When he refused to part with the daggers, Ravenwood must have decided the only way to acquire them was to make sure they passed into someone else's control."

"That's why Sir Malcolm was upset that the earl didn't leave them to his heir. If they'd gone to Algernon's son, he'd have sold them in a heartbeat," Julianne said. "Since they were a bequest to me, Sir Malcolm had to wait for my mourning period to end before he could even have Digory send a query about them." She turned the amulet over in her hand. "But how could this thing have caused Algernon's death?"

"The daggers possess a strong magnetism," Jacob said. "The iron circle acted as a target for the dagger's tip."

Early in their investigation, Jacob had said he knew what had happened in that locked study, but didn't know *how* it happened. Now that she was aware of his gift of touch and the visions that accompanied it, she'd trust his assessment without more details.

"So, Lady Cambourne, in light of this unsettling news, what do you propose to do?" Dr. Snowdon asked.

"With the boy held hostage, I haven't much choice." She slipped the slender pewter chain around her neck. The iron circle came to rest heavily between her breasts. "I'm going to Cornwall."

CHAPTER 27

"So nice to see you, Lady Cambourne," Sir Malcolm said to the wavering image in his gazing ball. The iron amulet over her heart amplified her life force. It allowed Malcolm to finally follow her movements by his art, even if Jacob Preston was in the same room with her.

Malcolm had wondered why Preston's presence had shielded her from his gaze. Now, thanks to Gilbert Stout, he knew.

He really owed the boy for the intelligence he'd brought him. If not for Gil, he'd never have guessed that Preston was a metal mage, one who drew information from ore. Preston also apparently cast back an aura that effectively covered him and whoever was near him from detection by Malcolm's gazing ball. Even now, Malcolm couldn't see Preston directly. With Lady Cambourne wearing the amulet, he caught glimpses of another being near her, an occasional flash of light only, but he sensed it was Preston, based on the countess's expressions and actions.

He wondered if Preston was aware he possessed the shielding power. It might simply be as unconscious an act as breathing for him.

It was a pity Malcolm couldn't turn him into one of his followers. A man who could divine another's secrets simply by touching a metal object was a valuable tool. Then, too, it was useful to know that Preston could be debilitated by direct contact with metal.

So many interesting possibilities there.

Yes, he hoped it wouldn't be necessary to kill Gilbert Stout. The boy had done him a better turn than he knew. But of course, if it came to that, Malcolm wouldn't lose sleep over one less street rat in the world.

Not a wink.

Even though time was pressing, Jacob insisted they make a few preparations before journeying to Cornwall. His artisan friend fashioned a strongbox lined with thinly beaten platinum to house the two daggers from his safe with plenty of room for the other four to be added. Jacob ordered thick workmen's leather gloves for himself and a steel mesh corset for Julianne to wear beneath her clothes.

"This is miserable," she said from behind a dressing screen as she tried on the barbaric garment. "Are you sure it's necessary?"

"You only need wear it when we are near the daggers." One corner of his mouth kicked up. "Or when you want to keep me at bay."

"In that case, I'll never wear it," she said, but her attempt at lightening the moment had a forced quality. In the end, she packed the corset with the rest of her things for the trip.

He ached to take her in his arms, but the iron amulet emitted a booming reproof each time he tried. Jacob was willing to suffer for the joy of touching her, but he didn't dare become incapacitated at a time when she might need him to protect her, so he shunned the metal's reach as if it were the pox.

Lord Kilmaine lent them his coach and driver, and they set off for Cornwall as the weather turned sharply colder. The only advantage to the frigid temperature was that it made the roads hard and rutted instead of muddy and impassible. George Snowdon canceled his appointments and insisted on accompanying them, reasoning that he'd have ample time to study the manuscripts further when they stopped each evening.

Fenwick traveled with them, too, seated beside the driver, the stinging wind and snow flurries lashing him. He proved as sturdy and capable on the road as when he served in Jacob's house, bespeaking their rooms at coaching inns and tirelessly tending to their comfort at the end of each day's journey.

When this sorry business was over, Jacob promised himself he'd see to a generous increase in Fenwick's pay.

Three days out from the city, they bounced along past winter-brown meadows and forests of naked trees. George had succumbed to the rocking of the coach and, head tipped back, snored like a rasping two-man saw.

Julianne sighed and let the curtain drop, plunging them into semi-darkness. "I wonder how young Gil fares."

"We're doing all we can for him." Jacob wished he could offer her more comfort, but truthfully, he gave the boy only one chance in three of making it through this debacle, even if they turned over the daggers. The problem with kidnapping and extortion was that it forced one to deal with a person without honor.

Sir Malcolm couldn't be counted upon to keep his word.

"It's like losing Mary all over again," she whispered.

Jacob should have realized she'd empathize with a boy who was so alone in the world. She'd never found her sister. Failing to help another orphaned child tore open that old wound.

She balled her fists in her lap. "And once again, it's my fault."

He started to protest, but she wouldn't hear him.

"If I hadn't come to you for help, none of this would have happened," she said miserably.

"If you hadn't come to me for help, *we* wouldn't have happened either." Jacob took her hand. It was the only sort of touch the iron circle didn't torture him over and it was fitting for a fellow to at least hold the lady's hand when he proposed. "When this is done with—"

"Please, Jacob." She put her fingertips over his lips. "I love you so. Never doubt it, but I can't think farther than the next milepost. So long as Ravenwood has that poor boy . . ." Her voice cracked with emotion and she couldn't finish her thought.

If they weren't able to save Gil, would she blame him? Or herself? Would the death of the lad hang over them like the sword of Damocles, threatening any hope of a future together?

Jacob kissed her gloved fingertips and winced inwardly at the jolt the iron circlet shot through her and into him. He'd never been affected by metal without touching it directly and it was damned inconvenient for his sensitivity to tick up now. The amulet had evidently bound itself to Julianne so thoroughly, touching her was the same as touching the cold iron. His only consolation was that Julianne didn't feel the metal's malevolent barbs.

That dubious treat was reserved for him alone.

"Very well," he said. "To business, then. Where are the other daggers hidden?"

Her mouth tightened in a hard line. "With Algernon. I slipped them into the foot of his casket before he was buried. At the time, I blamed his obsession with them for his death, so it seemed appropriate for him to take them with him. But it turned out to be a good place to hide them. No one would think of searching for them there."

Jacob nodded. "George, Fenwick, and I will take care of retrieving them then."

It was better for Julianne to remember her husband as he had been, not the rotted corpse they would dig up.

"I'll have to come with you," she said. "His grave is unmarked. As a suicide, he was denied burial in the churchyard and his son refused to even erect a stone for him. But I know where he lies."

"When we're done with Sir Malcolm—" This time he was quick enough to place a finger on her lips to hush her before she could interrupt him again. "You and I will visit the vicar and show him the iron ring. Once he realizes your late husband didn't do away with himself, the earl can be moved to the churchyard where he belongs."

Her sad smile squeezed his heart. She'd come to him with two requests—to find the remaining dagger and clear her late husband's name. He was determined to fulfill them both.

She laid her head on his shoulder. "Thank you, Jacob."

The iron slammed repeated flashes of pain into him, but nothing could induce him to push Julianne away. Instead, he bore up under the metal's thrusts, taking comfort from the fact that while his shoulder smarted, he didn't suffer from any visions and thus wasn't likely to lose consciousness. And having Julianne so close was more than worth the trade.

What doesn't kill a body makes it stronger, George always told him.

By those lights, he'd be a veritable Hercules by the time they reached Cornwall.

Julianne glanced at the note that a liveried footman delivered to the Dowager's House shortly after she and her party arrived. The stone cottage was large enough to be a manor house on a lesser estate and her stepson must have sent servants to scrub regularly because the place was spotlessly clean.

Not out of respect for her, Julianne was sure. It was simply that the new Lord Cambourne believed everything about the estate was a reflection on him. Including the people connected to the earldom.

How like her stepson to begin their reunion with a heavy-handed summons.

"Will you be pleased to send a reply, milady?" the bewigged footman asked. He shifted his weight from one foot to the other, clearly unhappy to be thrust into the middle of a family squabble between his betters.

"Yes. Tell the earl not to trouble himself on my account," she said, wondering if the new Lord Cambourne were the sort to shoot the messenger. For fear of that, she tempered her reply and didn't add that they wouldn't be there long enough to bother the earl. She'd stay only as long as it took to retrieve the daggers and receive the instructions Sir Malcolm had promised about how and where to exchange them for Gilbert Stout. "However, we'll need supper for five—myself, my two guests, and two servants. I'd like it delivered and served here in the cottage. If you could see to it yourself, I'd be appreciative."

"Of course. I'll handle it personally," the footman said with a hint of a smile. What the earl didn't know wouldn't hurt the help. "But his lordship was most insistent on speaking with you, milady."

"Then you may tell him he might call upon me here tomorrow at two o'clock," she said, pointedly ignoring her stepson's demand that she present herself before him immediately. "It's a long journey from London and I confess myself done in. Lord Cambourne and I will be more likely to come to a complete understanding if one of us is not dead on her feet."

The footman smiled, inferring she was prepared to make herself agreeable to his employer after a decent night's sleep. She hoped the earl would take that as a signal she was ready to capitulate. In truth, the only understanding she'd leave her stepson with was that it would be an exceedingly cold day in Hades before she bent to his demand that she marry someone of his choosing.

After the footman left, Julianne turned to Jacob, who waited for her at the foot of the stairs with the carpetbag that held the platinum-lined box.

"May as well not get too comfortable," she said. After tomorrow, Lord Cambourne was likely to restrict her movements. He might even refuse her the right to visit her husband's grave. "We'll have to visit Algernon's grave this night before his son arrives on the morrow. I have a feeling after his lordship and I have our little tête-à-tête, we'll be far less welcome guests than we are now."

"Have you a place to keep the boy under lock and key?" Sir Malcolm asked the quaking innkeeper.

The man's Adam's apple bobbed nervously, but he nodded. "We've a smokehouse in the back what's not in use now. Should do in a pinch."

One of the many advantages of being the Grand Master of the secret sect within the Order was that his followers' influence reached throughout the entire countryside. The innkeeper was second cousin to the woman who'd served as Lady Cambourne's guide at her initiation. Reportedly, he owed the woman a sum he could never repay. Her letter promising to see him thrown into debtor's prison if he failed to assist Sir Malcolm without question insured that even in distant Cornwall, Ravenwood was not without those who would do his bidding.

The innkeeper led him up to the chamber that was supposedly the best available. Inspection by the light of a kerosene lamp revealed it was sparsely furnished, and only marginally clean. Barely fit for human habitation. Still, it would have to do. Malcolm needed to be near Cambourne and this place was just over the hillock from the earldom's border.

"The missus will be bringing ye the supper soon as it's ready," the innkeeper said. "Is there aught else I might do for ye, sir?"

"Yes," Malcolm said. "Get out. And see to it the boy remains where you put him or else"—he let the threat hang in the air for a heartbeat or two, then continued—"I shall be most displeased."

The man stammered his assurance that no, of course, the boy would be right there when Sir Malcolm had need of him and for him not to worry about it a bit. The innkeeper backed out of the chamber professing his complete cooperation. Malcolm could still hear his nearly incoherent mutterings as he made his way down the uneven stairs.

Even though he was road-weary, Malcolm unpacked his gazing ball and set it up on the rickety table. Natural light was best for viewing, but in a pinch, he could see Lady Cambourne by the yellowish haze emitted by the lamp.

"So you, too, have arrived at your destination," he said to the image in the ball. The trip from London was tiresome, but he'd been entertained by glimpses of Lady Cambourne. He still couldn't see Jacob Preston clearly in the shimmering orb, but he sensed his presence with the countess almost continually and had decided how to use him.

He'd given a lot of thought to his next gambit in this game of brinksmanship. After seeking out several metal workers, he'd not found any who knew how to work an alloy with the unusual properties that his studies led him to expect the daggers to have. Malcolm decided he would make rejoining the blades into the staff of power Jacob Preston's problem.

Besides, based on what he'd read in the partial manuscript

Lady Cambourne had absconded with, when the daggers were originally cast, it was through a combination of metallurgy and the magic art of a metal mage.

He unpacked his traveling desk and wrote out the exact specifications for the binding. The wind howled outside the shuttered window, sending enough air through the leaky casement to make the lamp flicker.

"I'm still the binder," Malcolm said to the Watchful Eye as he sanded the drying ink and folded the instructions. "My will is what joins the blades together. I set my seal on these instructions. See?"

He melted a glob of red wax on the note and pressed his signet ring into it.

"I am the binder," he repeated to the spirits of the air. "Jacob Preston can't bear the touch of metal, so he can't wield the rod. The power of the staff will answer to me."

Why would a man rejoin the blades, only to give the Staff of Merlin to another? The question popped into his mind and swirled around it, taunting him. The powers were testing him to see if he were worthy of the staff.

"A man can be persuaded to do almost anything," Malcolm said as he looked back at the wavering image of Lady Cambourne in his gazing ball. "All one need do is find the proper motivation. I am the first cause. I am the mover. My command binds the daggers together again."

The wind moaned like the souls of the damned. Malcolm took it as a sign that the powers recognized him as the Binder and ultimate wielder of Merlin's Staff.

CHAPTER 28

Jacob insisted on waiting till moonrise to set out for Lord Cambourne's grave. He didn't want to draw attention to their activities and bring down the wrath of the current earl in the process. The estate was large enough, and the grave far enough from the Dowager's House, to require use of the coach.

"Algernon is buried in the woods at the top of the next rise." Julianne pointed out the coach window as they plodded along the narrow ruts.

Her husband had planned this drive through his sprawling estate as a pleasure path. Even when his age prevented him from riding horseback, he still enjoyed traveling a circuit of his land by carriage. The drive led past the duck pond, meandered through a meadow dotted with sheep, and finally wandered into the deep woods.

When Algernon had been denied burial at the church, Julianne had hoped her stepson would build a small mausoleum beyond the extensive gardens and hothouse. Tucked away, it needn't have marred the sweeping views from the manor, but it would have made the grave more readily accessible.

Instead, he wanted his father's body as far from the main house as possible, out of sight and out of remembrance. The new Lord Cambourne had let the pleasure path his father had designed go untended over the last few years. In another five, the drive would be overgrown and unrecognizable. No one would be able to find his father's grave.

Fortunately, the gigantic old hemlock still stood at the top of the hill. It was her guidepost. Julianne had made one last trip to the site before she left for London to look for the final dagger. In some ways, it seemed fitting that Algernon rested in the land he loved, but the location of his grave was so remote, so desolate, standing over it never failed to make her chest ache over the injustice.

She knew, without needing proof, that he hadn't taken his own life. But even if he had, she'd never understand why that should obliterate his memory in the minds of his family and friends.

Jacob rapped on the coach ceiling and the driver reined the horse to a stop.

"We're not there yet," Julianne said.

"We're close enough to walk from here." Jacob opened the door and handed her out. Fenwick leaped down from his perch beside the driver and unloaded a collection of shovels and picks from the boot. "Once you show us where the grave is, I want you to return to the coach. You'll be warmer."

She nodded in understanding. He was trying to spare her, but her imagination was probably worse than reality. "Thank you for doing this for me."

"Haven't you realized yet that I'll do anything for you?"

Words caught in her throat, so she pressed a kiss to his cheek. She'd spend the rest of her life making sure he didn't regret it.

Then Julianne turned to the matter at hand. She squeezed her eyes shut, trying to remember her husband's face. To her surprise, she found his image had grown hazy in her mind, all the little details that make a person unique fading into the mist. She could remember only that he was a good man, a decent, gentle, scholarly sort who, through no fault of his own, had gotten involved in matters beyond his understanding.

If her memory of Algernon's face was faulty, her recollection of his gravesite was crystal clear. She led the four men unerringly to the spot. Ten paces from the north side of the hemlock's thick trunk, there was a man-sized indentation in the winter-hard turf. In two years, the disturbed earth had shrunk from a mound to a sunken, compacted spot. The bare tree limbs rattled in the wind overhead, clattering like a dance of old bones. Shadows wavered in the moonlight like disembodied wraiths caught between this world and the next. Julianne's teeth chattered and she tried to convince herself it was from the cold.

Nothing remained of the hothouse roses she'd left on Algernon's grave at her last visit, and she had nothing to leave for him now. Instead, she was going to take.

"I'm sorry," she whispered to Algernon's ghost and turned back to the coach, clutching her cloak about her in the stiff wind. Her husband had been murdered, disgraced in death, and now his grave was being desecrated.

When she heard the strike of picks and the bite of shovel blades tearing into the earth, she lifted her skirts and ran the rest of the way back to the coach, grateful not to watch.

The Kilmaines' driver offered to help, but even with four able-bodied men digging, it took a long time to hack through the hard ground to the depth of Lord Cambourne's resting place. In the time since his death, the woods' roots had burrowed back into the space above him and formed a living fibrous shield for the dead.

They toiled on as the moon sank in the west and Fenwick lit a lamp to shed light on their work. Despite the cold night, all four men had shed their jackets and were sweating profusely by the time Jacob's shovel struck Lord Cambourne's simple pine casket.

"More light," Jacob ordered and Fenwick lifted the kerosene lamp to throw a yellow halo around the deep hole. In short order, Jacob cleared the surface of the casket and pried up the edges of the lid.

"Allow me," George said, and shouldered Jacob aside. "I'm more accustomed to this sort of thing, old chap."

Jacob was grateful to his friend. Not because he was the squeamish sort. It was simply that the idea of grave robbing sent a superstitious tingle down his spine. He knew the blades were there. He'd been hearing their soft hum for the last half hour, but actually taking them from Julianne's husband made him uncomfortable. He was beginning to feel he owed the old earl a debt he couldn't repay.

"They should be at the foot of the casket," Jacob said as he lifted the lid.

"Right-o," George said, his voice as cheerful as if they were playing whist at White's and he'd just been dealt a winning hand. "Here they are. One, two, three, and four."

He plopped each leather-encased dagger on the grave's edge as he counted them off. "Let me check one more thing."

George bent over the earl's body and pulled back the rotting fabric of his waistcoat and shirt to expose his breastbone. Something metallic glinted in the lamplight. "Ah, as you thought. He's wearing an amulet just like the one the countess now bears."

If the daggers hadn't been sheathed in leather, Jacob was convinced they'd have traveled up Lord Cambourne's dead body to lodge between his ribs afresh. With four of the murderous blades loosed from the coffin, he wasn't willing to trust Julianne's safety to old leather or the metal mesh corset he'd insisted she wear. The diabolical blades fed on human blood and misery. They needed to be destroyed, but all he could do now was contain them.

"Fetch the box, Fenwick."

His man ran back to the coach to retrieve the platinum-lined strongbox from the boot. The coach was parked a quarter of the way down the hill on the other side of the massive hemlock, so Jacob couldn't see it from Lord Cambourne's grave. And fortunately, Julianne couldn't see the desecration from where she waited, though he knew it troubled her all the same.

Damn Ravenwood for putting them through this.

"Do you want this amulet too?" George asked, pointing to the iron circle on the corpse's chest.

"No, leave it," Jacob said. "It's done enough damage." He wished he could persuade Julianne to remove the one she wore, but she was adamant about not allowing additional harm to come to Gil if she could help it. Jacob closed the lid on Lord Cambourne's casket, climbed out of the grave, and tossed a shovelful of dirt back into it. "Let's finish the job."

"Mr. Preston!" Fenwick's voice cut through the night. "Oh, sir, come quick."

Jacob dropped the shovel and sprinted back to the coach. Fenwick stood by the open door, his face drawn in dismay. "What is it, man?"

"I heard someone moaning and thought Lady Cambourne might be ill, so I cracked the door to see, but . . ." He gave a helpless little wave of one hand toward the interior of the coach and the moaning started afresh.

Jacob pulled the door open. Gilbert Stout squirmed on the tufted velvet squab, bound hand and foot, with a gag between his teeth. Julianne was nowhere to be seen.

"Gil!" Jacob worked the gag out of his mouth. "Where's the countess?"

"I'm right sorry, guv," the boy said. "Sorry as ever I can be. He plopped me down here and then he took her."

Jacob made short work of the knots at the boy's wrists and ankles. "Why didn't she cry out?"

"Maybe she didn't have a chance." George stooped to retrieve a white handkerchief that had been dropped on the ground near the coach. He gave it a sniff and then jerked his arm out stiff, holding it as far from his face as he could. "Chloroform. She was asleep in seconds. Fiendishly clever of him."

"How long has she been gone?" Jacob surveyed the winding trail they'd taken into the woods, but saw no one.

"Long enough," Gil said. "I been making all the noise I could for hours it seemed like, but didn't no one hear me till Fenwick there."

Between the wind and the rustling wood and the exertion of digging, none of them would have heard anything less than a full-throated scream. Maybe not even that when the wind kicked up. Jacob gritted his teeth in frustration. "I should have told the driver to remain with the coach." Instead he'd been grateful for another strong back to help dig up the grave.

"Don't blame yourself," George said. "Who could have predicted Ravenwood would do such a thing? And why? It's not as if we weren't trying to meet his demands."

"As to that, I guess he's changed his demands, seein' as the countess is a more important hostage," Gil said with a tight-lipped scowl. "He stuffed this note in my pocket before he left. Reckon it explains why he took her."

Gil dug into his trousers and came up with a much folded piece of foolscap, affixed with a wax seal.

"Cheeky bugger," George said when he saw the seal. "Not even trying to hide his identity."

"Why should he? He knows we won't go to the authorities lest he harm Julianne." Jacob ripped open the note and tried to read it in the lamplight. He was so angry, he couldn't make his eyes focus. Amid the spidery handwriting there were diagrams and dimensions and snippets of Latin interspersed with English. "This makes no sense. Where does he want us to deliver the daggers?"

George took the note from him and held it up to the light. "Not the daggers. He wants you to have them rejoined into a single staff, according to these specifications. Then you're to deliver it to the Giant's Dance on the twenty-first of December at sunset."

"Giant's Dance?" Jacob said, anger making his neck heat, despite the raw coldness of the night. "What the hell is that?"

George shook his head. "You never did pay attention in history class, did you? It's the old name for Stonehenge, of course. I always did think those monoliths were surely connected somehow with Druids."

"We're going to need a smith," Jacob said, trying to focus on how to meet Ravenwood's demands when all he really wanted to do was strangle the man barehanded. "And a damn good one."

"There's a fellow in the village near here," Lord Kilmaine's driver said. "I grew up on a little barony in the next shire and brought the estate horses to him to be shod each spring."

"I misspoke. We'll need someone with more skill than it takes to shoe a mare," Jacob said. The alloy was such a hodgepodge of metals, with different tensile strengths and melting points, he didn't see how the ore could be brought back together once the daggers were melted down. "We'll need a miracle worker."

George turned the note over. "Oh, there's more." He read the few lines of script and looked up at Jacob.

"What?" Jacob demanded, slamming the side of his fist against the coach in impotent rage. The horse shied at the blow and might have bolted if the driver hadn't caught his halter and calmed him. With effort, Jacob swallowed back his anger. It wouldn't help Julianne one bit.

"He wants you to wear something until you deliver the staff," George said. "And he threatens harm to the countess if you fail to comply."

"Believe him, guv," Gil piped in.

"What is it I'm to wear? A jester's cap? A highwayman's mask?"

George shook his head. "The old earl's amulet."

CHAPTER 29

Julianne forced her eyes open and stared up at the high coved ceiling. A watermark snaked down one smooth stone wall. She was lying on a narrow string bed, strung so tight there was no softness to the mattress at all. She didn't recognize the austere furnishings and had no idea where she was. Even wondering made her feel as if her head were about to explode. She loosed a deep sigh.

"Welcome back, Lady Cambourne." The silky bass voice slid over her like a serpent gliding over a garden wall. "I began to fear I'd overdosed you. So nice of you to finally rejoin me."

She struggled to sit up and discovered she was shackled with heavy manacles at the wrists and ankles. Snippets of memory sliced into her mind—a cloying scent, a nightmarish ride slung over a saddle bow as if she were a sack of potatoes, and the tattoo of horse hooves on hard turf. The hooves still pounded at her temple. The rest was nothing but blackness, deep and brooding, an oblivion from which no light escaped.

She lifted one hand to her head and the clank of her chains sounded unnaturally loud. "It doesn't appear you gave me much choice."

"None at all." His laughter was even more disturbing than

his voice. The sound danced on her last nerve and made her stomach roil.

She shielded her eyes against the light filtering through the window behind him. Dozens of green glass panes filled the opening. The colored glass, stone walls, and general draftiness meant she was probably in some sort of medieval solar. There was only one door leading from the circular room.

"Where am I?"

"At the country estate of one of my followers. I apologize for the inadequacy of your accommodations, countess." Sir Malcolm was seated at an escritoire before the window, poring over an old book. "But if you think this room is deficient, you should see the dungeon."

A foul metallic taste coated her tongue. He'd drugged her with something vile. She fought the urge to shudder and glared at him instead. "May I ask why you've done this?"

"You may ask, but I should think it would be obvious," he said, closing the volume and setting it aside. "I require the cooperation of Jacob Preston. Taking you prisoner is just the incentive he needs to accomplish his task. Would you care to see what progress he's made?"

Her heart leaped to her throat. If he was planning to take her out of the room, she might find a way to escape. But she didn't want to seem too eager, so she merely shrugged.

"Not curious? You astound me." He reached under the escritoire and pulled a round object from the leather bag.

She blinked hard, thinking whatever he'd used to drug her was making her imagine things. The man seemed to have an honest-to-goodness crystal ball.

He positioned it on the small desk, so the green light hit it just so. From deep within the orb, swirls of color coalesced into figures. Gingerly, Julianne eased off the bed and, though her ankle shackles were attached to the frame, she advanced as far as her bonds allowed.

The image in the ball came into sharp focus. She sucked her breath in over her teeth. She could see Jacob clearly in the crystal, encircled by flame and steam. Worse, he was also surrounded by metal objects of all sorts, knives and pitchfork tines and plowshares. She touched the iron amulet that rested over her heart.

Jacob was wearing an identical talisman. His jaw was set like granite, but he gave no outward sign the amulet hurt him. Julia knew better. She felt his agony as if it were her own.

"Jacob will do whatever you bid simply because you have me. There is no need to force him to wear that iron," she said, shaking with fury. "Why are you doing this?"

"Because it amuses me." Sir Malcolm smiled at her, like a cobra smiling at a caged mongoose. "You should be pleased. His willingness to bear pain on your account shows a depth of feeling I'd not suspected he possessed. But the truth is, there is another reason for him to wear the talisman."

"You hope it will make one of the daggers kill him as it did my husband."

"You wrong me, milady. I hoped when I sent the amulet to Lord Cambourne that he would be the one who possessed enough magecraft to find and reunite the daggers into the staff of Merlin. Sadly, your late husband was judged unworthy for such a task." Ravenwood leaned forward to peer into the ball. "I only hope Preston fares better. For your sake."

"I'm telling ye, guv, no matter what I try, there's no way to melt them daggers into an alloy I can work. The magnetism is all gone too." Gershom Flagg met Jacob at the open door to his forge with a bucket in his hands. Heat poured around the soot-covered, half-naked smith in waves. "For the life of me, I don't know how anyone fashioned 'em in the first place."

Jacob looked down at the smelting bucket filled with half-melted ore. "It's the iridium. I feared this would be the case. You'll have to raise the temperature of your forge."

Mr. Flagg shook his head sorrowfully. "I've done all I know to do. Ye've paid me better than a king and no mistake—all them gems from the hilts will set me and the missus up for the rest of our lives and our children's lives too, like as not—but I reckon I'll have to give 'em all back now. It just can't be done."

The song of the dagger metal curved around Jacob's ear. He expected it to taunt him, but instead the ore's voice beckoned him on, tempering its usual belligerence with soft persuasion. If he didn't know better, he'd suspect it was trying to tell him not to abandon hope. The amulet at his chest began to join in the song.

"There must be a way," Jacob said, stepping past the smith into his metal-filled shop, something he'd never have dreamed of doing, in response to the metals' chorus.

"Preston, wait." George put a hand to his shoulder, trying to stop him. "There's no need for you to—"

"No, I'm all right." Jacob appreciated his friend's concern, but he felt compelled to go forward despite any pain he might suffer for it. He grasped the platinum head of his walking stick in a white-knuckled grip and continued to advance toward the forge.

Since he'd been wearing the iron amulet, indeed since Julianne had slipped its mate over her head, he'd been in constant pain, but amazingly enough, it was bearable. He was almost coming to embrace the discomfort because it meant he was still alive, still conscious and yet in close contact with metal for longer than he'd ever attempted before.

Granted, the thin lawn of his shirt separated his skin from the iron amulet, but all it protected him from was any vision the metal might try to crowd into his mind. It was no shield from the iron's voice or the scraping of its little ferrous talons.

The fire leaped higher at his approach and then subsided to a white-hot glow. The amulet grew warm on his chest and his pain level ticked down several notches. The tension in his shoulders relaxed visibly.

"Fascinating," George mumbled. "If I didn't know better, I'd say that amulet is acting just like a vaccine."

The doctor was right. Jacob was able to bear more proximity to metal than ever in his life, but he sensed there was something more the amulet was trying to share with him. So he slipped it down his collar and inside his shirt. The metal radiated heat over his bare skin. All his senses went on high alert.

The brightness of the forge fire made him stagger back a step and he felt an instant connection between the circle of iron on his chest and the metal of the daggers. Colors brightened and he could actually see waves of magnetism return and grow. Power washed over him, pulled from every scrap of metal in the shop. It flowed through his body and out his fingertips.

"Hold there!" Gershom Flagg cried. The smelting bucket tried to pull itself from the smith's strong hands, and he struggled to keep it from floating across the space toward Jacob.

Jacob lifted a forbidding hand and the metal in the bucket settled. Then without adding a particle of heat to the container, chunks of unmelted ore began to sweat drops and slide into the rest of the liquid. The forge fire flared behind Jacob and then simmered to glow with shimmering heat. The metal whispered secrets, in a language of flashing images and ancient music, but Jacob's vision didn't tunnel, and he was able to bear up under the ore's message without succumbing to either pain or weakness. Instead, strength gathered in his limbs.

He wasn't sure yet what it meant, but his way ahead seemed a bit less murky. Instead of fighting the ore or surrendering to its ravaging power, for the first time in his life, Jacob was in control of it. With one hand extended toward the smith and the dagger ore, he closed his eyes and concentrated on the contents of the smelting bucket. When he opened them again, the metal bubbled in completely liquid form.

Jacob met the wide-eyed gaze of the smith. "Try to cast the staff again now, Mr. Flagg."

The crystal orb nearly shattered with blinding light, then went completely dark. No amount of fiddling or adjusting its position would bring it back to a state of receptivity.

Malcolm barely resisted the urge to send it crashing to the stone floor. The amulet had been working perfectly. He'd been able to follow Preston's movements from the instant he'd slipped the pewter chain over his head. Now the gazing ball was a cipher. One moment he was able to see Jacob Preston in minute detail and the next, his ability to view anything was completely obliterated.

"What happened?" Lady Cambourne asked, her lovely face drawn with concern. "Is Jacob all right?"

Malcolm cocked a brow. Preston was playing with power beyond the dreams of mortal man. There was every possibility it had sucked him out of this world completely. Yet another reason Malcolm decided to let the metal mage handle this delicate and dangerous undertaking.

But he didn't need to let Lady Cambourne guess that he'd lost the ability to keep watch over Preston.

"I decided you've seen enough," he said as he packed the blackened sphere back in its bag. "You'll learn soon whether or not he's been successful." He cast a dark glare at her. "I have no idea if you are of a religious bent, Lady Cambourne, but I advise you to pray to whatever Deity you hold dear that he was."

Chapter 30

"Here we are, Lady Cambourne," Sir Malcolm's voice rumbled next to her ear. He removed the blindfold, but when she looked out the coach window, all she saw was a wind-swept, snow-covered plain. "Just a brief walk now and your journey will be done."

She was still shackled, so he had to lift her down from the coach. He wore his red hooded robe and golden domino over his heavy greatcoat. Julianne would have been grateful for the extra layer of warmth, but she was given no such consideration.

A long row of carriages was stopped along the country lane, the horses' heads down and tails tucked against the wind. Wherever they were bound, she would have witnesses. Someone would surely object to seeing a countess in chains.

Sir Malcolm propelled her over the frozen ground with one hand to her elbow and the other on the small of her back. She was forced to mince along due to the leg irons, and she kept her eyes cast down to avoid tripping. The ground sloped upward and when they crested the small rise, she finally looked up.

Gray obelisks rose three times a man's height in the remnant of a circle.

"Stonehenge," she said softly.

"Ah, you know of it then," Sir Malcolm said. "I keep forgetting your late husband was something of an antiquarian."

"I know enough to know it probably wasn't built by Druids," she said, her teeth chattering when she paused for a frosty breath. "According to the earl, their rites were held in groves."

"Astute, as always. You're right, but our land is dotted with stone rings, all acknowledged places of power," Sir Malcolm said. "It's fitting to make use of the largest of them for this particular rite. The staff of Merlin is being bonded to its new master. Nothing less than the most auspicious place will do."

Her heart sank. The carriages along the road must have brought his trusted followers. The likelihood that any would object to her ill treatment dwindled with each step.

Snow crunched underfoot as they passed through the broken outer ring of megaliths and around the circle of smaller blue stones sprouting from the wintry earth. A horseshoe of trilithons curved around the inner portion of the space, brooding over a rather ominous-looking slab of granite. The sinking sun sent long shadows cutting across the ground. A dozen of Sir Malcolm's black robed, masked minions crowded within the horseshoe, their breaths rising in the crisp cold like a conclave of dragons.

"On this shortest of all days, the dying sun heralds the death of the old order of things," Sir Malcolm said, his voice echoing against the granite giants. "We hail the new power rising, the power we will wield."

And by "we," he means "he," Julianne thought. He wasn't the sort to share.

"But for power given, payment is required. And the only currency the spirits accept is blood." Ravenwood turned to the two nearest, and largest, of his followers. "Bind the lady to the altar stone."

A cold lump of terror lodged in her belly. She'd played

Jeanne d'Arc once and theatre critics said Julianne True went to the stake with a saint's fortitude and dignity. But this was no play. And Julianne was no saint.

She fought. She screamed. She tore at her captor's iron-fisted grips.

In the end, someone cuffed her across the temple and the world went black. When she came to herself, her spine was pressed against cold granite. Her shackles had been removed and replaced by leather straps, but she was still bound, hand and foot, unable to move, barely able to draw a deep breath.

Oh, Jacob.

She'd never hold him, never see him again. All the days of loving that might have been marched before her, their unfulfilled promise gnawing at her insides like a cancer. Then her anguish was overwhelmed as fear smothered all hope.

Jacob advanced through the circle of stones, following the crushed down snow. His nostril hairs froze with each breath, but his heart was hammering so hard, he didn't feel the cold. He'd glimpsed Julianne, bound to the slab of granite inside the innermost ring of stones. Every fiber of his being urged him to run to her, but he forced himself to walk around the henge to enter as the others had. Ravenwood's lot was chanting, a low drone that made the iron amulet at his chest throb in sympathy.

Jacob had come alone, as he'd been ordered. If he tried to burst into the circle and free Julianne now, he'd be overwhelmed by numbers. To even the odds, he'd have to force Sir Malcolm's hand somehow.

The deep shadow cast by the standing stones sent a shiver over his soul. In a snippet of memory, he heard his old vicar intoning, "Yea, though I walk through the valley of the shadow of death . . ." The Psalmist claimed to be unafraid, but Jacob doubted King David had faced this sort of evil. Given a choice, Jacob would rather have faced a giant with nothing but a slingshot if it meant Julianne wouldn't be threatened by the outcome.

His gaze cut between two of the sarcens to where Julianne lay helpless. Her face was strained with terror, but she bit her lip to keep from crying out. Anger and fear warred with each other in his gut and heated his neck, but he bridled himself. It wouldn't help her if he lost his head. This was about power, and right now, the only power he possessed was self-control.

He entered the inner horseshoe, stopping in the center where the last ray of sunlight shot between two stones and across the space. The chanting stopped.

"Jacob!" Julianne cried out. At a signal from Sir Malcolm, one of his followers gagged her.

A muscle ticked in Jacob's jaw, but he forced himself to stand still. Much as he wanted to, he couldn't run to Julianne. He had to make Ravenwood come to him. Alone.

Jacob twisted off the head of his walking stick and pocketed the platinum sphere, a last touch of beneficent metal. Once the staff had been cast from the daggers, he'd had his rapier removed and the cane's hollow core expanded to fit the new rod of metal. He drew it out and held it up for all to see.

"The Staff of Merlin," Sir Malcolm said with reverence. Then he fisted his hands at his waist. "The skin of animals is not fit to touch it. Remove your gloves."

Jacob swallowed hard. Damn Ravenwood for using the metal against him.

When he curled his bare fingers around the staff, a current of power surged through his body, centering hotly around the iron amulet on his chest. Strangely, he didn't feel as diminished by the metal's touch as he expected. At least, he wasn't sucked into another vision. He remained firmly anchored in his present reality. The lance of pain to his brain was still as sharp, but he was able to bear it.

He'd bear anything for Julianne.

His jaw set in a ridged line, Jacob staggered a step. His shoulders sagged. "Ah, I see your pain," Sir Malcolm said. "Give me the staff, and I promise you will very shortly feel no more."

"If you want it, come and claim it."

Sir Malcolm laughed. "We are many. You are one. Why should I?"

"How else will you know if you deserve to have it?" The man couldn't very well ignore that kind of challenge before his followers, so Jacob pressed his luck to add, "And be sure to wear the other iron amulet as well, just to make it fair."

Ravenwood glared at him for a moment, then raised his hand in a forbidding gesture.

"Everyone stay back." Sir Malcolm ordered. His dark eyes glittered in the slits of his domino. He stooped, removed the talisman from Julianne's neck and slipped it over his own.

Jacob barely contained his relief. Now if the staff got away from them, there was little chance it would target Julianne as one of the daggers had targeted her husband through the iron amulet. Though that was cold comfort so long as she was strapped to a stone altar.

Malcolm stomped to Jacob and grabbed the rod. The man's eyes flared.

"So," Jacob said softly, "you feel it too. Quite a rush of power, isn't it?"

Sir Malcolm tried to jerk the staff away, but he couldn't pull it free. "Let go, damn you."

"I can't," Jacob said. "And you can't either."

Sir Malcolm tried to force his fingers open, but couldn't.

"My friend deciphered more from the manuscript, and he says when two claim the rod's power, the staff has to choose." Jacob gave the length of metal a hard yank, but Sir Malcolm and he were both stuck fast. "You and I are bound to it, till the staff makes its choice."

"Then I'll help it along."

Sir Malcolm grasped the staff with his other hand as well and began trying to whack Jacob with one end. Jacob held him off and began shoving, but neither of them could gain much traction in the snow. Jacob threw himself sideways to the ground and they rolled in a tangle of kicking legs.

They came to a stop with Sir Malcolm astraddle Jacob's chest. He bore down on the staff against Jacob's windpipe.

Stars wheeled across his vision. Darkness gathered at the edges, but if he let himself slip into oblivion, Julianne was done for. Jacob fought for a breath. Then he bucked and struggled and managed to toss Ravenwood aside, though they were both still bound to the staff. Coughing and sucking air, Jacob staggered back to his feet. Neither man gave ground. Light faded around them as the sun began to slip beyond the curve of the earth.

Then suddenly, Jacob felt the staff quicken. A low thrum vibrated up his arms. The staff turned of its own accord, the length stretched between them. The tip of the rod nearest Sir Malcolm slipped through the iron circlet on his chest. Jacob felt the rod moving inexorably toward his foe, but he was unable to either shove it forward or hold it back.

"No!" Ravenwood shouted and began trying to push the rod away. Malcolm staggered back till he was flush against the stone illuminated by the last ray of the sunset. The tip of the staff wasn't sharp, but it pressed against his sternum with enough force that Jacob heard the bone crack.

"Help me, Preston," he cried. "You can have the damn thing."

A ripple of disapproving murmurs rose from Malcolm's followers. Evidently even Druids scorned bald-faced panic.

Jacob braced a foot against the sarcen and pulled with all his might, but he lost his grip as the staff released him. He sprawled backward into the snow, then scrambled to his feet. The staff glowed red gold for a moment, then it flared to white.

Beams shot from the end facing away from Malcolm. The bolt of light careened across the center of the circle like horizontal lightning. Jacob dove back down as the energy crackled over his head and singed his jacket. The acrid smell of scorched wool invaded his nostrils.

Screams jerked Jacob's head around. The fiery bolt had engulfed the black robe of one of Ravenwood's followers. The man writhed on the ground while another beat him to extinguish the flames. The rest of Ravenwood's crew ran shrieking back to their waiting coaches. Once the fire was out, the final two of Malcolm's sect deserted him, peeling off their tattered robes as they ran. Playing at power was one thing. Actually experiencing it was quite another.

Sir Malcolm struggled with the rod whose tip was still pressed against his sternum. "I don't want it," he screamed. "Take it back."

When the sun sank completely, the tip of the staff fell into shadow. Sir Malcolm was able to wrench it away from his breastbone. He reared back and threw the staff like a javelin at Jacob. It roared in a tone so low Jacob felt, rather than heard, it rattling inside his chest. The iron amulet on his chest burned. The staff flew straight for him.

In that slice of a moment, Jacob was acutely aware of myriad things—the puff of his last exhaled breath hovering in the air, the blood pounding in his ears, the piteous sound of Julianne's muffled sobs. He was going to die and there was no help for it.

And Julie would die with him.

"No," he bellowed and pulled the platinum head of his walking stick from his pocket. It wasn't much, but it was all he had. He hurled it toward the oncoming staff with every ounce of will in his heart and force in his body.

The two airborne objects connected with a ringing smack.

Then the rod flipped in midair and streaked back to Sir Malcolm. It rammed through the center of his amulet, through his body and buried itself in one of the sarsen uprights so deeply there was no sign of its passage but the small pock-mark opening.

A look of utter surprise lifted Malcolm's features, then the light went out of his eyes and his body crumpled to the snow. As Jacob watched disbelievingly, Ravenwood's body froze solid. Then, from deep inside the stone, the staff began to sing. The song increased its vibrations till Jacob was forced to his knees, hands clapped over his ears. Sir Malcolm's corpse shattered into snowflake-sized particles and fluttered away to the east in a driving wind.

"Looks like the Staff of Merlin chose you," Jacob murmured. Then he sprinted to Julianne and removed her gag. "Are you injured, love?"

"No, I'm all right. Oh, Jacob," she sobbed. "You came for me. Again."

"More than that, I'll stay for you," he said as he unbound her and took her into his arms. "If you'll have me . . ."

She covered him with kisses and they held each other in the growing dark. Her exposed skin was blue with cold, but her kisses were hot. He peeled off his jacket and wrapped it around her, unwilling to break the joining of their mouths for longer than a few seconds. He'd expected to lose the staff, his life, Julie's life, everything to Sir Malcolm.

Instead, the whole world was in his arms. He'd never known such completeness, such utter grateful relief. He buried his face in the sweet jointure of her neck and shoulder, content simply to breathe her in. Finally, he raised Julianne to her feet.

"We'd better go. George and Fenwick will be along with the coach soon," he said.

Julianne cast a questioning look at the obelisk where the rod had entombed itself. "You won the Staff of Merlin, fair and square. There's probably a way to pry it free."

"Not one that doesn't involve splitting that sarcen into rubble." The only trace of the rod was a small entrance hole and the stone was liberally marked with small pocks from centuries of wind and rain. No one who hadn't seen the metal shoot into the stone would ever know it was there.

"Don't you want power and wealth and long life?"

He flexed his fingers and felt a residual tingle of the staff's force in them. "I have more power than I need. If you love me, I count myself the wealthiest man in England. Marry me, Julie."

She stretched up to kiss him, her eyes glistening with unshed tears. "I love you with my whole heart. Yes, I'll marry you, Jacob."

"Then leave the staff where it hides." He picked her up and cradled her in his arms as light snow began to fall around them, crisp and cold and clean. "The only long life I'm interested in is the one I'll spend with you."

Did you miss the first book in the series, ***Touch of a Thief***?

Only once more, Viola vowed silently. Though, like the Shakespearean heroine for whom she was named, she'd miss wearing men's trousers from time to time. They were ever so much more comfortable than a corset and hoops.

From somewhere deep in the elegant town house came a low creak. Viola held her breath. The longcase clock in the main hall ticked. When she heard nothing else, she realized it was only the sigh of an older home squatting down on its foundation for the night.

The room she'd broken into held the stale scents of cigar smoke and brandy from the dinner party of the previous evening. But there were no fresh smells. Perhaps Lieutenant Quinn had taken Lord Montjoy up on his offer to introduce Quinn at Montjoy's club that evening.

Probably visiting a brothel instead. No matter. The house was empty. Why made no difference at all.

She cat footed up the main stairs, on the watch for the help. The lieutenant hadn't fully staffed his home yet, but had brought a native servant back with him from India. During the dinner party, Viola had noticed the turbaned fellow in the shadows, directing the borrowed footmen and giving quiet commands to the temporary serving girls.

The Indian servant would most likely be in residence.

So long as I steer clear of the kitchen or the garret, I'll be fine, Viola told herself. She knew the stones would be in Lieutenant Quinn's chamber.

Her fence had a friend in the brick mason's guild who, for a pretty price, happily revealed the location of the ton's secret stashes. Town houses on that fashionable London street were all equipped with identical wall safes in the master's chamber. The newfangled tumbler lock would open without protest under Viola's deft touch.

She had a gift. Two, actually, but she didn't enjoy the other one half so much.

Slowly, she opened the bedchamber door. *Good.* It had been oiled recently. She heard only the faint scrape of hinges.

The heavy damask curtains were drawn, so Viola stood still, waiting for her eyes to adjust to the deeper darkness. There! A landscape in a gilt frame on the south wall marked the location of the safe.

Viola padded across the room and inched the painting's hanging wires along the picture rail, careful not to let the hooks near the ceiling slide off. She'd have the devil's own time reattaching them if they did. With any luck at all, she'd slide the painting right back and it might be days before Lieutenant Quinn discovered the stones were missing. After moving the frame over about a foot, she found the safe right where Willie's friend had said it would be.

Viola put her ear to the lock and closed her eyes, the better to concentrate. When she heard a click or felt a slight hitch beneath her touch she knew she'd discovered part of the combination. After only a few tries and errors, the final tumbler fell into place and Viola opened the safe.

The dark void was empty. She reached in to trace the edges of the iron box with her fingertips.

"Looking for something?" A masculine voice rumbled from a shadowy corner.

Blast! Viola bolted for the door, but it slammed shut. The Indian servant stepped from his place of concealment behind it.

"Please do not make to flee or I am sorry to say I shall have to shoot you." The Hindu's melodious accent belied his serious threat.

Viola ran toward the window, hoping it was open behind the curtain. And that there was a friendly bush below to break her fall.

Lieutenant Quinn grabbed her before she reached it, crushing her spine to his chest. His large hand splayed over one of her unbound breasts.

"Bloody hell! It's a woman. Turn up the gas lamp, Sanjay."

The yellow light of the wall sconce flooded the room. Viola blinked against the sudden brightness, then stomped down on her captor's instep as hard as she could.

Quinn grunted, but didn't release his hold. He whipped her around to face him, his brows shooting up in surprise when he recognized her. "Lady Viola, you can't be the Mayfair Jewel Thief."

"Of course, I can." She might be a thief, but she was no liar. "I'd appreciate it, sir, if you'd remove your hands from my person."

"I bet you would." The lieutenant's mouth turned down in a grim frown and he kept his grip on her upper arms.

His Indian servant didn't lower the revolver's muzzle one jot. "Did I not tell you, sahib? When she looked at the countess's emeralds, her eyes glowed green." The servant no longer wore his turban, his coal-black hair falling in ropy strands past his shoulders. "She is a devil, this one."

"Perhaps." Quinn lifted one of his dark brows. "But if that's the case, my old vicar was right. The devil does know how to assume pleasing shapes."

That was a backhanded compliment if Viola ever heard one. She hadn't considered Lieutenant Quinn closely during the dinner party. She had little time for men and the trouble they brought a woman. Once burned and all that. She'd been intent on Lady Henson's emeralds. Now she studied him with the same assessing gaze he shot at her.

Quinn's even features were classically handsome. His unlined mouth and white teeth made Viola realize suddenly that he was younger than she'd first estimated. She doubted he'd seen thirty-five winters. His fair English skin had been bronzed by fierce Indian summers and lashed by its weeping monsoons. His stint in India had rewarded him with riches, but the subcontinent had demanded its price.

His storm-gray eyes were all the more striking because of his deeply tanned skin. They seemed to look right through her and see her for the fraud she was—a thief with pretensions of being a lady.

And try these other great titles available from Brava!

Sweet Stuff by Donna Kauffman

Double Fudge . . . Toasted Coconut . . . Key Lime . . .
Strawberry Cream . . .
Every bite is a mouthful of heaven.
And the women of the Cupcake Club are bringing their appetite . . .

Riley Brown never imagined she would find her bliss on Georgia's quiet Sugarberry Island after years of Chicago's city life. With a new career and fantastic new friends, she's got it all—except for eligible men. But a gig staging a renovated beach house delivers a delicious treat—six feet of blue-eyed, gorgeous writer as delectable and Southern as pecan pie. Quinn Brannigan has come to Sugarberry to finish his latest novel in peace, and suddenly Riley has a taste for the bad boy author that no amount of mocha latte buttercream or lemon mousse will satisfy . . .

Riley's friends are rooting for her to give in to her cravings and spice up her life, but it's Quinn who needs to learn that life's menu just might include love, in all its decadent, irresistible flavors . . .

Matthew by Emma Lang

It is a vast spread in the eastern wilds of the newly independent Republic of Texas, the ranch their parents fought for . . . and died for. To the eight Graham siblings, no matter how much hard work or hard love it takes, life is unthinkable without . . .

In the wake of his parents' murder, Matthew Graham must take the reins at the Circle Eight. He also needs to find a wife in just thirty days, or risk losing it all. Plain but practical, Hannah Foley seems the perfect bride for him . . . until after the wedding night. Their marriage may make all the sense in the world, but neither one anticipates the jealousies that will result, the treacherous danger they're walking into, or the wildfire of attraction that will sweep over them, changing their lives forever . . .

GREAT BOOKS, GREAT SAVINGS!

When You Visit Our Website:

www.kensingtonbooks.com

You Can Save Money Off The Retail Price Of Any Book You Purchase!

- **All Your Favorite Kensington Authors**
- **New Releases & Timeless Classics**
- **Overnight Shipping Available**
- **eBooks Available For Many Titles**
- **All Major Credit Cards Accepted**

Visit Us Today To Start Saving!

www.kensingtonbooks.com

All Orders Are Subject To Availability.
Shipping and Handling Charges Apply.
Offers and Prices Subject To Change Without Notice.